PRAISE FOR (

MW01167503

Praise for *The Last Madam*

"In this world, there are great characters who have no idea that they are great characters, and great characters who are fully aware of their greatness. Wallace must be counted among the latter. She had the wit of Dorothy Parker and the instinct for self-dramatization of Tallulah Bankhead." - *Michael Lewis, The New York Times Book Review*

"Christine Wiltz has done a remarkable and rare thing: she has captured perfectly the essential earthy complexity of the most fascinating city on this continent. The Last Madam is an exhilarating mardi gras of a book." - *Robert Olen Butler, Pulitzer Prize winning author*

"Wiltz elevates [an] impeccably assembled historical narrative above its elementary bawdy elements into something more elegant and fragile: the resurrection of a secret world like those uncovered by Luc Sante and James Ellroy." - *Publishers Weekly*

Praise for *Glass House*

"*Glass House* is far more than a story about one city. It's about the fear and rage and desperation that are destroying us as a people and a nation. New Orleans itself becomes a living, wounded presence as pervasive as the smell of Confederate jasmine or the reek of garbage cans behind the Convent project. I have never read a better depiction of the tormented American heart." - *James Lee Burke*

"It is the painful and unflinching honesty with which Wiltz confronts the issue of crime and fear of crime that give her novel its strength and power...A novel that needs to be read on both sides of Convent Street." - *The New York Times Book Review*

"Wiltz' expertly paced story sustains real entertainment while causing readers to search their hearts for their own hidden version of Convent Street." - *The San Francisco Chronicle*

SHOOT THE MONEY

A novel by
Chris Wiltz

Copyright © 2012 Chris Wiltz
ISBN: 978-1-62467-112-8

Premier Digital Publishing
www.PremierDigitalPublishing.com
Follow us on Twitter@PDigitalPub
Follow us on Facebook: Premier Digital Publishing

To
Marigny Goodyear,
who is always an inspiration,
and
Charlotte Schultz,
who gave me that fateful copy of
The Long Goodbye.

ONE

At 3:00 a.m. Karen Honeycutt woke up in a freezing hotel room above a casino in Biloxi, Mississippi, the song "Fifty Ways to Leave Your Lover" running around her brain. The light from the muted TV flickered around the room. She was in bed alone, though she hadn't been when she went to sleep. She got dressed and headed downstairs where she found Jack O'Leary in the casino bar with his face smashed into that of a petite blonde wearing a dealer's uniform.

Karen had thought about leaving Jack many times during the past year, but that didn't keep the bottom from dropping out of her stomach as she watched the spectacle taking place at the end of the bar. Jack sat on the edge of a padded stool, his back against the bar lip, the blonde standing between his legs. She fingered his salt-and-pepper pony tail with one hand and pushed against his crotch with the other. Jack's hands slid down her rear end and pulled her tight. His tongue tangoed in her mouth. The only other spectators were a couple at a table across a wide garish path of red and yellow floral carpet, and the bartender who was taking a cigarette break. The couple looked too tired or too broke to care, the bartender too bored.

A surge of anger carried Karen a step forward, putting her inside the open door of the lounge. She stopped. She might want to consider her options, not limit them with a conversation that began, "You asshole."

She turned and made her way back through the casino, walking past rows of slot machines, roulette and blackjack tables. The constant hum of the vast room with the overlay of plinks and plonks that sounded like a shifting heap of trashed xylophones made Karen's ears feel as if they were crawling up her scalp. She couldn't think again until the elevator door closed and insulated her from the noise.

"…Make a new plan, Stan, just get yourself free." That song, still playing in her head. She must have heard it on some oldies station, the only ones Jack listened to, as they sped across Alligator Alley, fleeing Miami twenty-four hours earlier. God, but she was sick of Jack's lifestyle. The late nights, the gambling, the drinking, the lowlife Jack hung with, and now a new act to add to his repertoire—running for your life in the middle of the night.

And where had he decided to stop and think over their final destination? A half-put-back-together casino on the Gulf of Mexico where nine months earlier hurricane Katrina had ravaged the coast for miles, where Karen had developed a sense of excruciating fatigue, a lethargy so profound that all she could do was read the latest Poppy Z. Brite novel and gaze out at the treacherous water.

Karen was ready to get herself free. She wanted to go back to New Orleans, her home town, but she didn't have enough money on her to pay for a Greyhound bus ticket. That reminded her of something Jack had said at three o'clock yesterday morning when they were still at their nice town house in Coconut Grove. The conversation wasn't one they'd ever had before, yet at the same time it was a typical conversation between them. He'd shaken her awake, and as she opened one eye to look at the clock, he switched on the lamp and blasted her with light.

"Damn it, Jack. Could you give me some warning about the light?"

"Get up and throw some things in a suitcase. We're taking a

2

trip." He talked to her from the bathroom as he emptied the medicine cabinet into a plastic grocery bag.

"What trip?"

"What?"

"Where are we going?"

He didn't answer, as though he hadn't heard her. She could be right in his ear and he wouldn't answer, unbelievably aggravating the way his mind was always somewhere else. If she repeated the question, he'd turn around, look at her, and say, "What?" and she'd have to repeat it again. She lifted herself on an elbow and watched him move into the bedroom and stuff his socks and underwear into another grocery bag. When it was full he tied the plastic handles together.

She waited. Several moments later he said, "Vegas," then, "I don't know. Come on, baby, get the fuck up. Pack a suitcase. Okay, pack two." As if she'd protested.

"We only have one," she called after him as he took all the plastic bags and dropped them in a pile at the top of the stairs. Back in the bedroom, he slid the suitcase from the top shelf of the closet and flipped it open on the bed for her.

"Jack, what's going on? I have a job, remember? I'm supposed to open the shop today."

His answer was to start taking his clothes to the car by the armload. Karen pushed back the covers, and as she sat up, hunched her shoulders and held her crossed arms tight over her chest, a defense against the assault of the air conditioner. The first thing Jack did when he entered the house was lower the thermostat to sixty. He was always hot, as though the blood boiled in his veins.

Karen walked over to the closet, and slid the mirrored doors so she could view her end of it. She sat back on the foot of the bed, despondent. She had no idea where to start.

Jack took the stairs two at a time. "Come on, sugarpie," he said

3

breezing back in. Mr. Efficient. The Good Humor Man. "No time to ponder. Just start dumping things in bags. You can fill the trunk of the bird." The turquoise 1958 Thunderbird convertible Jack had bought off eBay.

"It's Solo, isn't it?" Karen said. "You pissed Solo off."

Jack was out of the bedroom and down the stairs with another armful. Karen began taking her best clothes off the hangers, the Versace and Gaultier outfits Jack had given her as peace offerings, folding each one, laying it just so in the suitcase. She heard the car door slam, and he was back, framed in the bedroom doorway, watching her.

"You're gonna have to move a little faster than that."

Karen heard the edge of annoyance in his voice. "This is as fast as I move at this time of day," she said, mild and calm because she knew it would irritate the crap out of him.

She zipped the suitcase and packed a large tote with some casual pants and T-shirts. She filled a couple of grocery bags with cosmetics and hair stuff, then went down to the living room. Jack, with all four bags, started out to the car.

"I want to bring the commode," Karen said.

Jack dropped the suitcase. "*What?*" he said over his shoulder, his hand on the doorknob.

"And my library table."

These were the only antiques Karen had ever bought, the commode a particularly nice piece with a marble top and deep cabinet underneath.

"Christ," said Jack and opened the door.

Karen followed him outside to the slot where the car was parked in front of the town house they rented. "We can get a U-Haul," she told him.

Jack opened the trunk and put the bags and Karen's suitcase in it. He walked over to her and put his hands on her shoulders. "Look, baby, those are just things. We can always get other things."

"Getting things is time consuming. It consumes my time. I already found things I like. Anyway, a U-Haul will cost a lot less than replacing them."

"You're missing the fucking point, Karen. We have to go *now*."

"No, I'm not missing the *fuck*ing point, Jack. The fucking point is I want to take my antiques with me. You're taking your antique," meaning the car.

He dropped his hands to his sides. "You can sound so goddamn *reasonable*—you know, practical, and then, what, you think we can get out of here without a car? I'm supposed to leave it? Give me a break, Karen. It's the only goddamn car we have."

"I was just trying to make a *point*, for Christ sake."

"We can sit around here and jaw this thing to death, but if they get here before we leave..." He trailed off, flipped his hand, drew a finger across her neck.

"You're saying they'd kill us? Are you talking about Solo?"

He gave her a stone look then let his eyes sweep the row of houses behind her. "This is not a good place to talk, sweetface. Let's just get in the car."

"No. I'm not going. Why would Solo kill *us*?"

Air rushed from Jack's wide nostrils. He nodded toward the front door, and Karen followed him into the living room.

"You know how Solo's always so well-groomed, expensive suits, shoes, four hundred dollar haircuts, not a hair out of place...you know he has his chest waxed?"

"What does that have to do with..."

"So listen." He spoke low, as though someone was in the room with them. "He wasn't always so perfect. When he was five he saw his father stabbed to death, then he found his mother—she'd either OD'd or she was murdered too. Solo became a homeless, barefoot boy of the streets. He was half naked—the only clothes he had to his name were some nylon shorts with the Miami Heat logo on them..."

"Okay, that's it, Jack, just stop. Nylon shorts with the Heat's logo? You are so full of shit..." She waved a dismissive hand at him and started to turn toward the kitchen.

He grabbed her by the wrist. "Wait, listen, this is not a joke. He ate scraps from garbage cans, he smelled like a wet dog. Around Little Havana they started calling him *Perro Chico*, you know, Dog Boy..."

"For Christ sake."

Jack tightened his grip. "When he was seven he was adopted by the Allapattah Boys. They treated him like a slave, made an ass-wipe out of him until someone started making hits on the Latin Lovers. The rival gang. At first it was on the gang's dogs. He'd leave the dog's head on the door step, throw the body in a dumpster. Soon *Perro Chico* became a lieutenant and started killing the Lovers themselves, only they never found the bodies, just the tongue in the victim's refrigerator."

"That's disgusting, and I don't believe a word of it. Let me go."

Jack held tighter. "Do you want to take a chance it's not true? People don't change. He might change his clothes and act respectable, but he's still an Allapattah on the inside. He's gonna be over here looking for me and he's gonna torture you until you tell him. And if you can't tell him, even if you can, he'll cut your fucking tongue out."

They stood for a few seconds, tense, staring at each other.

"Okay, I'll go, but I still don't believe you. Let me go get some things. There's still a lot of space in the trunk."

"Space isn't the consideration here. Time is."

"I'm just going to get some sheets and blankets, a few pots..."

"Karen, just go get in the car."

She tried to pull her arm away, but he had it in a bruiser grip. "That stuff costs a fortune! You said I could fill the trunk."

"What am I trying to say here?" He got right in her face. "*Money's not a problem.*"

Karen stood there thinking that this business about money not being a problem was the most worrisome thing Jack had said. Money was always a problem, especially if Jack said it wasn't.

"Can we just get the fuck in the car, Karen?"

"*After*," she said, twisting her arm out of his grip, "I get my purse."

—⚹—

Once they were out of the city, racing across Alligator Alley through the Everglades to Naples, Karen remembered her red dancing dress—a Donna Karan, bias-cut silk—that was at the cleaners. Jack liked to buy her clothes when he was flush, but this one, her favorite, she'd bought for herself from the boutique where she worked. Used to work.

She looked over at Jack. The wind whipped through the convertible and messed with his mane of hair. He caught the pony tail and pulled it alongside his neck, then pushed it down inside his shirt. He was something like twenty years older than she was. Pushing fifty, unless he was lying and even older. And he was plenty vain enough to lie. He spent more time in the bathroom working on his hair than she did. In some ways, he was younger than any of the guys she'd dated before him. He had the radio up loud. His head bobbed in time to the music. He drummed his fingers on the top of the steering wheel. He looked like a man who didn't have a care in the world.

Karen had once thought he was so wise and powerful; she liked the age on him. Now she saw him for what he was, a gambler, an alcoholic, and a cokehead. She could feel the frustration and disappointment of the past years roiling around inside her. All the late nights, all the waiting she'd done, all the unsatisfying conversations about where Jack had been and what he'd been doing, having to be nice to Jack's friends, like that lowlife Solo Fontova and his gang of Cuban thugs. She knew they laughed at her anger and the way Jack mollified her with money and gifts and called her baby, sugarpie…Once upon a time, a long time ago, she'd liked those little endearments, but now they made her skin crawl.

She could feel her throat closing, hot tears gathering, the wind blowing them out of the corners of her eyes, along her temples, into her hair. It made her furious, everything she had left behind, that everything always had to be Jack's way, and that here she was getting ready to cry over it all when she damn well should have known better than to let Jack sweet talk her into giving up a good job in New Orleans and going to Miami with him.

She could feel the anger pushing up through her chest, opening her lungs like a bellows, and ripping through her tight throat.

"My red dress!" she wailed into the wind, surprised at what had come out. The tears broke loose.

Jack turned down the radio. "What?" he said.

When Karen got back to the hotel room, she went to the top dresser drawer where she'd seen Jack put a stack of bills. She picked it up, a shorter stack than it had been, and rifled it. A few fifty dollar bills, but mostly tens and twenties, not more than a thousand altogether. If money wasn't a problem, where was the rest of it?

A couple of long strides brought Karen to the closet in the short entrance hallway. She slid open the door and went down on one knee in front of the safe, putting the bills from the drawer on top of it. Jack was superstitious about numbers. They called out to him, they came to him in dreams. He had visions of numbers, overheard them in conversations, bet them. But for the burglar alarm at the town house or to access messages or use the ATM,

8

he used 2580, a straight shot down the number pad, no patience for anything except all night poker games and sports on TV.

Karen's finger went down the middle row of numbers on the safe. She pulled down the handle, but the safe didn't open. She read the directions. You needed six numbers. She tried 258000. Nothing. She tried several variations and lost track without a system. Maybe he'd used his birthday. She punched in the date. It didn't work. "Lying bastard," she said and went down a year at a time until he'd now be sixty-five. Her palms were beginning to sweat. If Jack's tongue had gotten tired, he could be on his way to the room. Her back and neck crawled in anticipation of him walking through the door. She rushed to it and put on the chain.

Kneeling in front of the safe again, she rubbed her cold hands together, cupped them, and blew into her palms. Now that she'd gone this far, Karen wanted out badly, away from Jack, and to get back to New Orleans, back to her old life. She hoped it was still there, not blown apart by the hurricane. She had no new ideas so she played with Jack's speed code, this time systematically, double two, double five, double eight, then alternating. She scored beginning with the double zero and putting the code in backwards.

The lever engaged, the door opened, and Karen saw a gym bag stuffed into the safe. She fell backwards pulling it out, righted herself, and unzipped it. It looked like mostly tens and twenties, but as she sifted through the bills, several fifties and hundreds rolled to the top, the money jumbled together, as though Jack had won the big pot at the poker game. But if he'd won it, where did Solo Fontova fit in?

For now, Karen wanted to get out of the room fast, not to think too hard about anything except that it looked like enough money to set her up in New Orleans, which her mother had told her had gotten expensive since the storm—high rents, big energy bills, and pricey, if available, services. She zipped the bag closed, grabbed the bills on top of the safe, and started to throw them inside. That's when she saw the black gun lying on the safe's dark floor.

She stared at it, not sure why she was hesitating, getting more nervous by the second. She picked it up, the decision more about not wanting to regret leaving it, not for a second thinking she might regret taking it. She dropped the short stack of bills in its place, closed the safe, and ran into the bathroom. She swept her toiletries from the counter into a hotel laundry bag, zipped her leather manicure case, and put it and the gun in her purse.

With both the gym bag and her purse slung over her shoulder, she unchained the door and looked up and down the empty hallway. Rolling her suitcase behind her, she eased through the door, held it until it closed with a soft snick, then dashed to the end of the hall and took the stairway to the floor below. She'd noticed a service elevator down another hall. She rode it to ground level. A startled employee waiting for it retreated a step when he saw her. She asked him how to get out the back way.

The salt air tasted like freedom. She walked along a makeshift breezeway for staff that connected the offshore casino to the land hotel, and when she reached the shoreline, went down a few steps to the beach. The heels of her sandals sunk into the sand. She took them off and walked out to the packed sand where she stood for a moment, looking out over the Gulf. Karen wished she'd found the guts to leave Jack after one of his three-day blowouts or one of his three-football game Sundays rather than after seeing his big hands cover the petite blonde's ass in a smoky bar. She liked his height, six feet four, and the feeling that he towered over her; at five eleven, not many men did. But she didn't mind standing eyeball to eyeball with a man either. So Jack could have his little blonde. He'd be one of those ridiculous tall men who run around with women that stood as high as their rib cage, good height for a low sucker punch.

She was wasting time. She thought about going back to Coconut Grove to get her things, but only briefly before she began to walk up the beach to the front of the hotel to look for a cab. This was going to have to be a different kind of freedom. Like the Janis Joplin song—nothing left to lose. From what she'd heard, she'd be in the same boat as most of the people in New Orleans.

TWO

Earlene Dick sat in the front of a flat boat that crawled through duck salad and alligator weed in a shallow pond, fogging the humid night air with its thick, foul-smelling smoke. The boat's engine sat up high out of the water and could have been a large lawn mower motor given how it sounded. It was attached to a hydraulic pump and powered a large steel wheel, rather than a propeller, that pushed the boat through ankle-deep mud at the bottom of the shallow pond. The only sound Earlene could hear over its loud drone was the sonorous call of the bullfrogs.

A fat cushion of clouds hid the stars. Every now and then the full moon burned through and illuminated the small levee separating the pond from the adjacent rice field. The headlamp Earlene wore kept the black water lit. A water moccasin slid past the boat. Behind the snake, coming up on the left, two eyes glowed red just above the water line. She leaned forward, careful to keep her light on them, and as the boat drew level, she reached out and plucked the frog from the water. The frog tried to make himself skinny so he could slip through her grip and leap to freedom, but Earlene's hand closed firmly around his bulging stomach. Through his sleek skin, not slimy in the least, she could feel the crawfish he'd swallowed whole. She held him over the side of the boat while he peed. No matter what, the frogs always seemed to be smiling. She'd have let him go if it weren't for Raymond, her brother, and her boyfriend Daniel, who were in the boat with her.

And her plan, which had been two years in the making.

Earlene had chosen June 1, the opening day of frog season in southwest Louisiana, as the day she would end her life. She got a thrill thinking of it in such harsh, dramatic terms. Earlene Dick of Mamou would be dead.

"Lookit little sister," Raymond yelled as she reached over to put the frog in the nearly full mesh sack hanging from the boat's console. "Biggest frog of the night."

Daniel, a frog in one hand, moved up behind Earlene and wrapped his other hand around her breast, jiggling it. "That's not the only thing she's got that's the biggest," he yelled back to Raymond.

With her forearm, Earlene pushed his hand away. She hated the way they talked about her as though she wasn't there. The talk, of course, was mostly lewd and crude. For once, she held her tongue. This would be the last time she had to hear it.

Raymond's headlamp spotted a frog close to the bank of the far levee. He guided the boat toward it, and when it got too shallow, he waded out into the water. Earlene pulled the end of a pint of generic bourbon she'd taken from her father's stash out of her bag. Earl stayed too drunk to miss it. She gave it to Daniel, then held it out to Raymond as he clamored over the side of the boat with the frog.

"I got a full Wild Turkey in the truck," she told them. She knew that would get them moving. Otherwise, they might want to start another sack, and Earlene still had something she wanted to do before she ended it all.

They had one frog-hunting ritual left to perform before they left the pond. Earlene turned to face the front of the boat. Raymond pulled roughly at the top of her T-shirt. A frog slid down her back got hung up on her bra, then jumped around, trapped inside her tucked shirt. When they were kids Earlene used to scream as if they were murdering her. The past couple of years, ever since she'd come up with her plan, she just pulled her T-shirt out of her jeans and yelled at whoever had done it to grow up. Tonight she didn't say a word. She lifted her shirt and let the frog jump into the black pond water.

"What the shit you do that for?" Raymond yelled, greedy for every last frog he could get at the end of the night. He leaned over and pinched her upper arm so hard she knew she'd have a whopper of a bruise. Her arms were covered with purple and yellow marks. But, again, she didn't yell. She wondered if Raymond would be sorry tomorrow. Probably not.

"Let's go drink some Wild Turkey," she said. He gave her a look of fury and jerked the boat across the pond diagonally in the direction of Daniel's pickup.

At the house, they hung the sack of frogs under the shed and sat out beneath the huge oak tree to drink. Earlene knew the pint would have to be gone before she and Daniel could get rid of Raymond. He was on the outs with Bernie Habetz, his girlfriend and Earlene's best friend, which was just as well, since if Bernie had been with them she would have known Earlene was acting odd.

Earlene drank more than she wanted just to kill the bottle faster. She wanted to make love to Daniel one more time before it was all over. She still loved him but not as she once had. He wanted to get married, but she didn't want to become the wife of a rice farmer. It's what her father had been before her mother died and he'd sold the farm to his brother. Now he was drinking up the money while Raymond paid to borrow land from Uncle Dudley and grow his own rice, struggling for every dime, and he didn't even have a family yet. Daniel would be better off, working his father's land and flooding the fields to make crawfish ponds after the government told him he couldn't grow any more rice. Then he'd sell the crawfish in the spring, and Earlene would spend every summer frying the frogs they caught in the crawfish ponds, no doubt a brood of brats around the kitchen table. No way she could live that life.

—∿—

Raymond finally staggered off, barely conscious, banging the screen door loud enough to wake the dead. No lights came on, so Earl had probably passed out on the sofa in front of the TV. Earlene and Daniel crawled into the back of the pickup, under the camper top. She helped him pull off his cowboy boots. They managed to pump up the air mattress, but by the time they were finished it was the only thing pumped.

"In the morning, Earlene," Daniel whispered and released a truckload of alcohol fumes. "Wake me up before you go."

She traced his spine down his long muscular back. She'd told him she had to work the 7:00 a.m. shift at the grocery store where she stuffed boudin sausage and made andouille po'boys for lunch. No one would miss her until they missed their fried frog-leg supper that night.

Earlene waited until Daniel started making soft snuffles, blowing air with a "puh" after each one. Another reason not to marry him: He was going to rumble like a Harley before he was thirty.

She kissed his forehead and ran her fingers through his mink-like black hair, then she was over the tailgate and creeping into the house through the back door. She heard voices, the TV, its volume turned low. The only light in the house was from the screen. The living room smelled like a closed bar, stale smoke and recycled alcohol vapors. Earl was draped over the sofa, one hand dangling above an ashtray full of butts. He'd been watching a Western, the only movies he really liked, with the exception of Patton. Earlene turned the volume up a tad.

She hit the bathroom first. From under the sink she took out a large box of Tampax. She'd hidden her money in it, the only place she could think of that Raymond and her father, with noses like bloodhounds, wouldn't sniff out the cash. It had taken her two years to save $2400. Twenty dollars a week like Baptists tithing.

From under her bed Earlene slid a suitcase she'd packed six weeks ago, though the contents had changed several times since. She winced at the scraping sound it made over the floorboards, as heavy as if a body had been stuffed into it. Carefully, she maneuvered it through the doorways, stopping in the living room with a thought to kiss her father good-bye. But if he woke up for even a few seconds she might not be able to walk away from his sad brown eyes. She went on through the kitchen, banging the suitcase against a chrome dinette chair. This was followed by a loud exchange of gunshots. Earlene froze. She didn't think she'd turned the TV up that loud. She heard Earl stirring on the sofa and jumped when he yelled out, "Keep it down, will ya?" She waited, but just as she moved, Earl called, "Earlene, is that you?" When he didn't get an answer, he said, "Goddamn kids," in his surly way. She hated it when he cursed. The sofa creaked as he turned. After he settled down she took her time getting through the back door and down the steps.

At the end of the concrete patio Earlene passed the sack of frogs, the plastic-coated mesh tight against their soft white bellies. A few throats pulsed here and there; by morning they would appear comatose in their captivity. She took the bag down and with a knife she found in the shed, cut open the top. She watched the frogs wobble and hop in drunken zigzags across the concrete and into the grass, off in search of another pond and another meal until the next time they were mesmerized by the drone of a boat engine and the hard glare of a frogger's headlamp.

Maybe there was a lesson here about not getting mesmerized by bright lights and the unfamiliar noises men make. She shook the last frog free of the bag and considered it the last act of her life in Mamou.

Peewee Meeker turned on his car lights and flashed them at Earlene as she walked along the side of the road. She dropped the huge suitcase in the tall grass as though trying to hide it. He'd scared her.

He stopped on the shoulder and got out of the car to put the suitcase in the trunk of his Malibu. He was the only male Earlene knew who didn't drive a pickup.

"I thought you were going to wait for me in the parking lot at school." Mamou High, their alma mater.

"I'm sorry, Earlene. You were late. I got worried."

"I said I'd meet you around two. It's two fifteen. That's still around two."

"Sorry." Peewee lived up to his name, meeker than anyone ought to be.

Behind the steering wheel, Peewee looked shrunken, like a kid. He was half a head shorter than Earlene and fit into her shadow; twenty-two years old and he still had acne. Tonight he'd glued his hair back with some kind of smelly pomade or maybe he'd slapped on a cheap after-shave.

"What's that smell?"

"Canoe." When Earlene wrinkled her nose, Peewee said, "I'll smoke a cigarette."

Earlene watched him light up. No matter how old he was, she decided, he'd always look as though he was trying to be cool when he smoked. But when it got right down to it, Peewee had been the only person she trusted enough to ask for a ride to Lafayette. If she'd have asked Bernie, there'd have been a million questions, then before she could get on the bus, Bernie would have flapped her mouth to Raymond. Friendship changed after your best friend fell in love with your brother.

Peewee didn't ask questions; he was too glad to be in Earlene's company. He'd had a thing for her since grade school, from the time they both started taking a lot of abuse because of their names, Peter and Dick. They couldn't beat people up the way Raymond did. They avoided each other because together they were the Penises. Even Raymond laughed. But it had created a bond between them so that by the time Peter became Peewee, because of its supposed size, and Earlene developed a couple of attributes that made the boys think of her in an entirely new way, they became friends. Raymond asked her why she still fooled around with the little pipsqueak. Earlene didn't bother to tell him that Peewee was into something other than football, sex, and hunting.

He was into music. He had some nice jazzy piano music playing. Earlene asked him what it was. "Ellis Marsalis," he told her.

They were cutting it close to go through Rayne to Lafayette, but Earlene wanted to see the frog murals one more time, the last time. The closer they got to Rayne, the slower Peewee drove.

"We're not gonna make it if you don't kick the speedometer up, Peewee."

"Sorry, Earlene." The car shot forward.

"You don't have to apologize every time I say something."

She'd have sworn he almost said "I'm sorry" again. She supposed she shouldn't protest since he was the only penis-equipped person she'd ever heard apologize—so much that it could be aggravating. He rolled his hand through the air, an I'm-sorry gesture if ever she'd seen one.

"I been thinking, Earlene." He backed off the gas, as if he couldn't talk and accelerate at the same time. "I'm taking you this far. Just let me take you where you're going."

She didn't answer. They were in downtown Rayne, empty as a church on Saturday night, coming up on the bullfrog that looked as though he were jumping off the wall of the building at you. Her favorite, the frogs in court, the judge frog wearing a long curly white wig, a whole jury of frogs, was painted on the wall of the courthouse. Peewee stopped in front of it.

Earlene stared at the mural. "Let's go," she said abruptly, sorry they'd come through Rayne. Nothing was going to stop her, sure as hell not premature homesickness.

They drove a few blocks, but she couldn't shake it. They passed the Chamber of Commerce. The big billboard had a light burned out, but she knew what it said, "Rayne. Frog Capital of the World. Home of the Rayne Frog Festival."

She squeezed her eyes shut. She could see RAYNE written on the inside of her eyelids. A thought came to her that edged out all her anxiety. Rayne. She could call herself Rayne.

For months Earlene had been looking for a new name. She wasn't starting her new life with the old one. Since Raymond was first-born, she'd asked her mother any number of times why she just couldn't have name him Earl Dick, Jr. and gotten it over with. Her mother said she didn't understand it either, so wistful sometimes that Earlene thought she must have had a lover name Raymond who'd either died or jilted her.

She'd be Rayne. Or Raynie. She needed a last name. She'd had a Marilyn Monroe fixation since she'd been a child. A few years ago when her mother was talking about Jeanne Moreau it had occurred to Earlene that all the most famous actors had names that ended with an "o" sound—Monroe, Moreau, Harlow, Brando, Garbo, DeNiro, Pacino, Paltrow…She wanted her new last name to end with an "o". Like LeBeau. Too masculine. Thibodeaux, too Cajun. Theriot, same problem. LeVeau, pretty, but veau in French had something to do with cows. From a dick to a cow. Not great.

"You hear what I said, Earlene?"

"Yeah. But you'd never make it to work on time. I'm going to California."

"Bullshit!" He turned up the sound. "That's George Porter."

He punched the next track. "Dr. John," he said and punched the next one. "Kermit Ruffins." He called out the names of the groups, "Walter Wolfman Washington. Papa Grows Funk. Los Hombres Calientes. Johnny Vidacovich. John Boutte. Dumpster Funk. Rebirth Brass Band. Clint Maedgen."

"Haven't heard of half of 'em," said Earlene.

"But you will. It's all New Orleans music. That's where you're going—New Orleans. It's where your mother wanted to go. The most glamorous city in Lou'siana. If she'd've gone there, she never would've married a rice farmer. Remember? You told me everything she ever said."

"I never should have told you anything."

"Well, you did, and I'm still the only one who knows, right? But, what, are you crazy? Why are you going now?"

"What do you mean?"

"June first, you know, hurricane season? The place could disappear off the face of the earth this time."

"Then I'll just disappear with it, Peewee. You're not going to talk me out of it, so let's not talk until we get to Lafayette." She turned up the volume, folded her arms, and stared straight ahead.

Peewee maintained silence for all of ten seconds before he turned the sound down. "Let me take you down there. I won't needle you."

"Raymond's going to beat the shit outta you, and you'll tell him where I am."

"He'll have to beat me unconscious. Come on, Earlene, how would he ever figure I know? I mean…" He flipped his hand toward her, then himself. "Huh?"

He had a point.

"What about your parents? Where do they think you are?"

"Out. Driving around, hanging out. Are you kidding? They don't give a shit where I am as long as I'm out. If I'm out all night, they'll hope I'm knocking someone up."

Kids in Mamou lived at home until they got married. By day Peewee sold guitars at Savoy's. At night he stayed in his bedroom, wore earphones, burned CD mixes, practiced guitar riffs. A loner. A weirdo.

"You really won't make it to work tomorrow, Peewee."

"I took the day off."

She gave in. He gave her a crash course in New Orleans music for the next three hours, until they got off the spillway and the sun was barely lighting the sky on the eastern horizon. From the Interstate, passing through the Metairie suburb, they could see the backs of storm-scarred shopping centers, gaudy billboards for casinos in Biloxi, some that leaned at awkward angles, a few large pieces of twisted steel that came from—where? There was a church with its steeple hanging upside down, and as they got into the city, the rubble, the vacant houses and boarded up buildings, the scalped Superdome... It was a city she could see had been changed by a horrific event, and she didn't know what it had looked like before. Her stomach lurched with the strangeness of it all, with the uncomfortable feeling that the city she was moving to was not the same city Earlene had wanted to make her new home.

Then she remembered she wasn't Earlene. She was Raynie...

The name she'd searched for—the "o" name—was suddenly there. Devereux, exotic but still graceful, the name of the old man who'd given her Willie, a frog he'd raised on his frog farm on the outskirts of Rayne. Willie won the frog-jumping contest at the festival that year; then got disqualified because he was a farm frog. She'd been just a kid; she cried. "He's still a real frog," she said. Mr. Devereux told her not to worry. Willie would jump far, far away from all those fools.

Raynie Devereux. She said it to herself three times, caving to superstition. It worked. She definitely felt different.

THREE

Karen was on the bus from Biloxi to New Orleans when she decided she'd be damned if she'd abandon all her stuff in Florida. Good stuff too—the best cookware, Egyptian cotton linens, down pillows, and her antiques. She didn't feel like starting all over, living in a place with a mattress on the floor, pillows instead of a sofa, no rugs. Winters in New Orleans, the cold seeped up through the floorboards and tiles of the old houses. Your feet felt it unless you wore Canadian mountain boots. Maybe she'd spent too much time in sunny Florida. Or maybe she and Jack had played house too long.

Around noon she checked into Mary Pat's Sun and Moon, a bed and breakfast on N. Rampart Street. The first thing she did was dump the money out on the bed and count it. She stacked it. She counted it again. She couldn't believe it—$56,000 and change. Solo would want Jack's nuts for this. What could he have been thinking?

What was she thinking?

She was too tired to think. She lay down on the bed with the money and let her mind wander. She wondered when Jack would have gotten around to telling her about the money, the way he would have told her. He would have waited until she'd gotten over being hustled out of Miami at three in the morning. Then he would have staged a scene, champagne in the hotel room, maybe a present—something outrageous, like the time he hired the guy in the red leather jockstrap to deliver a dozen roses and sing "Thank Heaven for Little Girls" in a thick New Orleans accent trying to sound French, followed by a half-second strip show, which made her run from the room.

Or there was the time after an argument when they'd first moved to Miami. She told him she wished she'd never laid eyes on him and cried because she was homesick. She came home from work the next evening, found the living room lit with dozens of candles, and Fats Domino belting out "Walkin' to New Orleans" on the stereo. Jack came into the room stark naked except for a gold turban like a genie's and bands of bells around his ankles, carrying a couple of Schnapps shots like Tom Rivers used to serve at the Ace, the bar on Dumaine Street in the French Quarter where they'd met.

He was insane. Karen had no doubt that he could have made out with the blonde in the bar one night, then concocted something dramatically romantic for her the next. As she fell asleep she saw herself lying in bed, Jack straddling her, and from his hands, money and rose petals floating down to cover her....

She woke with a start nearly ten hours later. The room was dark, and she hugged the edge of the bed, one bent elbow and crooked knee off the mattress, sleeping as she had been living, on the edge. At night she retreated to the edge to stay away from Jack's long limbs flailing about, and slept in protective position, body curled in on itself, one arm covering her head in case a rogue elbow entered her space. The silence around her seemed strange. Even if Jack wasn't snoring or grunting as his big body thrashed, his breath rasped loudly in and out of his large nostrils.

The smell was missing, too, the straightforward smell of sweat overlaid with a slightly sweet bitterness that reminded Karen of anise. She drew a deep breath and thought she got a whiff of it, a scent as dark as his olive skin, as mysterious as what went on in his mind.

She shuddered, as if shaking off any longing she still felt for Jack, and turned on the bedside light. She must have thrashed quite a bit herself. Some of the money had fallen to the floor. From her position half off the mattress, she picked up what she could before she slid to the floor to look under the bed. She stuffed all the money back into the gym bag and hid it behind her suitcase in the closet. When she lifted the suitcase, she heard the gun clunk in it.

A couple of years with a man, and she wasn't sure what he'd do when he found her, which wouldn't take long. She knew she wanted the money and didn't regret taking it, considering that it came from that slimeball Solo Fontova.

Just thinking about Solo raised the hair on the back of her neck, his thick-skinned face that looked as though it had been beat out of shape with an oiled meat mallet, or maybe the oil leaked from his expensive hair-do, swept back and polished with gobs of extra-shine product. Whenever they met he held her fingers as his beefy lips brushed her knuckles and told her what beautiful hands she had. A perfect gentleman, excused himself if he said fuck in front of a woman. A self-described businessman, his short, hard-gutted body in two-thousand-dollar expertly tailored iridescent suits, his feet in sheer-striped hose and eight-hundred-dollar alligator loafers. No pointy-toed shit kickers or guayabera shirts for Solo. His pocket handkerchief always matched his colorful silk shirts, which he wore with the top two buttons undone to give the ladies a glimpse of his immaculately waxed chest. Big thug in Little Havana, running his security company, his biggest client his own gambling enterprises. But an Allapattah Boy? Had he really left the tongues in refrigerators? Jack was so full of it...

But Solo was Jack's problem. She'd figure out what to do about Jack when he showed up. Until then, Karen decided to take $5000 of the money to rent an apartment and get to Florida.

The rest she'd put in a safe deposit box first thing in the morning. She would need a visible means of support. She showered, got dressed, and walked over to La Costa Brava to see if LaDonna Johnson would give her back her old bartending job.

—∿∿—

The street action in the Faubourg Marigny, behind the French Quarter, was not as heavy as Karen remembered at eleven o'clock on a Saturday night. At the top of Frenchman Street, the Hookah Café and Mona's were open, both restaurants that Karen liked. Next door was a new place, Ray's Boom Boom Room. The music was loud and people were packed in. Karen walked by slowly. This looked like the hot spot on the street. There was no one hanging in front of the Blue Nile, and when she got to it she saw it was closed, the front windows boarded up. Something like a shock wave went through her system. She picked up speed, anxious to get to La Costa Brava, wanting to make sure it was still there.

Karen didn't want anything to be different. She wanted the same life she'd had before Jack, with all the familiar people and places, the Marigny a hip scene for locals, not just another tourist trap like most of the Quarter had become, and as she walked beyond the Blue Nile, she walked into her past. Behind the large ground-floor windows of the buildings down Frenchman were the same old haunts, with their peeling paint facades and chipped plaster showing blackened brick. From their doors came live music—reggae, Latin, and African—and good old rock 'n roll at d.b.a.

When she got to La Costa, Karen could see through the window at the left that LaDonna had less than half a house of late-night diners. She went through the small front foyer into the bar on the other side. The battered wood floor creaked familiarly under her feet. As her eyes adjusted to the dim light, that old feeling of possession swarmed her. She'd put in her time on both sides of the bar as well as most of the tables that lined the walls. Under the low ceiling, the jazz from the back room mixing with smoke and talk, it was a good place to hunker down, figure out the meaning of life, catch up on the local gossip.

The lone bartender moved fast to serve a healthy crowd, though nothing like the Boom Boom Room, that didn't leave much space down most of the length of the bar. He had that kind of cool about him that he didn't seem rushed or harried, plenty of time to joke around with a couple of women seated about center, who looked as though they'd reached their final destination for the night.

Karen stood back watching, realizing she had it in for this guy on two counts: one, he was working her old job; two, he was too good looking in that bad boy way, with his messy dark hair, face unshaved, the sleeves of his plain black t-shirt rolled up and tight around his well-developed biceps. Benicio del Toro came to mind, or a darker version of the young Marlon Brando, though not quite as brooding. Karen credited herself with having learned a few things during her years with Jack. One thing, if a guy was that good looking and heterosexual, he was bound to be a bastard.

She pushed her way up to the bar, right next to the two women. The one closest gave her a look and leaned toward her friend. Karen kept her eyes on the bartender and felt pleased when she drew him right to her.

"Get you something?" he said.

"No thanks. Is LaDonna upstairs?"

"Who's asking?" He let his eyes drift down, away from her face.

"Karen Honeycutt. I used to have your job."

People were moving to the back room where the late show was starting, Delfeayo Marsalis, always drawing a good crowd.

The waitress from the back, who was standing at the end of the bar, shouted, "Luc, two Matadors, a blue-cheese martini, one Coke, Heineken, and a Turbo Dog."

He started moving, but staying close enough to say, "Oh, yeah, hard-ass Honeycutt I heard they called you. When you were manager."

Karen stared at him.

"Just kidding," he said and lifted his chin toward the stairs at the back of the room. "LaDonna's in her office."

Karen unhooked the velvet rope and went up the narrow staircase, hidden from view of the bar by a wall. At the top of the stairs, she opened a bead-board door and entered a long hallway. Second door on the left, she knocked once, followed by three rhythmic taps, wondering if LaDonna would remember.

LaDonna called out, sounding surprised, "Who's that?" then, "Enter."

Karen opened the door to see LaDonna get up and nearly knock a stack of papers off the edge of her piled-high desk. Her gold bangle bracelets rattled on her wrist.

Big smile showing her large white teeth, she said, "Hey, girl," and the two embraced. LaDonna, a head shorter than Karen, though she never seemed to be looking up at anyone, held her by the shoulders. "You're not so good at keeping in touch, honey."

"I feel bad about that, LaDonna. It's been way too long."

The smile shrunk. "Longer than you can count in real time, I'll tell you that."

"Is your house still there?"

"Hell no. It's a pile of sticks. They still sittin' out there. I just thank the Lord Jesus my mama and daddy didn't have to see this. Would've broken their hearts."

"I tried to reach you after the storm. I knew the 9th Ward went under. I wanted you to come stay with me."

LaDonna laughed, deep and rich. "I should've headed your

way, but let me give you the short version of what happened after Katrina.

"First, we commandeered a tour bus, king size, to get us out of town. We go East to head West, 'cause that's what the radio told us to do, and that takes so long we run smack into that Hurricane Rita when we stopped at my cousin's house in Erath. We gathered up the cousins and hauled ass to Lake Charles and kept on going to Houston. Then we couldn't figure what to do with the bus. So we turn around and start back. We stayed on FEMA's tab at a motel in Beaumont for a couple of days, took a detour to my other cousin's in Lake Arthur where we scraped flood sludge out of her house, de-slimed back in Erath, and then we decided we didn't care what was goin' on in New Orleans, we said, we are goin' home."

"Who's we?"

A question that threw LaDonna into distraction. "Oh, uh, musicians from the Lower 9, people hanging around the Marigny, anybody who wanted to come."

"So all that's *after* Katrina? Why didn't you evacuate?"

"Honey, you are a New Orleans girl. You have to ask that question? We were open for business the Saturday night before. Everybody's in a party mood. When C. Ray gave the evacuation order, they were all at a football game. Maybe half the ones who bothered to watch the weather left. The others, well, you know how it is. If they're young, they're immortal; if they're as old as me, they say they went through Betsy, so they sure as hell ain't leavin for this."

"Did you manage to get anything out of your house?"

"Nope, stayed here the night the bitch hit so I'm down to my undies. If I didn't have this club…Push some of that crap off the sofa and tell me about you. I can't talk about this shit."

The house phone rang and LaDonna went to the wing chair behind her desk. "What now?" she said wearily, listened, then said, "Tell the asshole those were the last two entrées, we're out of food, he should try the Marigny Brasserie a couple doors down."

Karen saw that the past nine months had put a few strands of gray in LaDonna's black hair. She still wore it pulled back, a cascade of tiny braids down to the middle of her back. She'd lost a few pounds, which looked good, but the difference wasn't in her looks so much as in her eyes. They had dark circles under them and they were flat and slow, without their usual quick interest. She sat tiredly in the big chair. Karen had never seen LaDonna slouch before; her normal posture was bolt upright, at the edge of her seat, taking care of two or three things at once.

She hung up the phone. "Why can't people think on their feet any more? So tell me, you visiting or you back for good?"

"I'm back. You were right about Jack. I believe the term you used was lowlife."

"I could have said worse, but, girl, he had to have something going for him. What was it, a couple of three years? That's a long time at your age."

"Yeah. I've been wondering since I left him why I ever thought it was a good idea to go off with him in the first place." Karen shook her head and laughed. "He smelled good?"

"There's something to that," LaDonna told her. "Oprah, Dr. Phil, somebody said for men it's the visuals attract them to women; for women, it's smell. Anyway, there no wrong decisions, only decisions."

"Who said that?" Karen got a visual of the money all over the bed at the Sun and Moon.

LaDonna sighed. "I don't buy it either." She stared off at the corner of the room.

Karen didn't know what to say to LaDonna. She was different, changed by what she'd gone through or still in shock. LaDonna had never talked much about her personal life, though she was interested in Karen's. She had a quick wit that deflected questions so that Karen never felt they were equals that way, LaDonna also being her employer and older, roughly Jack's age. Now they had time and a catastrophe separating them. But until Jack came along with his slightly bowed legs, crooked smile and hot sex, LaDonna had been the final authority for Karen. In the three years she'd worked for LaDonna, she'd learned more from her than she had from her own mother. Then Karen had found out that it wasn't just men who didn't always think with their brains.

She cleared her throat. "I notice you seem a little short-handed downstairs." Most nights the bartender didn't work alone, never on weekend nights. "Could you use another bartender?"

LaDonna turned to her. "Business is off. I don't use more than one bartender 'cept for Friday and Saturday nights. One of them didn't make it tonight." She thought for a moment. "What I could really use, some office help, move some of this paper around like you used to."

"No manager?"

"I had to let her loose. Listen, the way things are, I can't pay you what I used to, but I could use some part-time help in the dining room. The tips could make up the difference. You up for that?"

So because of Katrina, LaDonna had money problems. She'd had those before, but it had only made her work harder. Maybe the answers weren't so simple now.

"Sure," Karen said. "Give me a few days to get a place and get my things from Florida."

"Florida? I thought you went to Detroit."

"By way of Memphis. It's a long story. We'll need a couple of drinks."

"And a fast car, sounds like."

—⁓—

Karen stepped from the brilliant Florida sunshine into the darkened townhouse. She didn't remember drawing the curtains. That thought became secondary as soon as the cold air laden with the smell of food hit her. Her sensory confusion lasted only a split second, but she still didn't bolt fast enough.

For a big man, he was quick, his thick arm across her collarbones, a long blade nudged up against her cheek. He kicked the door shut. He was shorter than Karen but twice as wide. He pushed her into the dining room, talking up close to her neck, black beans on his breath.

"You try to run, I slice your face."

He increased the blade's pressure against her cheekbone and used a cell phone with his other hand. He fired a rapid burst of Spanish, part of which she understood: "The girl is here." Perhaps he also made a suggestion to disfigure her now rather than later.

Karen could hear Solo Fontova's voice. "Solo!" she called out.

The Cuban moved the blade—she knew him, one of Solo's thugs, Ernesto—and she felt its razor edge break her skin. She wanted to whimper but decided against it.

He ended the call, removed her purse from her shoulder, and shoved her toward a chair. "You sit," he told her.

Karen put a finger to her cheek and felt the blood. She turned around, walking backwards the last couple of steps to the chair, not wanting her back to him. He was interested in her purse. He slung it on the table, and holding it and the knife in one hand, began to go through it. He found the manila envelope at the bottom, took it out, and smirked at her when he saw the money, his eyes not meeting hers but lingering on her chest. His jaw hung open. With his undershot bite he reminded Karen of a Bullmastiff. The latest *Perro Chico*? She expected him to drool. He was young, not twenty, maybe not a day over seventeen, eighteen. It was hard to tell, with his chunky build and pockmarked face like Solo's.

Fifteen minutes they waited in the dining room, Karen so tense she clutched her hands together until the antique diamond dinner ring Jack had given her felt as though it was cutting into her finger.

Solo arrived, mean and sober looking, but saying, "Karen, how nice to see you."

He was dressed in one his suits, a shiny green reminiscent of lagoon scum, double breasted with a chartreuse silk shirt, gold cross hanging over his waxed chest, and matching pocket handkerchief, a power suit in the world of Miami thugs.

"What's all this about, Solo?"

He smiled and said, his Cuban accent and his important, busy man shtick making his English quick and precise, "You want a little verbal sparring, I can indulge you."

"Your *man* here cut my face."

"I see that. A little nick, nothing much. Ernesto takes his work very seriously. He gets carried away sometime. But he has a very steady hand, I assure you."

"I'm bleeding."

"Karen, let's not make a big deal."

He handed her his handkerchief. She hesitated, but Solo was the dry-clean king. Still, she blotted her cheek and laid the handkerchief on the table nearer Solo, folding it over to hide the blood, obscene against the parakeet-bright square of silk.

He said, "We can be very quick here. I want to know where my money is, so I want to know where Jack is."

"I have no idea where Jack is."

"I'm sorry to have to say I do not believe you."

He picked up her right hand, just as he'd done from the first day they'd met. He held it as if he might kiss it, his large manicured thumbnail shining under the globe light over the table. "Your hands, they are still most remarkably beautiful. I tell 'Nesto, I don' recall more beautiful hands. Isn't that right, 'Nesto?"

She saw it coming and tried to wrench her hand away, but 'Nesto had it, twisting her wrist painfully. She didn't cry out but couldn't stop a small noise in her throat.

"You are brave, Karen. I hope you are not also stupid," Solo said.

'Nesto laid her hand palm up on the dining room table. He flattened it, spreading her fingers. His huge paw was sweaty, grubby; he breathed hard and fast, like a big dog. He held the knife blade snug against the tip of her pinkie, its edge across the back of her nail, like a scallion he was about to slice.

"I ask you one more time, Karen. Where is Jack?"

"The last time I saw him he was at a casino in Biloxi. The Isle of Capri, I think."

"The last time. When is that?"

"About a week ago."

"I think, Karen, you move closer to the truth, but you aren' there yet."

He closed his eyes. 'Nesto angled the blade and with a deft flick cut off the tip of her fingernail into the quick. She cried out, but it sounded more like surprise than pain. The pain, though, was rather stunning. She wasn't sure she had any of her fingernail left. She saw blood on the blade as 'Nesto lifted it.

"'Nesto, he will give you a very nice manicure. Maybe I don' have to tell you what he'll do if he runs out of fingernails. Surely that will not become a problem."

Karen shook her head. She saw tongues instead of fingers spread across the table.

"I didn' think so. Where is my money?"

"I know where some of it is…"

'Nesto moved the blade to her fourth finger and another nail sailed through the air. Her cry this time was more of a breathless moan, and her eyes teared. She started talking loud and fast. "I took five thousand dollars Jack had in the dresser drawer at the hotel. The rest of it he locked in the safe. I never saw it. I would have taken all of it if I could have opened the safe." She nodded toward the envelope on the table. "What's left of the five is in there. Take it."

Solo didn't so much as glance at the envelope. He drew his brows together, perplexed. "Why did you take this money?"

Karen didn't meet his eyes. She said just loud enough for him to hear, "Because I caught him making out with this little blond bitch in the bar, and I was pissed."

Solo threw his head back and laughed. "Ah, the woman's revenge. So you jus' leave? Like that?" He snapped his fingers. "You don' make big trouble in the bar, fight with the other woman? With Jack?"

"They were busy. They didn't see me."

"Truly, Karen, you are a most remarkable woman."

Karen looked at him. "Jack's crazy—you know that. No telling how many women there've been. You should've seen the fight after he didn't come home once for three days. I broke every dish in the house, a few things I really liked. I decided not to get mad that way anymore. I started acting like nothing he did bothered me, you know? But the blonde. I'd never seen him with another woman. It did something to me. I took the money. I spent it on an apartment and a plane ticket."

Solo motioned to 'Nesto to release her hand. Karen rubbed her wrist but couldn't bring herself to look at her mutilated fingers. They were still bleeding, a small pool of blood on the table. Solo, always the gentleman, picked up his handkerchief, flipped it to spread it open, and presented it to her. She wrapped her fingers and cradled them in her other hand.

Solo fingered the manila envelope. He didn't look inside but held it, felt its weight. He tossed it back on the table.

"To show you what I think of you, Karen, I don' ask you to return the money, the five thousand dollars. You keep it." He gestured toward the living room. "Move your furnishings. Start a new life."

He held out his hand and the well-trained 'Nesto handed Solo Karen's plane ticket. He handed it back to 'Nesto who shoved it into Karen's purse. She made a face, disgust that his grubby hands were on her things.

"New Orleans. What's in New Orleans?"

"That's where I'm from."

"Where you met Jack."

Karen nodded.

"Jack with this blonde," Solo said, "is not the last you'll see of Jack."

She shrugged. "I guess he could find me without any trouble, but a couple of years ago we left New Orleans almost as fast as we left Miami. Maybe he won't think it's a good idea to find me."

"He will want to, then he gets his money back or whatever he decides because you spend his money."

"But he has the rest of the money. A lot of money."

"Yes, very much money. But his woman left. She does not even fight for her man. This makes him feel maybe he is not much of a man."

"You think you've got Jack figured?"

Solo lifted a shoulder. "I know what it is to be a man."

The bozo was perfectly serious. "I see," said Karen.

"What you maybe don' see is that if you don' call me as soon as Jack finds you, you have a bigger problem than Jack."

He reached inside his jacket and held a card out to her. A business card, for fucksake. Solo Fontova. Security Specialist. Phone number, cell phone, pager, fax number. No address.

"All I have to do is call you, and I'm off the hook?"

"That's it. You earn your money."

"What will happen to Jack?"

"That is up to Jack—whatever he has done with the money."

"You know, Solo, Jack didn't talk much about his business—your business—very much."

"Of course not."

"I don't even know how much money was in the safe. A lot, I guess, because when we left here, Jack told me not to take anything, you know, any of our possessions, money wasn't a problem."

Solo found this most amusing. "For Jack, money is always a problem." He said something in Spanish, and he and 'Nesto laughed.

Karen waited, their amusement wearing thin, and said, "How much money did he take, Solo?"

Solo stared at her, a woman speaking out of place. She stared back. Just when she thought he wouldn't answer he said, "Sixty thousand," made a guttural throat noise as he waggled his hand in the air, said, "give or take, mostly give," and raised his eyebrows at her.

"*Madre*," she said, eyes wide.

Solo pulled out a dining chair and put his foot on it, exposing his sheer-striped hose, so straight and smooth that Karen wondered if he kept them up with garters. He leaned on his knee, which put him closer but still looking down at her. "You would like to know how he got it, wouldn't you, Karen?" He paused, but not waiting for an answer, enjoying her rapt attention, increasing the suspense. "He saw an opportunity and he took it. In this case, a very stupid thing to do."

That night Jack had provided the "security" for one of the men at the poker game. An important man, Solo said, meaning rich.

"What is it you call the suckers?" Karen said. "Marks? Fish?"

"We don't have marks or fish," Solo told her patiently, but she could tell it riled him. "We have only players. You read too many books, Karen." He glanced over his shoulder at the bookshelf stuffed with her paperback thrillers.

This man, the player, was the big winner that night, going all-in on the last hand. Jack put the sixty-plus thousand in a duffle bag and with his gun at his side, walked the man to his car. That was the last Solo had seen of them. Next thing, Solo gets a call from the player. He's in the hospital. Had a heart attack out by the car that night. Jack drove him to the hospital, told him he'd hold the money for him until he got out. He's getting out, he tells Solo, and he wants the money.

"No problem, I tell him, except I discover Jack is no longer in Miami."

"So you had to make good," Karen said.

Solo closed his eyes briefly, his way of nodding. "I will have to, yes."

"But you haven't yet."

"It is the only way to get him to come back."

So the fish could lose the next time, nothing left to chance, not that anything had been left to chance the first time. Jack had told Karen enough about his "business" dealings. She said, "He might not come back anyway, Solo. Too much booze, too many broads and cigarettes for his heart."

"I have my reputation to protect."

And your ass. Karen said, "You see, that's where Jack has an edge. He doesn't care about things like reputations. He's a type T personality."

"What is this, type T?"

"T. For thrills."

—⟨⟨⟨—

Karen walked to a drugstore a couple of blocks away, her two fingers wrapped in Solo's blood-stained handkerchief and a dishtowel. When she'd finally looked at them she'd been relieved to see a good part of the two nails still there, but where the quick was exposed, it hurt too much to think about getting a couple of customs glued on yet. She got gauze, adhesive, and Neosporin, a butterfly bandage for her cheek, and a look from the cashier. After the movers left Karen went straight to the airport, not in the least sorry to leave Coconut Grove behind.

It wasn't until she was settled on the plane that she had a chance to think about what she'd done. She'd convinced Solo that she knew nothing about the money, and except for the fingernails, it hadn't even been hard, just talking fast and acting scared. Not that it was all an act; 'Nesto and his knife had scared her plenty. But not enough to give up the money. Not enough to really believe Solo would amputate her fingers or her tongue. He was far too fastidious. Jack was such an ass.

The plane took off, and she experienced a moment of lightheadedness. What she'd done, it wasn't like her, and that was exactly why she liked it. The lightheadedness was a rush of exhilaration.

The staff at La Costa Brava might have called her a hard-ass, but that was about work, running a tight operation, because in that business inattention to details and not keeping track had a way of making money disappear. Outside of work, she'd been a pushover. All Jack had to do was look at her, those puppy-dog eyes…except that was the excuse, not the reason. She'd been restless, bored, and being in love was action. Danger was action too. All in one package—Jack.

So what about Jack? Would she really be able to hang him out there, wait to see what Solo would do? She knew she wouldn't; she'd give Jack the money.

Karen ordered a bourbon and soda, and as she sat sipping it, she admitted to herself that she'd crossed the line from watching danger to putting herself in the way of it. Was she still so bored that she needed a change from following the action to being it? Maybe action was addictive that way. Maybe that was Jack's problem, always looking for his next fix of exhilaration. She wondered if that's what Jack felt, exhilaration, after he saw an opportunity and took it. She also wondered if it made seeing the next opportunity easier. Her line of thought got broken because something else occurred to her. She'd forgotten her Donna Karan dress at the cleaners after all.

FOUR

Raynie Devereux walked the streets of the French Quarter. She had to find a job, and she had to get out of that rat-hole where she was living. For one thing, she couldn't cook there—just a back room in a deteriorating house on Esplanade, a hole in the roof over the stairway, for which she paid an extravagant hundred and seventy-five dollars a week, bathroom down the hall. And the other people who lived there were weird. Worse than weird—scary. They wore black all the time, dyed their hair black, painted their fingernails black and wore black lipstick, even some of the...What should she call them? They weren't boys, but they certainly weren't men, and to call them guys seemed... too wholesome.

The couple next door, though, had been nice to her during the thunderstorm the previous afternoon. The roof had begun to leak over her bed. Raynie had moved it, but the room was situated that the best she could do was shove the bed against a wall so only a corner of the mattress got wet. The girl found a bucket for her in a closet downstairs then asked her if she wanted to go to a party that night with her and her boyfriend.

She beckoned Raynie into their room, one of the large front rooms of the house with two windows that stretched from the floor almost to the high ceiling, an alcove with an ancient rusting refrigerator not as tall as she was, a tiny stove, their own bathroom. The paint was peeling from the walls, the mantel full of candles and crosses and strange objects, a dead rat painted with stars and stripes dangling above it. Between the windows a plastic baby doll was nailed naked to a cross, one blue eye open, a hole where the other eye should have been. The other eye, glued on top of the cross, stared from under its fringe of lashes. Raynie nearly ran from the room.

Then the girl sat down on the unmade mattress on the floor where the boyfriend lounged with his big black boots on the dirt-gray sheets. She leaned into him, crossing her ankle over her knee, her black skirt falling between her legs. Her eyes closed. She smiled as his fingers with their black nails drifted slowly up her arm. Their sensuality made Raynie feel weak, she wasn't sure with what. She just had to get out of there.

As if the girl could hear her think she said, "Come sit with us, stay a while."

Raynie didn't know if she was being invited for a threesome. She was both curious and afraid. Fear won out; she told them she had to go.

"Come with us tonight," the girl said, her eyes fluttering. The boyfriend smiled—no, it was more of a smirk—at her.

"I'll see," Raynie murmured and turned to flee.

"We'll knock on your door before we leave," the girl said.

As she closed their door, Raynie saw the girl bend her head back, exposing her neck, the boyfriend's large-knuckled hand loosely circling it, stroking it.

In her room, Raynie felt agitated. She wanted to leave, walk until she got distracted by the street action, until she calmed down, but it was still raining too hard. She sat in the straight-back chair, her feet propped on the small wobbly table, the only other furniture in the room besides the bed and a bureau, and listened to the rain on the roof and the ping in the old galvanized bucket.

As soon as the rain stopped, Raynie left and stayed out until after ten. She wandered up and down the streets, looking for

HELP WANTED signs. She saw none. Then she sat in front of the cathedral at Jackson Square and listened to the street musicians. When she got back to the rooming house, she crept up the last few stairs after she saw light through the transom above the couple's door.

When the knock came, it jolted her awake, nearly midnight. Raynie lay rigid, her heart pumping so hard she could hear it. They knocked again. Her heart revved for fifteen minutes after she heard them leave, the lug soles of the boyfriend's boots thunking down the staircase.

She had trouble getting back to sleep. She blamed it on the heat, oppressive even though she lay in her underwear by the open window. But she couldn't get the image out of her mind— that big hand with its slow light touch on that long stretch of neck. The agitation set in again. How could they be so scary— and so sexy?

Daniel's hand, her neck: Raynie, sad that it wasn't exciting without the look of sexual abandon on the girl's face, cried herself to sleep.

—⚋—

Raynie's feet in their strappy, high-heeled sandals, her toenails painted cherry red, were tired. She walked up Royal Street, stopping in at the shops she'd passed up the first week she was in town, choosy before she'd been humbled by hearing, "Nothing right now; you know, the storm; business is slow; don't know if we can stay open; maybe in a couple of months," too many times. She was starving when she got to the newsstand at Canal for a morning paper. At a nearby coffee shop she looked for a bulletin board, hoping to find a woman in the Quarter who needed a roommate, but this shop didn't have a board. She pulled out the Classifieds and put them aside, too weary to look at them, too afraid that she was close to the last resort—grunge work in some two-star hotel or washing dishes in some dirty restaurant kitchen. She sipped a cup of coffee and slowly ate a large bran muffin, the cheapest item in the display case.

Desperation was not far away. Restaurants and cafés were eating her money, but loneliness was gnawing her spirit. She'd have gladly paid to talk to Bernie, even Peewee, but she knew if she called, she'd end up going home. Raynie was more homesick than she'd ever imagined, and she'd told herself many times over the months she'd planned her escape that she'd be lonely for a time, maybe a long time. She didn't want to give up for that reason. She told herself she wanted the comfort of home without having to be there.

Not that she particularly wanted to be here. She looked around the coffee shop—a seedy looking character, greasy hair, ripped khaki pants, his grimy fingers sunk into the cheese center of a Danish; a possible tourist couple, in shorts and new sneakers, but tourists were in short supply, one reason she couldn't get a job.

What could her mother have been talking about—such a glamorous city, so exciting, when she'd only been here as a child? Could the hurricane really have changed the city that much? She rested her chin in her palm, forgetting her muffin and coffee. Okay—she could imagine it being exciting, glamorous, just not in the present circumstances, the city's or hers. Imagine—dressed up, on the arm of a man in a well-cut suit like she saw in the magazines, walking along the lamp-lit, European-looking streets, dining in a crowded, expensive French Quarter restaurant... No, that was not her vision; it was her mother's.

Maybe she didn't want to be anywhere. Those months after her mother died, when she cried at night and asked, "How could you do this to me?" by which she meant leave her, only fourteen years old, to take care of two men who couldn't do a thing for themselves in a house. She'd thought about Marilyn Monroe killing herself when it all got to be too much.

Raynie's vision as she sat in the coffee shop on Royal Street? Her own naked body sprawled on the bed in the lonely, dingy room on Esplanade, the sheets twisted around her.

Raynie sighed. Death, especially suicide, was no more appealing to her now than it had been then. She had a zest for life she couldn't deny. She finished her muffin, poured herself a cup of milk from the serve-yourself stand when the girl behind the counter wasn't looking, and opened the Classifieds.

The ad caught her eye immediately, hostess at a restaurant on St. Louis Street, Le Tripot, around the corner, no more than two blocks away. She'd passed it last night—not the kind of place to put a HELP WANTED sign in the window.

APPLY IN PERSON, AFTER 2:00pm

Raynie folded the paper. She checked her watch. Less than three hours to figure out how to land this job.

—ഝ—

Raynie's eyes went out of focus, watching the Mississippi River from the Moon Walk. If she took it in from bank-to-bank, looked at it whole as it meandered its way along, pretty and tame as could be, a light lapping against the rocks under the boardwalk that went out over them. If she narrowed her gaze, she could see strange currents, some that seemed to go upstream, some that went down. They'd meet in a swift whirlpool that closed in on itself and disappeared. Treacherous water.

For pity's sake, what was she thinking? She had fifteen minutes before she walked over to Le Tripot. The only plan she'd come up with was to get there early. Beyond that, her brain refused to work. It drifted along with the river, random thoughts that disappeared like the whirlpools.

Her moment of panic ebbed as she remembered something

she'd read in an old magazine her mother had kept devoted to Marilyn Monroe on the twenty-fifth anniversary of her death, a reminiscence by one of Marilyn's friends who called her Norma Jeane.

Not long after *The Seven Year Itch* opened, the two women were walking along Fifth Avenue. Norma Jeane's friend, amazed, said, "I can't believe it—no one recognizes you!"

"That's because I'm not *her*," Norma Jeane said. "Watch."

Before the woman's eyes, Norma Jeane changed. "She became *Marilyn*. Her face got...soft, her eyes dreamy. She moved an entirely different way. We hadn't gone ten steps when people started turning around, staring. Then they realized who she was, and I thought we were going to be mobbed. We escaped into Bergdorf Goodman's."

Raynie sat up straight on the bench. What would happen if she tried that? She stood, smoothing her straight black skirt over her hips, stretching the ballet neck of her close-fitting sleeveless top wider across her shoulders. She wasn't as voluptuous as Marilyn— she thought of herself as more cat-like than bombshell. Her hair wasn't blond, but its dark brown made a nice contrast against her fair skin, and it fell in a wave above her blue eyes.

She started walking to the restaurant. She put one foot directly in front of the other to give more movement to her hips but felt like a slouchy runway model, not a sex goddess. She tried a little hip swing, but that felt slutty and silly. She pulled her shoulders back. Her neck got long, her head lifted. That was more like it. Interesting—the shoulders seemed to make it all work. This felt saucy, sexy, but she had no idea if this was the walk that turned Norma Jeane into Marilyn. Maybe it was all in her head and she only looked ridiculous. She lengthened her stride a bit. People were beginning to look. Even a couple of women. They didn't smile at her, but the men did. She tried a few variations—more hip, one shoulder raised, more bounce in her step, a toss of her hair as she looked left, then right at the intersection. Plenty of eyes on her. The hips, the shoulders, the hair—maybe none of that mattered. Maybe the *only* thing that mattered was in her head.

—⚊⚊—

Raynie breezed into the restaurant. The man behind a red buttoned leather, semi-circular counter just inside the door glanced up from the computer.

"I'm Raynie Devereux," she said, hearing her voice as a little breathy. Oddly, she didn't think he heard it that way, yet the effect... She had his full attention and struggled for a moment to keep her eyes on him. "I'm here for the hostess job. I'm a little early."

"That's fine," he said. "Why don't you sit over there?" He walked with her to a table for two in the front window, pulled out a chair for her. "Can I get you something to drink?"

She asked for a Coke. He went to the bar on the other side of the door. Raynie was concentrating too hard on herself to notice the red velvet curtains at the windows, the miniature Tiffany-type lamp on the table, the nude paintings, or the shadow-boxed corsets that hung on the dark red velvet-flocked wall behind her. She did notice the man—good-looking, smooth, sophisticated, beautifully dressed in a suit and tie, the tie snug against his collar, not a visible wrinkle—and if she didn't stop noticing she could end up tongue-tied. He was too old, anyway, a good fifteen years older than she was, maybe more. She adjusted her top over her shoulders, keeping that feeling in them even though she was seated, and took a deep steadying breath. She wasn't leaving this restaurant without a job.

The man slid the Coke in front of her and sat down opposite. He told her he was Pascal Legendre, the owner, and wanted to know if she was from New Orleans.

"I am now." Raynie told him how she'd always wanted to live here.

He was amazed that she'd picked this moment in time, when the city was still on its knees from Katrina, to make the move.

She put her elbows on the table, closer to him, and rested her chin on her clasped hands. "It doesn't matter when I got here, I'm here for good," she said. "I'm not just a good-times girl."

He smiled. Behind her the door to the restaurant opened. Mr. Legendre excused himself, and as he walked toward the door, Raynie turned to see two young women, one with long blond hair and a lot of makeup, wearing a very short, very low-cut dress. After her, the other couldn't help looking a little frumpy in her flat shoes and below-the-knee skirt.

The women were there about the job. Raynie turned back to face the interior of the restaurant. She was seriously sweating the blonde when she heard Mr. Legendre say, "Thanks for stopping by, ladies, but the position's been filled."

Karen walked over to La Costa Brava just before five o'clock. A two-top and a four-top were occupied in the dining room. At the four-top were LaDonna and two men in business suits, drinks and papers in front of them. If LaDonna looked at her as she passed in front of the window, it was a mere glance, her attention back to the GQ type doing most of the talking. The other one reminded Karen of a thug, Solo-genus, his back beefy under his dark jacket, not much of a neck. He rivaled Solo for best dressed, worst looking. His pitted nose was a real honker, brow bone of a cave man, one little pig eye darkly glinting from under that ledge.

"Who're the suits?" Karen asked Luc. She sat on the edge of a bar chair, liking the way he started making her a double cappuccino, her five o'clock habit, before she asked.

"Don't know. LaDonna's been in a seriously foul mood since I got here. Then they walk in. I make them as developers. It's just a matter of time before the Marigny goes the way of the Quarter—boutique hotels, condos, and theme cafés."

Karen shook her head. "Don't even say it. Hotels on Esplanade, but not back here. I haven't gotten the impression that LaDonna wants to sell. Did she say anything?"

He steamed the milk and put the cappuccino in front of her. "No, but the way she's been biting everyone's head off, she's acting like they might give her a cool million for the club if no one fucks up around here." He folded his arms, putting a little more distance than just the bar between them. "Is that why you're here? To make sure no one fucks up?"

"Are we back on the hard-ass thing?"

He unfolded his arms and leaned his hands on the bar. "Nobody really called you that." He smiled.

It was the first time they'd talked alone. Karen had watched him flirting with women all week. She wasn't sure if he was flirting now, but she liked his smile, his confidence, and she could feel something give inside, soften for him. She didn't like that. She was going with her first instinct: a good looking bastard.

"And I'm not really here to see that no one fucks up." She stood and finished off the cappuccino. "Fuck up all you want. For all we know, LaDonna's selling the place."

She set the cup on its saucer and stood, hanging her bag over her shoulder.

He pushed off the bar, arms folded again. "So what are you doing here?"

"I'm on at six, in the dining room."

"I'm out of here at seven. Meet me for a drink when you get off."

She hadn't expected that. "Where?" Then, "I might be tired.

I'm not used to the routine yet."

He flipped open a La Costa matchbook and wrote inside the cover. "My cell number. You might need to wind down." He pushed the matches across the bar, not handing them to her, but making it her choice. He kept his eyes on her, no smile, not at all flirty.

She took a step back from the bar, pushed the chair in. As she turned away she reached back for the matches. "Don't wait up or anything," she said and pocketed them.

—⚏—

Upstairs, Karen found the piles of paper on LaDonna's desk much the same as she'd left them the day before, the stack of unpaid bills with Karen's notes headlined URGENT on top. Some of the invoices were dated three months ago; most were to suppliers, the most alarming a few thousand to the liquor wholesaler.

Karen threw her purse on the sofa and sat with her feet on the edge of the coffee table. She'd spent every day for a week since she got back from Florida sorting LaDonna's papers, filing, looking at spreadsheets, and throwing out junk. Until LaDonna sat down with her, she couldn't do much more. From what Luc had said about LaDonna's mood, she was glad she'd been at her apartment, waiting for the moving van today. She hadn't rushed to the club but unpacked some boxes and made up her bed.

She called down to the dining room to see if the rest of the wait staff wanted to split her tables tonight. She needed a visible means of support, not to work herself to death, though the chances of that were slim if business stayed this slow. They wanted the tables, which they'd had before she came. LaDonna didn't need extra help in the dining room. Karen wasn't sure why she'd hired her.

She heard LaDonna on the stairs, then going down the hall to the room she used as her bedroom, a storage room with boxes pushed out of the way to make room for a mattress. She came into the office, looking nice in her summer dress, but also tense and tired.

"Girl, this has been a day," she said. She threw some papers on the coffee table then fell on the sofa, kicked off her heels and stretched her feet across the table. Head back against the cushion, eyes closed, she said, "You on tonight?"

"I gave my tables away."

LaDonna turned her head toward Karen to look at her.

"You said it yourself. Business is slow. You don't need me down there weeknights."

"I know, but I want you to work here, and eat and pay your rent."

Karen hesitated. "I think you have other things to worry about."

LaDonna turned away.

Karen said, "I think you need to at least look at those bills."

"You're right, honey. I'll get to 'em tomorrow." She closed her eyes again.

Karen thought that was her cue to leave. When LaDonna called her honey instead of girl, a certain tone in her voice, she seemed to be putting age and distance between them, telling Karen she was too young to be her confidante. Karen sat there until she worked up her nerve to say, "You know, my name's Honeycutt, not honey." LaDonna opened her eyes, gave Karen a hard look. "What's going on around here, LaDonna? Some of those bills are months old. You owe the supplier so much I'm surprised you have liquor down there."

"I changed wholesalers."

"Duck and run—yeah, that'll work."

"I'm paying cash for everything now."

"Uhm." Karen changed tactics. "You look nice in that dress. What's the peplum—thirties, forties? Shows off the weight you've lost."

"Ramon bought me this dress. After the storm."

"For fucksake, *Ramon*?"

"Yeah, Ramon…" LaDonna blinked rapidly. A solitary tear ran from her eye into her hair.

"Shit, LaDonna, I'm sorry."

"Don't be—Honeycutt. Just give me those Kleenex."

Karen got the box from a shelf behind the desk. "No, really, LaDonna," she said handing it to her, "I shouldn't have said that. If I'd been thinking, I would have figured you have a man problem."

LaDonna wiped her eyes and blew her nose. "Not any more, I don't. Son of a bitch been gone six months. What I got is a memory problem. I can't forget. No age or memory jokes either. I'm in mid-life crisis. I'm sensitive at the moment."

"Does that mean he left you for a younger woman? Or was he younger than you?"

LaDonna narrowed her eyes. "Both."

"How much younger?"

"Twenty-two years."

"Whoa," Karen said, rocking back into the sofa. "That explains the mid-life crisis but not the money crisis." She sat up again. "Or does it?"

"We had a goddamn hurricane." LaDonna's eyes filled, her voice wavered. "You get any smarter I'm gonna have to ask you to leave."

Karen put a hand on her arm. "You already decided you were going to tell me. Back when you asked me to do the office work. So tell me."

LaDonna wiped her eyes and laughed. "What? You grow balls while you were with Jack O'Leary?"

"A man like Jack, a woman needs a couple."

FIVE

Raynie walked down Decatur Street from the Canal Place Shopping Center, shoulders back, hips rocking and hair swinging. Inside the shopping bag she carried was a slinky calf-length black skirt slit to mid thigh and two halter tops, one a deep red, the other a leopard print, that she'd bought for her new job at Le Tripot. Mr. Legendre had told her the restaurant's name meant bawdy house in French.

She turned on St. Louis, heading for the Napoleon House down the street from Le Tripot. She'd have a drink to celebrate her new job then treat herself to dinner at the soul food restaurant around the corner from the rooming house.

Not yet six o'clock and already there was a line outside Le Tripot. Mr. Legendre had told her she'd have to handle the people who tried to move to the head of the line by claiming they'd made a reservation. He said they could get loud and hostile. Raynie felt up to handling anything, anybody. She could see a younger man in shirt sleeves, a garter around his arm, behind the leather counter checking the reservations list, a couple standing in front of him. He picked up two menus, and Raynie watched until he led the couple out of her line of vision before she crossed the street. She didn't see the cowboy come out of the side door to the restaurant and follow her into the Napoleon House.

He was on her heels when she stopped a couple of steps inside the door to let her eyes adjust to the shadowy world of the nineteenth century. All the tables were taken. Cocktail hour rowdiness bounced off the high ceiling and yellowed plaster walls. The best seat in the house was open, though, the chair at the end of the bar where she could sit up against the peeling wall and watch the crowd.

Raynie put her shopping bag on the chair next to her, ordered a Pimm's Cup and unzipped the little black purse she had slung diagonally across her chest. The cowboy strolled over, but there was too much noise for Raynie to hear his boot heels on the tile floor. He waited until she became aware of him.

"Oh," she said and moved the bag, putting it on the floor in front of her chair, glancing at him as he said, "Thanks—" lots of twang—but all she needed to see was the cowboy hat. Too much like home. She counted a few bills from her purse, zipped it and sat facing the bar.

The bartender returned with Raynie's drink, the cowboy ordered a Molson's then asked her, "What's that you're drinkin there?"

"Pimm's Cup," Raynie said without looking at him. She concentrated on getting a grip on the cucumber slice garnish.

"What's Pimm's Cup?" he said managing to get two syllables out of Pimm's.

Raynie looked up from her drink. "You're putting me on, right?"

"No, ma'am. I never heard of Pimm's Cup before."

"That's not what I mean," Raynie said. "That drawl—you sound like a bad movie or something."

"Well, ma'am," he said sitting a little taller, "I don't know what movies you been watchin but this's how we talk in Longview, Texas."

"Oh, now I've hurt your feelings," Raynie said. She was enjoying the mean streak she'd discovered in her new personality.

"You cain't hurt my feelins, ma'am. Not someone's pretty as you."

"You know, if there was a seat left in this place, I'd move. I came in here to have a drink all by myself. Then go home. All by myself. Not get picked up. Get it?"

The cowboy lifted his hands from the bar in protest and swiveled back and forth in his chair, saying no with his whole body. "Whoa there, little lady."

"For pity's sake—whoa there, little lady?"

"I'm sorry, ma'am, I really am…"

"Little lady? Ma'am? Everyone talks like that in Longview, Texas?"

He stuck a finger under his hatband and pushed the hat up on his head. Not a bad looking guy, if you liked cowboys.

"Well…" He considered her question. "Maybe not ever'one… Hey, how 'bout we start all over and this time I won't try to pick you up." He stuck out his hand. "My name's—"

Raynie lifted her hands as he had. "Whoa there, little man." She gave man a cowpoke-worthy extra syllable. "How 'bout no introductions. How 'bout we finish our drinks, decide not to talk to each other so we can't say anything personal, then we go our separate ways. No muss, no fuss, no future." The cowboy stared at her. "Tell you what. I'll give you a couple of minutes to think it over. Don't let the bartender take my drink."

She picked up her shopping bag and headed to the ladies room. She'd only gone a couple of steps when the cowboy said, "Hey." Raynie turned to look at him. "I wasn't gonna give you my real name."

No way he was getting the last word. "That's what I mean about personal," Raynie said. "That's way more than I want to know about you."

She turned fast and walked off with a Marilyn flounce.

—⁂—

The bitch deserved what he was getting ready to do to her. Big time deserved it. He took the small brown vial out of his jeans pocket and unscrewed the cap. He put the cap between his thighs. The bartender was busy at the other end of the bar; the guy sitting next to him had his back turned so he could paw the girl with him. The cowboy took Raynie's drink from the bar and quickly dumped the powdered contents of the vial into it. He put it back on its wet napkin, capped the vial, took a long chug from the Molson. His chin resting in his palm, he stirred Raynie's drink, a few lazy circles of the long straw she'd left in the tall slender glass, a show of distraction for the audience he always imagined was watching him.

He had an idea. He thumped the back of the guy next to him with his forearm and got an unfriendly over-the-shoulder look.

"Hey," he said, "you got a pen?" No trace of a twang or a drawl, no extra syllables.

The guy hesitated before he took a pen from his shirt pocket and handed it to the cowboy, who then crowded him to reach a stack of napkins on the narrow apron of the bar.

He wrote on a napkin, "Nothing personal. See ya later gator."

He left the guy's pen next to the napkin and walked out to St. Louis Street. He crossed to the opposite side to position himself to see the bar through the French doors that lined the St. Louis side of the Napoleon House. The restaurant across St. Louis also had a row of French doors, but his best shot of the girl put him in front of a couple dining behind him, a pane of glass away. He edged down to lean against the piece of concrete wall between two doors. Now the light was reflected so he couldn't see the end of the bar. Anywhere he stood, people from both places could see him. He was sure the white cowboy hat glowed in the dark. He was almost itching with conspicuousness. He thought about tossing the hat in the trash can at the corner, but he'd just bought it that afternoon from Meyer the Hatter, and it hadn't been cheap.

Maybe he'd been hasty to leave the bar. He broke into a sweat when he realized he'd forgotten to tell the bartender the girl was coming back, leave her drink. His vial was empty; he'd crushed his last tablet.

A wave of anger made his skin feel hot and prickly. Where was the little bitch, anyway? Judas Priest, the amount of time women could spend in a bathroom. She could be in a line of women. He was on fire thinking the only thing to do was run back into the bar and save her drink, if it wasn't already down the drain.

Then he saw her coming from the direction of the courtyard. She looked as though she was heading to the door. "Son of a bitch," he said. A couple walking down the street gave him a wide berth. She hesitated a moment, changed directions and went back to the bar. The cowboy scraped his shoulder falling against the concrete, he was so relieved. He had saddlebags of sweat under his arms.

—⁂—

While Raynie put on some lipstick and fluffed her hair in the bathroom mirror, she decided she'd had enough of Mr. Longhorn or wherever it was he said he'd come from. She remembered when she'd sat in the courtyard once seeing a long brick-walled corridor with a gate to the street. She left the bathroom and cut through the courtyard only to find the gate locked. She'd have to go through the front room in full view of the bar. If he saw her and tried to follow...well, she'd think of something.

He wasn't at the bar. His beer bottle was pushed away as though he'd finished it; her drink—she hadn't drunk half of it— sat where she'd left it.

Raynie looked toward the men's room to make sure he wasn't coming out of it and went to the bar. She saw the napkin. What an idiot. But he was gone. She sat in the chair, put her shopping bag in front of it, and resumed her evening. She sipped her drink and watched the crowd. Most of all she enjoyed being Raynie Devereux who was much more real since she'd gotten a job. She thought about Earlene Dick. She was different now. The way she'd handled the cowboy. The way she didn't mind so much being alone. No, she was happy to be alone, to think about her new life that started tomorrow, but for tonight aloof, unapproachable, the mysterious woman at the bar.

It didn't last long. Raynie started feeling weird. Everything was getting kind of blurry. She thought for a minute she might fall out of her chair. One drink never did this to her. Maybe Pimm's Cup was one of those liquors that was a lot stronger than it tasted. When was the last time she'd eaten? That muffin? She couldn't remember. She didn't feel bad; she felt pretty good even if her equilibrium was off. She'd better get back to the rooming house and get something to eat.

She bent to pick up her shopping bag and had to hold on to the bar to keep from falling out of the chair. She got to the doorway okay but was confused about which way to walk. All she knew was she'd better walk. Her legs—hm, what were they? Slippery little devils. Like eels. Raynie got this image of herself walking down the street on two eels, each of them wanting to slither off in a different direction. Funny if you thought about it.

She went straight. She passed in front of the Royal Orleans Hotel. The doorman in full dress was her last memory. She wouldn't remember that he said, "Hey, baby, you okay?" She wouldn't remember the cowboy saying to him, "A little too much sauce. Couldn't wait for me to pay the bill." She wouldn't remember that the cowboy no longer talked with that drawl or that he put his arm around her to hold her up or that by the time they got to the end of the block and turned down Royal Street she tried to push him away.

She only tried once. After that it was all she could do to put one foot in front of the other.

SIX

LaDonna told Karen that when she met Ramon, she fell harder than she ever remembered falling before, even as a twenty-year old whose first big love was a musician who played at the club, the son of one of her father's old band members. He'd gone to New York to seek fame and fortune, which he never found, but wouldn't let her go with him. It seemed to her that she'd cried for a year.

Ramon had stars in his eyes too. He wanted to make films. After LaDonna told him about her famous first love, he decided to start his career with an hour-long docu-drama about a New Orleans musician and his band, a behind-the-scenes look at their personal lives and the business: plenty of music, sex, and show-stopping outfits.

"He said I was his muse, and I fell for it, Honeycutt, just like I was twenty years old all over again. He said if the band decided to leave New Orleans, we'd both follow them."

As plans progressed, Ramon got more ambitious: a series of shows—a chef, a club owner, a landlord—he'd pitch to cable TV to make seed money for a feature film.

"A landlord?" said Karen.

"Well, you know, he was spinning ideas. He's the inventive type, can make a day in the life of a landlord sound interesting—an apartment building, a couple of cross dressers, an exotic dancer, a dominatrix..."

Karen nodded. "I get it. The personalities and occupations change, but there's always, sex, music and outfits."

They had already started shooting when Ramon's money-man had trouble closing a deal and the cash flow stopped. Ramon asked LaDonna to fund the show until the deal went through. LaDonna took out a short-term loan, using the club as collateral. Along came Katrina. The money- man's deal never closed, and a few months later the bank called the loan. Karen wanted to know why they wouldn't roll it over.

"They did, but I couldn't make the payments. What we're saying here is no business after the floods."

"How much money are you talking about?"

"Fifty thousand. Ramon's sayin he should have some money for me by the end of the month. He's negotiating with Showtime. I'm sure he'll be wildly successful out there."

"Where is he?"

"L.A."

"Permanently?"

"Who knows? At least until Bebe Boudreau—the Zydeco musician? The subject of the pilot. Till Bebe calms down. Ramon ran off with some of his money too. And his girlfriend."

"So no more Bebe, no more docu-drama? I thought it was called a reality show."

"Who cares what the fuck it's called. It ain't hap'nin. There was nobody here to work after the storm. Bebe wasn't even here. He went back to Lafayette, to his roots, he said. Ramon hung for about a month, then he went to Lafayette, and took la *chiquita* to L.A. At least the first star didn't take another woman with him."

"But, still," Karen said, "same thing all over again."

"The way Ramon sees it, everything happens for a reason."

"What reason? New Orleans got wiped out because of all our sins and corruption? The Decadence Festival?"

LaDonna waved her off. "Ramon's not a religious fanatic. He

isn't talking about the big picture. He doesn't talk about anything but himself."

"What's he into? There are no coincidences, only signs?"

"That's not guy-think, Honeycutt. What he says, all this forces him to set the shows in a larger, more universal venue. L.A. He says he was headed there anyway."

"He explained this to you?"

"Uh-huh. The muse, remember? He got in a habit of telling me everything a while back."

Karen said, "Calling regularly, is he? He left, what, six months ago? Don't tell me—there's trouble in paradise. Bebe's girlfriend is homesick or something."

"She misses her mama."

"For Christ sake. How old is she?"

"Eighteen." LaDonna held up her hand.

"I wasn't going to say anything."

"Like hell. And speaking of mothers, yours dropped by a couple of weeks ago, a few days before you strolled back to town, come to think of it."

"The woman has radar," Karen said.

"Why didn't you tell her you were coming back?" LaDonna cut Karen a look. "Or is she psychic?"

"That's what she'd say. But let's not get off on her quite yet. What are you going to do about the loan? Can you go to another bank?"

LaDonna shook her head. "It's taken care of."

Karen glanced at the papers on the coffee table. "The men you were with downstairs?" When LaDonna didn't answer, Karen said, "Don't tell me you sold the place. Luc said you might."

That irritated LaDonna. "Luc Celestin needs to keep his stuff to himself. He's the only male busybody I know who isn't gay. No, I didn't sell it."

"Are you thinking about selling?"

"I don't know."

"Do you want to?"

"I don't know. I don't know what I want to do. It's everybody's problem around here. It's the Katrina effect."

"What you need to do is figure out if someone's ripping you off. The receipts look like most of the town's already evacuated for the next big one, but still, the liquor disappears."

"Maybe you can figure it out."

"Maybe you could give a shit, LaDonna."

"Maybe I will." LaDonna stood up and went to her desk.

Karen took her compact from her purse to check her makeup. LaDonna said, "You haven't called your mama?"

Karen got out a lipstick. "I'm not ready to have my life taken over by swamis and shamans and psychic healers yet."

"She says she's done with all that New Age crap. That's a direct quote. She's using her own name again."

Karen looked up from the mirror. "You've got to be kidding? No more Moksa Prana?"

"Nope. She's Judy Honeycutt, and she's an entre-preneur."

"Oh yeah? And what kind of business is Mom entrepreneur-ing?"

"Fixing up storm-wrecked houses."

Karen made a face. "She works for a contractor, has for years. How does that make her an entrepreneur?"

"She got her own contracting business. Brought the labor in here with her, good-lookin thing, lot of muscle, him hanging all over her. She said he convinced her. Otherwise, she thought about a day spa. Says she considered manufacturing wigs, maybe buying into a direct mail company, maybe taking over a car detail shop."

Karen put the last touch on her lipstick and snapped the compact shut. "There's always a world of possibilities with Mom." She went to the small bathroom off LaDonna's office and opened the door so she could see herself in its full length mirror.

"What's with all the mirror gazing?" LaDonna said.

"Luc offered to buy me a drink."

"Now there's a worthless hunk of stuff."

"It's something to do."

"At least he's your age."

Karen turned to her. "You know, I don't really think age is such a big deal."

"Good," LaDonna said. "You can try to convince me of that sometime."

Karen called Luc from LaDonna's office. LaDonna was sitting at the desk now. She said she was going to get some work done. She stopped shuffling paper to listen to Karen's end of the conversation.

When Luc answered his cell phone Karen could hear a lot of background noise.

"Hold on," he said. "Let me step outside so I can hear you."

She could hear his muffled voice talking to someone. She said to LaDonna, "He's with someone, maybe a date."

"I got to admit," he said a few seconds later, "I'm surprised you called."

"Of course you are. I'm supposed to be working."

"I mean I'm surprised—never mind. I'm glad you called."

"I'd be lying if I said I'm into spontaneity, although sometimes it works out," she said. LaDonna nodded her approval. "Where are you?"

"Harry's Bar."

They both waited for the other one to say something. Karen said, "We can have that drink another time."

"Hell no. I'm not going to give you time to change your mind. Give me half an hour, and we can have it tonight. Tell me where."

"I'll meet you there." Karen gave LaDonna a wicked smile.

"No. I'm ready to blow out of here."

"Do you know Tom River's Ace?"

"Right down the street. Half hour."

Karen hung up. "He's dumping a date to meet me."

LaDonna said, "Honeycutt, never let it be said I didn't tell you that when they're young snakes, they don't even know they're snakes yet."

SEVEN

The girl didn't weigh much, but she was going to be dead weight soon. The cowboy was at the corner of Royal and Dumaine, seriously regretting that he hadn't caught a cab when he was in front of the Royal O, even if he'd had do to it with that palace-guard doorman watching. He shifted her weight against him to get a better grip on her. Her right tit was proving to be a nice little handle, but he moved his hand below it so he could concentrate better. He wasn't sure he should take her to his apartment, which was five blocks away on Bourbon or just check into the hotel three blocks away at the corner of Dumaine and Burgundy. The real problem was what to do with her afterwards. He didn't want her to wake up at his apartment; if he checked into the hotel he could just leave her there. But how the shit was he going to explain her condition when he checked in? By the time he walked another three blocks he was going to have to sling her over his shoulder.

He had one more block before he had to decide. Judas Priest this girl was heavy. He got that feeling, his skin crawling with red ants. He clutched the girl so tight she moaned.

"Walk you stupid bitch," he said.

—◊—

On her way to meet Luc, Karen stopped at her apartment on

St. Philip to change out of her work clothes. She wanted to make it quick so she could get to the Ace a little early, do some catching up with Tom Rivers. LaDonna told her he'd opened soon after the storm, still the watering hole of choice for the people who worked at the TV station around the corner and the restaurant workers who came after hours to unwind.

She let loose her streaky blond hair from its ponytail, shed her jeans and La Costa Brava T-shirt, and put on a short red stretch skirt with a black top that laced up the back. She decided the outfit was too overtly sexy. She stood in front of her closet, staring into it, pushing a hanger back now and then. She took out a pair of pants, held them up to look at them and discarded them on the bed. She did the same with another pair of pants, a skirt and a couple of dresses. She checked her watch, said, "For Christ sake," decided to wear the red skirt, went to her dresser, and took a black spandex camisole from the top drawer. She put it on and over it a sheer T-shirt silk-printed with a woman smoking a long cigarette. The cigarette was a man. On top of his head at the glowing tip was a red rhinestone. In her hand the woman held a pack of cigarette-men, brand name Lumels.

Good outfit, but choosing it had used up most of the time Karen had hoped to spend with Tom Rivers. She raced through the courtyard and cursed the worn lock on the tall wood gate to the street that demanded a safe cracker's touch to open.

She turned up Bourbon to walk to Dumaine, not too many people on the street in this residential part of the Quarter. She'd walked a half block when she spotted a couple crossing Bourbon on Dumaine, a cowboy with a date who looked more than just a few sheets gone. Her feet managed a step now and again, but the man was mostly dragging her. He had to jostle her up the curb. Her head flopped forward, and she dropped the shopping bag she was carrying. The cowboy didn't see it.

"Hey," Karen called, "you dropped your bag."

He didn't hear her. They went past the corner building, and Karen couldn't see them. She ran to the corner and picked up the bag. The couple hadn't gotten very far. The girl was no longer on her feet at all; the cowboy had stopped to figure out how best to carry her.

Karen heard him speak roughly to her, calling her a bitch. He shook her. The way her head flopped she'd get whiplash.

"Hey," Karen called again, moving toward him.

The cowboy jerked around to look at her as the girl's head fell toward him. He cracked his jaw on the side of it. "Shit," he said.

As Karen came up, the cowboy grabbed the lower part of the girl's face. It looked as though he was going to try to twist her head off.

"What are you doing?" Karen said.

The cowboy stood still a second, then he shoved the girl backwards into Karen and took off running.

Karen struggled to keep herself and the girl upright. Even though she wasn't as tall as Karen and quite thin, Karen couldn't hold her for long. She tried to maneuver her toward the wall of a house only a couple of steps away, but she wasn't going to be able to carry her that far. She might drop her, crack her head against the stucco wall, or fall down with her.

She was trying to get her to the ground as easy as possible when she heard someone walking up behind her. She glanced over her shoulder to see Luc.

"Karen, what's going on?"

"Her date just unloaded her on me."

"You know her?"

"No."

Luc pulled the girl's arm around his shoulder. "Let's get her to the stoop there."

"If we put her down, I'm not sure we'll get her back up. My place is just around the corner on St. Philip."

"I hope she doesn't get sick all over us."

"She's not drunk. That guy slipped her something."

"Then let's call 911. Let them deal with it."

"Where will they take her? Where's the new Charity Hospital since the old one got flooded? Do you feel like spending the night at some hospital in East Fuckover? I don't."

"There's a charity hospital. I think they're using University Hospital. It's not far."

"They'll want someone to go with her."

"We don't have to go."

"Then what? She wakes up all alone tomorrow morning, no idea what happened to her? Let's go to my place."

Holding her arms over their shoulders, supporting her at the waist, they carried Raynie to Karen's.

When they got to the wood gate, Karen put the key in the lock and tried to get it to turn while supporting her half of Raynie's weight with her hip. She jiggled the key, worked it gently, lost patience, and gave it a vicious twist. "You try it," she said to Luc. "It needs testosterone."

First try, the lock turned. Luc pushed the gate open with his foot.

—⚇—

They dropped Raynie on Karen's bed, lifted her head so Karen could get the purse over it, and swung her legs up on the mattress. Raynie's skirt inched up her thighs. Karen pulled it down.

"Let's take her shoes off," she said and started unbuckling the one closest to her.

Luc lifted Raynie's leg. From under it he got the lace-up top Karen had rejected earlier. He rubbed it between his fingers and held it by its shoulder straps. "Nice little number. Not as cute as the one you have on."

Karen took it and threw it over the back of a chair. "There's a bottle of rum on a table in the living room. I could use a Cuba Libre," she said.

"Okay, boss." Luc left the room.

The red polish on the girl's toenails was chipped, the shoe Karen held was scuffed from dragging along the sidewalk. She watched the girl breathe, her breaths deep and even. With a soft moan, the girl turned. Karen gathered the rest of her clothes from the bed and tossed them to the chair. She listened to the girl breathing again, then she kicked off her shoes, picked up the girl's purse from the floor and opened the French doors to the courtyard. She crossed the courtyard barefoot to the living room where she opened the two sets of doors. The apartment was laid out in an L. Karen was paying more rent than she could afford without the money in the safe deposit box, but the private courtyard, like another room with all the doors open, was worth it. She turned on the ceiling fan, sat on the sofa, and emptied the little black purse.

A lipstick rolled out on the coffee table. There was a compact, a small box of soft brown eye shadow, an eyebrow pencil, a folding comb, twenty-two dollars, and loose change at the bottom of the purse. No wallet. Inside a zippered pocket was more money and a key. Karen was counting the money out on the table, six one-hundred dollar bills, when Luc came in with the drinks.

"She's not broke," he said.

"No ID," Karen said. She put all the makeup back in the purse, folded the money and zipped it along with the key in the inside pocket.

Luc handed Karen her drink and sat beside her. "What are you—Mother Teresa or something? Take care of the poor, the sick, the needy, bring home perfect strangers, put them in your bed?"

"Do I have to be Mother Teresa to help a poor kid who almost got raped tonight? I came along, it's up to me to help her. Do you have a problem with that?"

"Take it easy. So you played the Good Samaritan. It's not what I expected, that's all."

"You expected hard-ass Honeycutt to leave an unconscious woman on the sidewalk and go have a drink?"

"Why are you so pissed?"

"I'm not."

He'd hit a nerve, though, with that Mother Teresa stuff. The last thing Karen wanted to be was someone who took care of other people. The whole time she was growing up her mother had acted as if she was running some kind of missionary refugee camp, a string of needy people moving in and out of the house, most of them women. From her bedroom Karen would listen to them cry, her mother talking softly to them. There would be the occasional hysterical laughter then more crying. In the morning the house would smell like a Catholic church from all the candles they'd light to whatever saint needed to intervene. As the years passed they made a subtle shift into the New Age. They still lit candles and they still liked the Virgin Mary and the saints, but they began to talk about things like karma and becoming one with the universe, guru-talk. Karen's mother became a guru junkie. The most potent gurus were the ones who helped her get in touch with her spiritual self by screwing her all the way to enlightenment, liberation, reincarnation, whatever.

Karen said, "I'm not Mother Teresa, okay?"

"Okay."

"Or the Good Samaritan."

"Got it."

"Or hard-ass Honeycutt."

"I'm sorry I ever brought that up. I only heard a couple of people call you that."

"I believed you the first time."

They sipped at their drinks until Luc said, "Why did you call me tonight?"

"You offered to buy me a drink, remember?"

"Yeah, but you're not desperate for someone to buy you a drink, and you don't seem too interested in me. If you've been talking to LaDonna or looking at the paperwork, and you want to know if I'm stealing from the bar, I'm not."

"You just got more interesting."

"No offense taken. LaDonna probably doesn't remember, but I told her one of the bartenders was stealing. I didn't tell her I'd put my money on Little Joe, but I would."

Little Joe had been hanging around the Quarter since the sixties, an old hippie with his long hair and the faded tattoo of a peace symbol on his forearm.

Karen said, "You usually work with him on Saturday nights."

"I've never seen him pocket any money or even give a drink away. But sometimes I don't come in until the late shift on the weekends and he works alone a couple of nights a week. I say it's him because he's got the most opportunity. Zachary only works part time."

"Why do you think somebody's stealing?"

"Because LaDonna's always complaining that things are slow. She cut back on kitchen and wait staff, let one bartender go. If things are that slow why are we using the same amount of liquor?"

Karen nodded. "I'll take care of it."

He stared at her for a few seconds. "Where did you come from, Karen? All of a sudden you show up out of nowhere and start running the show. Not that somebody doesn't need to since Boy Wonder left."

"Ramon?"

"Yes, but we're talking about you."

She picked up her drink and settled back into the corner of the sofa. "Like you said, out of nowhere. I came back home."

Luc waited, but when she didn't say anything more, he said, "The way you talk, a little bored by everything, defensive but not giving anything up—if you didn't look so healthy I might think you just got out of jail."

Karen laughed. "In a way, I just did."

Luc waited again, then said, "But you'll tell me about that some other time."

"Maybe."

"Is this the way you flirt? A lot of women like to be aloof. They keep themselves at a distance, but you can tell they're interested by the way they look at you out of the corner of their eyes or the way they toss their hair or move a shoulder. Even when they're trying hard not to act interested, something gives them away. The way they circle a foot. Especially when they're wearing those beg-me-to-step-on-your-balls high heels."

Karen folded her legs up on the sofa. "You're showing off now."

They both jumped when the girl cried out from the bedroom. Karen ran through the courtyard and stood by the side of the bed. The girl had been restless, her skirt hiked up to her underpants, one arm flung over her head. Her cheeks were slightly flushed. She didn't look old enough to drink legally. Karen watched until she settled down into a deep sleep.

When she got back to the living room Luc had taken off his shoes, stretched his legs out, his feet on the coffee table, ankles crossed. Karen folded one leg under her and sat down. "She's still out."

"You really think she's okay, sleeping it off?"

"Probably."

"Probably. Is that good enough for you."

"Nervous, aren't you."

"Yeah, I suppose I'm nervous. Yeah. Definitely. An unconscious woman makes me nervous. What I don't understand, why aren't you nervous?"

"I've seen it before. She'll sleep eight or ten hours, wake up tired, and she won't remember what happened."

"This happened to you?"

Karen hesitated before she said, "When I was in high school. I used to sneak down to the Quarter with this fake ID I got from a guy on Decatur Street. I'd tell my mother I was spending the night out with a friend."

She'd only caught Karen once, and then she'd bought Karen's story that she'd changed plans, gone to another friend's house and forgot to call. Her mother let it go because she was tired of fighting and because she was giving her attention, most of it, to—who was it then? The Sikh? Maybe the swami. She always got the two of them confused.

"Did you remember the guy?" Luc asked.

"He's all I remembered, this nice guy, very polite, interested in everything I had to say—very seductive—until I woke up the next morning in a cab. The driver was hanging over the seat in my face, yelling, 'Young lady, we're in the Quarter. Any place in particular you wanna go?' When I tried to pay him he said my boyfriend had taken care of it."

She'd been too scared, too humiliated to ask the driver where he'd picked her up. Later, it made her feel dumb that she let fear and humiliation keep her from asking. She took a bus out to the lakefront and walked three blocks home, got her key from her bag—miraculous she still had the bag with her—and let herself into the lower duplex. When she opened the door, she expected fireworks. She could hear her mother on the phone in the kitchen; by her tone she could tell she was talking to the Sikh. She eased the front door closed.

Karen went down the hallway and opened the unlocked door to her bedroom. She closed the wide open window behind her bed. She took a long shower, hot as she could stand it, then in pajamas, she walked into the kitchen.

Her mother was still on the phone. "Hold on a minute," she said putting the phone under her chin. To Karen: "You're up early." It was ten thirty; Karen never got up before noon on Saturdays. Taking in Karen's wet hair, her mother said, "Are you going somewhere?"

"To bed. I'm not feeling so well."

"I'll be in to check on you," her mother said and resumed her phone conversation.

Karen crawled under the covers, thinking, not this way; it wasn't supposed to happen this way, until she fell into a fitful sleep.

Luc said, "Did you ever see the man again?"

"No, but I looked for him every time I went downtown. I didn't know what I'd do if I ever found him, but that didn't stop me from looking."

"You never told your mother?"

"I never told anyone."

Luc took his feet off the coffee table, drew one leg up on the sofa, his arm stretched along the back. He put his hand on her shoulder. "Do you want some help looking for the cowboy?"

Karen looked down. Luc's knee rested against hers. When she looked up she said, "You know what the guy was wearing who gave me the drug?"

"What?"

"A safari jacket."

EIGHT

Raynie slept fitfully all night, coming in and out of consciousness long enough to wonder where she was but not long enough to care before she'd fall asleep again.

On the white wrought-iron daybed at the far end of the long living room, Karen couldn't sleep at all. At first it was because of the girl's thrashing and moaning, occasionally calling out the name Daniel. Karen had checked on her several times, Luc's uneasiness over not taking the girl to the hospital attaching to her as soon as he left. Within the hour, though, the girl's eyes started fluttering, and Karen went back to bed, figuring the girl would get up early and in a panic.

Still she couldn't sleep for thinking about Luc, men in general. She was attracted to Luc and that annoyed her. She'd come home with the idea of staying away from men, not dating, see how several months, even a year or two, without a man shaped her. LaDonna had told her once that if she hadn't gotten a divorce, she wouldn't have become who she was. The last three months with Jack, Karen had thought about that a great deal. These days every woman was supposed to know that you shouldn't let your life be defined by a man, but she couldn't think of anyone who paid much attention to that, though they'd all say they did.

So let's say you avoided becoming defined by a man. The problem was how did you fall in love, give a relationship the attention it needed to thrive, and not become defined by it? Was the only solution to be alone?

Like LaDonna. Except that after seven long years alone, look what had happened to her. Maybe sex was like sweets: deprive yourself too long and all it takes is one irresistible confection, put together just so, one tiny taste, and you go on a binge.

Her mind floating amid these questions and their no-easy answers, Karen finally fell asleep. She woke up to see the girl standing over her, holding a bottle of Jack Daniels by its neck, like a club.

Karen sat bolt upright and screamed. The girl took a step back and screamed too.

Karen scrambled from the day bed saying, "Wait, wait, it's okay," and fumbling with the switch on the lamp next to the bed, nearly knocked it off its table.

Raynie crumbled to the floor. She sobbed as she clutched the bottle of Jack in her lap.

"Hey," Karen said softly. She reached down and took the bottle. "Come on, come sit on the sofa with me, we'll sort everything out."

"What happened to me?" She wiped the tears off her face with the back of her hand.

"Luckily not much," Karen said, "except that a man loaded your drink. Do you remember him?"

The girl let herself drop into the sofa. She didn't answer. Karen went off to the kitchen and poured a glass of orange juice. The hands of the big, blue rimmed wall clock above the stove moved to six o'clock. As Karen sat on the sofa facing the French doors, dawn was just beginning to turn the sky milky. She said, "He had on a cowboy hat," and held out the glass of juice.

The girl turned to her but didn't take the glass. "Who are you?"

"Karen Honeycutt. I ran into him dragging you down Dumaine Street. He wasn't talking so nice to you. When I asked him what he was doing, he shoved you over to me and took off down the street."

"I left the bar with him?"

"I don't know. Here." Karen put the glass of juice in front of her.

Raynie took it. "No, no I didn't. I left alone."

"And that's probably the last thing you remember."

"I was very woozy. And the drink. The drink tasted funny." She told Karen about going to the bathroom, finding the note from the cowboy. "Oh my God, I could have been raped." She looked at Karen. "I don't think I was raped." She seemed to be asking Karen for a definitive answer.

"I don't think you were. I think he was taking you somewhere, but you might want to get checked out."

Raynie nodded and looked away from Karen, embarrassed. She sipped the juice and put it on the coffee table.

"What's your name?" Karen asked her.

The girl's head jerked toward her. She looked perplexed, then she panicked. "My clothes, oh my God, I've lost my clothes. What day is it? If I've lost that job..."

"Hold it. I've got your clothes." From the bedroom Karen got her purse, shoes and the shopping bag. "Are these the clothes you mean? And it's Thursday, barely. Six a.m."

Raynie went through the bag. "Thank you, thank you. I don't know how to thank you."

"Just tell me you remember your name. There's no ID in your purse."

Raynie sat up straight. Karen watched as she composed herself, smoothed her hair back.

"I'm Raynie Devereux. From Rayne, Louisiana."

She told Karen she'd moved from the backwater to the big city to make a new life for herself, that she'd lived on a frog farm and didn't want to spend the rest of her life growing frogs, selling them, and frying up frog legs. Frogs were all that was left from

Earlene Dick's life.

"Who's Daniel?"

Karen watched as Raynie cast her eyes down. She picked up her purse and played with the toggle on the zipper before she looked up, frowning, and said, "Daniel? I don't know. Why do you ask?"

"Because you called his name several times last night."

Her face softened.

This one, though, was quick. She tilted her head and one side of her mouth tipped up, a playful, quizzical smile. "The man of my dreams?" She shrugged, unzipped her purse, and counted her money.

—∞—

Karen had thought a lot about money in her life, the usual—that there wasn't enough and how to get more of it. It had been nice, thinking of all that money in the safe deposit box, a different kind of feeling. It was as though she didn't have to scrounge any more, yet it wasn't freedom from worry because of Solo lurking with his unfailing memory, and it wasn't a lifting of the crushing weight of credit card debt; she barely maintained staying below max-out level. It didn't have to do with the ability to go shopping whenever she wanted. Karen hadn't spent a frivolous dime unless her two acrylic nails fell into that category, and in her mind they didn't.

What did it matter? The feeling was an illusion since she couldn't leave Jack to Solo and keep the cash, but she'd rented an apartment she couldn't afford based on something that felt all warm and fuzzy, for Christ sake.

Raynie zipped her cash into the inside pocket of her purse. "At least he didn't take my money. It's all I have left." She looked around the living room as if she was just now taking it in. "This is a nice place. Now that I have a job maybe I'll be able to afford something like this soon."

"Where are you working?"

"This'll be my first day. Le Tripot. Over on St. Louis?"

"I know the place. It's all decked out to look like a whorehouse. People like to say there're rooms on the third floor. I even know a few men who claim they've been upstairs with the help, but they're probably full of it."

Raynie looked faintly alarmed. "What are you saying?"

"Nothing. It's just rumors. You work there long enough, you'll find out."

"Maybe I don't want to find out."

"I mean, you'll find out they're rumors. Don't worry about it. It's a very hot restaurant right now. You'll do fine there. People tip well when their imaginations are engaged."

Raynie pictured men putting money down the waitresses' bras, snapping it under their garters. "I'm not a waitress," she said. "I'm the hostess."

"Even better. They'll be laying money on you to get them the best tables—next to Lulu White's corset, the painting of the redheaded nude…"

"What is it, some kind of men's club?"

"Believe it or not, women like to go as much as men. Watch the lunch crowd. Four-tops of women on both floors."

Raynie made a face. "That's weird."

"Yeah, but when you think about it, it's not any weirder than women who like all that gangsta rap about pimps and whores. Look, why don't you take a shower. I'll take you to breakfast. You'll feel a lot better."

By the time they finished pecan waffles, scrambled eggs, and a pot of coffee at Café Envie on Decatur, Karen had asked Raynie if she wanted to move in with her for a while. Raynie thought the daybed in Karen's living room was a luxury after the Goth mansion where the foot of her bed was always damp. As they walked over to Esplanade to get Raynie's things, she told Karen about the red, white and blue rat and the crucified doll in the next-door apartment.

But Karen had lived in downtown New Orleans too many years to be bothered by anyone's kinky idea of cool. What gave her the creeps was the hole in the ceiling straight through to the roof above the stairway, and Raynie's room, the dirt embedded in the floor, caked on the window sills, filmed over the glass panes, the grubby stained mattress, the mildewed bathroom down the hall. She'd lived in a few places that had the same stink—old house, mold, cockroach shit—but none that rivaled this, none with gaping holes in the roof, not even one of those blue FEMA tarps to cover it.

She started to wish she'd never taken the money from the hotel safe, because standing here in the middle of this squalid, expensive tenement room, she feared ever being without it.

—⁓—

Karen drove out to the suburbs to see her mother in LaDonna's Classic Silver Prius, which Ramon had insisted she buy so she could be environmentally conscientious like the Hollywood celebs he'd read about in *Us Weekly*. Driving to Metairie she thought about what would happen when Jack showed up, which she expected any time now. No matter where her thoughts turned— to handing the money over to Jack, the phone call to Solo, the showdown between Solo and Jack—her imagination stalled. It was all too unpleasant; her mind resisted believing that any one of these scenes could become reality. The only thing real was the money. She had held it in her hands, counted it, placed it in the safe deposit box, taken five hundred dollars out this morning after seeing Raynie off to Le Tripot. Real, yes, but elusive. Karen had never been able to hold on to money. It slipped through her fingers like slick well-dressed men.

Judy Honeycutt lived in a tan brick box of a house on a quiet street lined with similar houses, half dozen different facades and shades of brick if you counted. The roll-down steel storm covers over the windows of several homes had been there long before the hurricane. The owners had used them more for security than storms. As usual they were rolled down tight on enough houses to give the neighborhood a blank, uninhabited look. A few FEMA trailers sat in front of houses.

Her mother's block showed the mark of Katrina—trees cut to stumps, blue tarps flapping on roofs, landscaping a little rough around the edges, big brown spots on the lawns—but when Karen pulled up in front of her mother's house she saw that the patchy grass and the weeds that had once grown up close to the foundation had become a thick manicured lawn and flowerbeds. The best looking house on the block, gardenia bushes loaded with flowers and a young crape myrtle tree blooming near the curb. An overflowing basket of impatiens decorated the small concrete entranceway to the house.

As soon as Karen cut the engine, the front door flew open and her mother came running down the walkway to her. Gone were the flowing clothes Karen had last seen her wearing, that she'd worn for years, long black skirts and wide-legged pants with tunic tops and loose jackets in dull floral patterns that might have been inspired by turn-of-the-last-century upholstery. Today she wore a body-hugging sun dress, her preference still florals but not your grandma's sofa. A white dress splashed with bright red flowers, sophisticated, up-to-date. Now. Finally, she was showing her body, rich-bitch thin and hard from her yoga practice.

Gone too were the sturdy Birkenstocks and thick-soled walking shoes. The spike heels on her pink thong sandals tapped down the walk, red toenails glittering, and her hair, released from its messy barrette-anchored upsweep, swung free, grazing her shoulders.

As they embraced Karen said, "Mom, you're transformed. The only thing I recognize are your glasses." Her large thick-rimmed tortoise-shells.

Judy hooked her arm through Karen's to walk her to the house. "Karen, a woman needs to reinvent herself at certain stages of her life. She needs to…" her hand spiraled through the air "… recapture her youthful enthusiasm."

She stopped before the step to the doorway so she could face Karen. The sun made her red highlights, salon-bought reinvention, sparkle.

"You know how there are times in your life when possibilities are all around you, there are choices in front of you, but none of them seem quite right?"

Karen recognized the talk, what she used to call swami-talk, the calm, quiet tone that started out with a question then went into words of wisdom.

"That is a time when you must be still and be with yourself. It is not a time for decisions. You must sit and wait. I don't mean that you give up. You face the uncertainty and wait until you know deep down what is right for you."

It must have been ninety-eight degrees on the blazing concrete. Karen felt a bead of sweat work its way into her cleavage. "You know what Dr. Phil said?"

"No."

"He said there are no wrong decisions, just decisions."

Judy lifted her hair off her neck. "No decision is still a decision. It's a decision not to make a decision."

"You told LaDonna you were finished with all this New Age shit."

"You brought up Dr. Phil. Except Freud said that, not Dr. Phil. What's New Age about him?"

"The hell if I know," Karen said. "Do you think we could go inside, Mother? I'm frying out here."

—⚒—

Transformation continued inside the house. The kitchen was in progress, with the wall down between it and the den. The den's heavy drapes had been removed. Outside Karen could see that the old garage had been opened up on the yard side to become an outdoor party house. All it needed was a pool.

Judy was behind her, still talking about reinvention. "What I'm trying to tell you, Karen, is this is not about looks. It's nothing less than the entire psychological evolution of a woman, the next step to becoming the person she was always meant to be, her best person, not the person who's trying to meet everyone's expectations but her own."

Karen stared out the sliding glass doors to the yard. "Who's the new guru, Mom?"

"There is no guru. I know you think this sounds like the same old stuff..."

Karen turned to face her. "No, it sounds new. You were talking about *being*, not *becoming*, when Swami Heart Attack was hanging around."

Judy headed for the kitchen, her heels making a dinky sound on the new parquet floor, as if it was made of plastic.

"Harguchet, Karen, the man's name was Harguchet, and he's a brilliant Hindu thinker. And being and becoming can exist simultaneously."

"O-kay." Karen sat on one end of the sofa.

"If you'd just listen and stop being your flip self, you might find you're interested in this." Judy's heels ticked across the den to the sofa. She handed Karen a glass of iced tea.

"It's the constant excitement, that's all," Karen said. "It makes me tired." She said it and thought that she never gave her mother much of a break.

"I'm so sorry I bore you."

"Bored and tired are different."

"You've never had it in you to get really excited about anything. I guess that's what passes for cool these days."

Karen stifled a yawn. "Thanks. I don't need to be excited to be interested. Tell me what's going on."

Judy pushed herself into the corner of the sofa and sat up straight, her body wired with enthusiasm. "I got to Baton Rouge—you know, when I evacuated for the hurricane—and after the flood when I knew we couldn't come back for a while, I felt relieved; strange since I was as worried as anyone else about my house. I knew I'd have a job, and I knew I was supposed to feel lucky about that, but fifteen years of pushing paper at the construction company, I didn't want to go back.

"I needed a change, Karen, but not another paper-pushing job. I needed a challenge. I wasn't unhappy, but I didn't feel really alive any more. Not because of the storm. This had been going on for most of the year. It was time to be still. To go into the dark room and wait. The possibilities swarmed around me..."

Judy came out of the dark room with a clear decision to go into business for herself. She didn't know what kind of business. "You know how it is, Karen, when you ask for it, it comes to you."

Three days later it came to Judy in the form of Kirkley Hope— "I mean, can you believe his name, Karen?"—one of the young men who worked at the construction company and had also evacuated to Baton Rouge. Judy ran into him at a coffee shop. Over coffee, Judy told Kirk about her revelation. Kirk said he'd always wanted his own construction company. They got back to New Orleans as fast as they could.

"Honeycutt and Hope, LLC, and we're making money, Karen. I get the jobs, do the estimates, keep the schedule, and in my spare time—not much of that!—I'm taking a real estate course online. Three years I'll get a brokers license then we'll start building houses and selling them ourselves."

"Where'd you get the money?"

Judy grinned and shrugged, her hands palms up. "The money comes from wherever it is."

One of Judy's hardcore beliefs, inspired by the Swami Heart Attack, whose money had come from Judy's savings account. Karen stared at her, hard.

"It didn't take much money, okay? The cost of the LLC, signs to tack to the telephone poles, living on FEMA money. We took small, quick jobs at first. I'm telling you, Karen, the money is out there. We're not gouging anyone either, and Kirk and his guys are doing great work. No cut corners. Not one complaint so far. Here's the deal—I wouldn't be involved any other way. I don't like tainted money. It brings bad luck to anyone who touches it."

"Tainted money," Karen repeated.

"You know, money from a bad source, stolen money, ill-gotten…"

"Yeah, I know." Karen finished off her iced tea. "And what about Kirk?"

"You mean me and Kirk? He's *hope*lessly in love with me." Judy smiled. "But he's still in the guest bedroom. Right now, I'm more interested in money than men."

NINE

Pascal Legendre and his business partner James Johnpier lounged back in their well appointed office on the third floor of their restaurant. At the wet bar Pascal poured himself a small glass of Porto Rocha and a generous Glenlivet for Jimmy. Across the room, against the exposed brick wall, Jimmy lit one of his Cubans and stretched his arm along the back of an expensively distressed brown leather sofa. He had furnished the room with discards from his house: a large age-frayed Tabriz rug under an octagonal coffee table of glass and burled walnut, the leather furniture, and an antique cherry desk looking very old-world against the backdrop of shuttered French doors to a balcony. The amenities included a built-in limestone bar. Pascal put the Glenlivet in front of Jimmy on the table, the rug's medallion directly beneath its glass top. The man was ugly as New Orleans sin, his face under his prominent brow bone messy, as if he'd been given life before it had a chance to set properly. One of his dark murky eyes drooped as though trying to slide off his cheekbone; his nose had taken the dive into an off center bulb; his lips were puffy and asymmetrical. But it couldn't be denied that the man possessed a sense of aesthetics, precise and fine. He could definitely put a room together; with the assistance of a top designer from Houston, he'd put an entire St. Charles Avenue mansion together. It had been featured in *Architectural Digest*.

Pascal sat in a well-worn leather club chair and took a small sip of the port. "Are you giving odds on LaDonna Johnson?"

Jimmy puffed at the cigar. "She's a tough call. Fifty-fifty without knowing why she borrowed money in the first place. As far as I know, the woman runs a tight ship, just like her daddy did. Ole Toots Johnson had a sharp business head. You know why he bought that club?"

"No idea."

"Too damn young to know. He was marching with his band, Toots Johnson and the Midnight Revelers, at one of the night parades. Someone threw a brick, hit him square in the mouth. The way it scarred, he could never get the same sound out of his trumpet. He was one of those players his horn just poured honey. He opened the club, did so well he eventually bought the building."

"He named it La Costa Brava?"

Jimmy nodded. "He married an Isleños woman from St. Bernard. She always wanted to go to the Costa Brava, so Toots told her she could go every day."

"You know some weird shit," Pascal said.

"That's because I've been around a long time. I know this particular weird shit because I sold Toots the building. I've known LaDonna since she was, uhm, maybe fifteen and Toots had her working as a barmaid. That's why she called me."

Pascal tossed the bottom of the port down the hatch, got up and poured a bigger one in a small Old Fashioned glass. Jimmy had hardly touched the scotch.

"Let me make sure I've got this straight," Pascal said. "This is more of a personal favor than a business deal."

"Why would you think that? She's into us for fifty large. I must have been poor too long 'cuz I still think that's a lotta money."

"Right. Pocket change during a slow month."

"You're not gonna lose anything."

"I'm more concerned about what I'm going to make. At my age you had a multi-million dollar pipeline company."

"If you're trying to play catch-up, forget it unless you want to get into the oil business, and I got in when there was still wild-catters and independents a dollar a dozen. You'll do fine with your restaurants and real estate. The truth is nobody needs as much money as I've got. All I do is sit around trying to figure out what to do with it."

"James, you're full of more bullshit than anyone I've ever known."

Jimmy Johnpier grinned past his cigar. "And I'm in business with you. Must say something about yourself, Pascal. And here's the crux of it, my young friend. If LaDonna's got to go bust, I'd rather see you running La Costa Brava than anybody else. Got a soft spot for the old place. Met my almost first wife there."

Jimmy had been almost married three or four times but every time the woman got close to the altar something stopped her. Pascal didn't know if she realized she was seriously considering procreating with the ugliest man in New Orleans even if he was one of the richest, or if Jimmy had some kind of nasty pre-nup he whipped out a few weeks before the ceremony. Something to make sure she wasn't marrying him just for the money. Couldn't be, no. The man was a realist and like he'd said, he needed things to do with his money. A nice trophy wife contributed to the economy.

"But let's talk about something really interesting, Pascal, like that gorgeous girl you've got welcoming our valued patrons to our cozy faux bordello."

"Did you talk to her?"

"I stopped to look. I wanted to linger so I got her to call up here and tell you I was on my way."

"And I thought she was just being her efficient little self. Turns out she's pretty sharp. She was only here a couple of days, right?

And I see her, smooth as an old pro, slide a couple folded right down her cleavage from one of those real estate conventioneers to get him the eight-top under the big nude. And I know she handled him because first she shook her head like she didn't have anything. Then he starts to schmooze. She says something else and next thing, he's palming her the cash."

"She's the most beautiful girl I've ever seen."

"I'm trying to tell you there's more to her than looks. If you care."

"Sure."

Pascal recrossed his legs, ankle over knee, the foot going like it had a motor in it. "Get this. She calls herself Raynie Devereux. Says she's from Rayne, you know where that is? Grew up on a frog farm. But I had to get her social, the IRS forms and all, and that's when she had to tell me Raynie Devereux isn't her real name, though as soon as she gets the money together, she's going to change it legally."

"So where're you going? Her real name's a kicker, right?"

"Oh yeah. Real name is Earlene Dick." Pascal sniggered over his port.

Jimmy's face was as straight as his features allowed. "You are so fucking immature, Pascal. Damn straight that girl's got more than looks. That's real chutzpah. Leave the frog farm, change your name...new name, new life. I like that."

"What did I say? There's more than looks." Pascal tried not to laugh. "She asked me, please, never to tell anyone."

"So you never told me." Jimmy chewed the cigar end. "I bet I can get her to tell me."

Pascal stomped his wagging foot to the floor. "Ah ha, so he's in a betting mood now. Let's make this about what's really in a name, Jimsy. You think you can get her to go on a date and tell you dick?"

Jimmy smiled. He leaned over to roll his smoking tip in the

ashtray. He looked up from under that big brow bone. "Yes I do, dick face."

"One large says you can't. One large says you can't even get her to go out with you. Two large if you can get her to whisper Earlene Dick in your ear."

"You are cruisin for a losin, pawdna." Jimmy sat back, arm stretched again, smoke curling all the way up to the fourteen-foot ceiling. "Earlene Dick. Whaddaya know. I kind of like it."

Pascal made a rude noise, but Jimmy looked over at him quite contentedly, a fat-Elvis smile playing on his puffed lips.

He had propped himself against the leather counter, leaning on his elbow, one ankle crossed in front of the other, a jaunty look except he was the homeliest man Raynie had ever seen. Homely as a frog. And like a frog he always seemed to be smiling, at least on one side. He was waiting for her. She slipped behind the hostess station, her position there as comfortable now as home. Sometimes the lunch counter at the grocery store in Mamou would flash across her mind. She'd want to laugh. She'd come up in the world, little Earlene Dick, working in this classy restaurant, feeling as elegant when she left as when she arrived instead of going home smelling like a big old link of andouille sausage.

"Hi, Mr. Johnpier. Would you like dinner before the kitchen closes?"

"Thank you, dear, but Pascal and I had a few appetizers up in the office. Tell me your name so I don't have to call you dear and sweetheart and all those sweet-thangs that young women these days don't like."

She was so used to flirting with men who came into the restaurant alone or with other men, getting a little lagniappe as she thought of it, to pad her paycheck, that she almost went into Marilyn-mode. Unsure of what his relationship to Pascal was, she pulled down her shoulder and leveled her head. "Please call me Raynie, Mr. Johnpier. I'm Raynie Devereux." She put her hand out to him over the counter.

He took it and smiled at her, a big smile that gave him a face lift. "You'll be seeing far too much of me around here, so call me Jimmy."

He stayed another ten minutes, making small talk as the restaurant began clearing out, Raynie unapologetically interrupting to tell people goodbye. He told her he liked the way she made each exchange seem personal, that he didn't quite know how she did it because she said more or less the same thing to everybody. He said it wasn't easy to have a stand-out personal style based on being nice without being showy about it, people who acted nice but called all the attention to themselves doing it. He shrugged and said, "Maybe it has something to do with your looks," but didn't make a big deal out of it, turned his head and took in the action in the front part of the restaurant, a table of six getting ready to leave. Raynie let it pass; she didn't answer him and wondered guiltily if that didn't have something to do with his looks.

After he left, Harley Sands, one of the waiters who'd befriended Raynie and sometimes went with her for a drink after hours—the wind down, he called it—stuck his head around the piece of wall behind the counter. "How about I yell monkey throwing turds and get the rest of these people out of here?"

Since the wait staff wasn't allowed anywhere near the hostess station, Raynie walked over to him. "Harley, who's Mr. Johnpier? Is he a regular customer, Pascal's friend...?"

"You mean what happened to his face?"

Raynie put a hand on her hip. "Did I say that?"

"There I go, hearing things again. The word is he's Pascal's partner, only Pascal never says anyone owns the restaurant but him. If you ask me, which you did, I'd say he's the money man. Bought himself a place to hang out." Harley rubbed his fingers together. "Major cush."

Raynie felt every hair on her body stand at attention and had no idea why.

—m—

Avery Legendre, who had managed to lose his cowboy hat along with a few thousand dollars at the Venetian in Las Vegas, drove straight from the airport and parked his Jaguar XF at the Royal Orleans instead of the private lot near his apartment, in a hurry to get to Le Tripot so he could eat before the restaurant closed. Chef had threatened to quit if he ever raided the kitchen after hours again. Crashing from a two-day coke binge and drinking heavily, Avery had trashed the kitchen when he couldn't find a bottle of Ketchup. Two things he didn't eat without Ketchup, steak and eggs, and he'd cooked up both for himself near dawn in the empty restaurant. He didn't give a shit about the prima donna chef, but his fat monthly paycheck depended on the restaurant's four-star reputation, even if in his never-humble opinion, said reputation was inflated.

He raced the block to the restaurant and almost stopped dead in front of the glass doors. He had to do a double take—it was the girl, all right. She wasn't a customer either. She stood behind the counter, talking to the phantom of the opera, Jimmy Johnpier. He ducked his head and went in the side entrance, down the alley and past the door to the kitchen. Too furious to wait for the service elevator, he stomped up the stairs to the third floor and burst into Pascal's office. He stood across the room from where Pascal was working at the desk.

"When did that girl start working here?"

Pascal had glanced up when Avery threw open the office door.

He went back to checking the day's receipts. "Which girl would that be?"

"The one in front, Pascal. Don't act like you don't know."

Pascal thwacked his pen down so Avery could hear his annoyance. If his father had never married that gold-digger after the divorce, he wouldn't have to put up with this demented half-brother, and he would have ended up with a lot more money after the old man died. He reminded himself that he made plenty of money and that the calmer he stayed the quicker Avery would leave.

"We've hired a couple of new girls lately. If you mean the new hostess, she came on last week."

"She's gotta go. She's bad news. I'm not kidding, get rid of her."

"Bad news. Could you elaborate?"

"No. Just take my word."

"Hm. Actually, Avery, she's working out pretty well. What reason would I put on the pink slip?"

Avery walked over to the bar, the heels of his cowboy boots digging into the Tabriz. "Don't fire her. Just make her uncomfortable, you know, so she quits."

Pascal watched him make a drink. "So you know this girl."

"Yeah." He turned, took a sip of his drink. "We had a thing, got ugly."

Pascal nodded. "She shot you off the saddle, huh cowboy? Say, what happened to your hat?"

Avery got red. "You fucking prick." He threw his drink, along with the glass, into the sink. The glass broke. "If anyone did the shooting, I did. Fact is the little bitch is lucky she's alive after what she did. So just shut the fuck up."

"Get out, Avery, before I have you thrown out, you shit-faced lunatic."

"I'll get out when I'm ready. I own half this building, remember?

I need five grand against the rent you owe me."

"Buyout's still available. You could have cash within a week."

"You can't pay me enough for this rat trap. Five. Now."

"On the first. That's the agreement." Pascal went back to his receipts.

"I don't think you heard me."

Pascal looked up to see Avery holding a small gun on him. He must have had it down one of his boots. Pascal took out his checkbook.

As soon as he heard the elevator door close, Pascal picked up the phone but put it down before it reached his ear. He had in mind to call the cops, but he couldn't get a restraining order to keep his brother out of a building he half owned; he didn't think it was ever a good idea to call the cops, anyway. He wanted Avery out of this building and out of his life, permanently. That would take some serious thought.

TEN

It was the odd night when both Karen and Raynie were at home and awake at the same time. The late night air was cool and they'd opened the doors to the courtyard then sat on the sofa under the ceiling fan, sipping their nightcaps, as Raynie called them, which reminded Karen of her mother, who always made nightcaps or toddies for the bodies of the laughing and crying women. It also reminded her of the money club.

"Next Monday," she told Raynie, "my mother is having the monthly meeting of her money club. She's been nagging at me to come to it. She says it will change my life. Want to go have your life changed?"

"What do they do?"

"The way I understand it, they sit around, have drinks and dinner and talk about money—anything anyone wants to say about it. The theory is, if they think about money and learn about it, they'll get it."

"How do they learn about it?"

"They read books, and they have people come talk to them about it sometimes. My mother had a friend of hers who's an accountant talk to them about their personal finances. They had an investment broker once too."

"Those people," Raynie said with disgust. "You might as well go to the horse races."

"Sounds like you lost money in the stock market."

"Not me. My dad. He gave all his savings to his nephew, my Uncle Dudley's oldest boy—he worked for Merrill-Lynch—and he invested it in one of those dot-coms that went bust. It may be what killed my mother. She sure did think about money a lot, but she never got any."

Karen wanted to ask Raynie about her family, only every time she did, Raynie answered her vaguely and changed the subject. She tried to say something that would keep Raynie talking about her parents, like, "Your mother sounds like my mother."

Raynie's thoughts seemed to have already drifted. "I guess you think about money a lot when you don't have it."

Karen wanted to tell her that she had a lot of it at the moment, and she couldn't seem to think about much else either.

Raynie looked far out into the courtyard. It was quiet and still for a few moments, not even a car passing, as if the world had stopped around them until she said, "Have you heard of a man named Jimmy Johnpier? He's really rich. My friend at the restaurant, Harley Sands, says he's the richest, ugliest man in New Orleans, and he's pretty sure he's Pascal's partner in the restaurant. He's been coming in almost every night, hanging around, talking to me. I'm afraid he's going to ask me out."

"Why are you afraid?"

"Well, he's old…"

"And he's ugly."

"I hate to say it, but yeah, and besides, he's Pascal's partner, the silent partner, Harley says. That kind of puts me in a weird position."

"No it doesn't. Tell him no. Say no as much as you can. I hear it gets easier. Then you won't run off with a Jack O'Leary and find three years of your life in the trash can like I did."

"This would be more like flying off," Raynie said. "Jimmy has his own jet."

"For fucksake. You're gonna do it."

"No I'm not. I'm just telling you the man owns a jet."

"And next you'll tell me you feel fucking obligated to go out with him because he owns part of the restaurant."

"Karen, I have to tell you, you have the worst mouth I've ever heard on a woman."

Karen laughed. "And you, Raynie, are pretty fucking sharp the way you slide out of a conversation. So, look, do you want to go with me to Mom's money club? Think of it like this—you make your own money, there're no strings attached. You're your own woman, no ugly men required."

"Am I going to have to read anything?"

"You don't want to read *Think and Grow Rich!?* All you have to do is think and the money attaches itself to you." Karen held her hands out in front of her, beckoning the money. "It's one of the group's favorites. Okay, I can see that title isn't getting you off. How about Suze Orman, *The Courage to Be Rich.* The club likes her, and she's one of Oprah's favorites. No? I know—I've got this great thriller you can read called *A Simple Plan.* It's about these two guys who steal a bunch of money—guess from where. A plane that crashes! You won't believe how fucked up things get after that. Bad money, bad motivation, bad luck. This one will speak to you, I promise." Karen shuddered thinking about the book. All of sudden she couldn't wait for Jack to get to town so she could give him the money. Then she wouldn't have to worry about what bad luck the money might bring down upon her. She could go back to worrying about not having enough.

Raynie said she'd go to the money club with Karen if she tried not to say fuck for a week.

Karen said, "Deal. Now, want to help me catch a thief?"

—∽∾—

Raynie was in love with her new life. She loved working at the restaurant, and she was good at her job. After she told Pascal she preferred working the late shift, he arranged the schedule so she could work as many nights as she wanted. He liked her there on the busiest ones, and that made her feel important. She'd found two advantages to night work. She made more money on the side at night, and it left fewer of the lonely dark evening hours. Since she'd started the hostess job she hadn't been lonely at all. She felt no need for a love life. For the first time in years, her life not only didn't revolve around a boyfriend, but she'd been startled to realize she was happy without one. She had good action on her own, and now Karen had asked for her help figuring out how one of the bartenders at La Costa Brava was stealing. She was learning about a different kind of power than the kind you got from having a good-looking guy in love with you. This was hers alone, and it was heady stuff.

After work the next night, Raynie told Harley Sands they were on a mission. She told him about Little Joe the bartender and the disappearing liquor as they walked to Frenchman Street.

"I don't guess he's ever alone in the club," Harley said. "I heard of one guy who brought his own cash register."

"Karen thinks he's just pocketing the money, one for the bar, one for Little Joe. We need to pretend we're in love so he won't notice us watching him."

"Not mission impossible, but a dangerous mission, melove."

"Why's that?"

"Because if my skinny boat wants to take a ride to tuna town, it could get painful."

Raynie stopped walking. "Harley, half the time, I have no idea what you're talking about."

"I know. You're so sweet and innocent, your most endearing qualities."

"So what are you talking about?"

"Let me put it this way. If the purple-helmeted monster has his way, my wife will kill you and castrate me."

"Oh, for pity's sake!"

"You see. No one else I know says, oh for pity's sake. For fuck's sake, for..."

Raynie took off at a fast clip. "Let's just get there so we won't be the only people at the bar."

———ᴍ———

Even though the restaurant was shut down and the live music in the back room had ended over an hour ago, Little Joe had The Pretenders on at almost max volume, giving the audio-illusion of action. There were four people at the bar, a man and woman deep into getting-to-know-you, and two women in close conversation. Not a lone drinker in sight.

"Perfect," Raynie said.

The short end of the bar, with the only unobstructed view of the cash register when Little Joe stood in front of it, was the hinged lift-top entrance and the service station for staff. Raynie and Harley took the last two stools near that end.

Little Joe drew them a couple of beers and took the ten Harley laid on the bar to the cash register. His long hair streaked with gray was pulled back into a pony tail.

Harley nudged Raynie. "Skinny tail," he said up close to her ear. She scowled and nudged back, harder. "His, not yours." She pushed him and he caught himself on the bar, as if she'd pushed him off the stool. "The pony tail," he said, righting himself.

"I know."

"Needs new ink." He paused a beat. "Tattoos."

"I *know*."

The red and blue peace sign on his left forearm had blurred edges, as though it had nearly been scrubbed off. He'd ripped off his t-shirt sleeves, so the heart on the bicep of his right arm was visible. All one color, old-tattoo blue, Little Joe's heart belonged to Mother Fucker, one word on top of the other, ribbons curling from its sides around his arm.

"Must have been the coolest motherfucker in the French Quarter back in the sixties," Harley said.

Raynie wrinkled her nose. "Ssh. He's going to hear you."

"What? Do I smell bad?" He sniffed his armpit. Raynie pushed him off the stool.

Every time Little Joe opened the cash register he'd step to the side of it for a moment before he closed the drawer. They couldn't see what he was doing, but his hands never went to his pockets. For half an hour they watched, their heads close together and eyes on each other when Little Joe turned. He wiped down the bar's apron, washed some glasses. The two women left.

Harley swiveled his stool so he faced Raynie and draped his arms around her neck. He leaned in close to her and said that since they had accepted this mission to help stop the rash of post-Katrina criminal activity, he was taking the only opportunity he might ever have to soul- kiss her. Her lips latched to Harley's, her eyes slit, Raynie saw Little Joe lift the rubber mat next to the cash register, take several bills from under it, and put them in the back pack he had stashed on a shelf underneath. Then he emptied the tip jar. She closed her eyes and kissed Harley as soulfully as she knew how.

"Dee-vine," he said when she broke it off. "I'm in plenty trouble now." He looked down.

She patted his cheek. "No you're not." She put a five on the bar. "Buy yourself a, um, stiff drink. I'll be right back."

He groaned as she got up and went to the bathroom where she called Karen on her cell phone. "The cash is in his back pack, but first he puts it under a small rubber mat next to the cash register." She folded the cell, did a quick mirror check, and returned to the bar.

"Let's sit at a table," she said to Harley. He picked up his drink. Raynie ordered a Coke. The change from Harley's drink covered it, but she took out another dollar and pushed all the money toward Little Joe. He smiled at her. She didn't smile back.

As she followed Harley to the table, she turned enough to see Little Joe standing to the side of the cash register, which he hadn't bothered to open.

Raynie sat so her back was against the wall. She watched as Karen hooked the velvet rope in place and made her entrance. She glanced over at Harley, a shine in her eyes. She was going to enjoy this.

—⁂—

Karen ducked under the lift-top. Little Joe, cutting a lime at that end of the bar, stepped to the side, said, "Hey," and when she didn't answer, left the knife poised in the middle of a juicy wedge to glance over his shoulder at her. She walked the length of the bar to where the couple sat and said, "Last call, guys. We're closing down a little early tonight—got some clean-up to do."

Little Joe had just made them Tequila Sunrises. Karen poured the drinks into go-cups and they wandered out into the night. She slipped into a nook off the bar and switched off the music.

"Y'all want go-cups?" Little Joe called to Raynie and Harley.

"They're with me," Karen said as she moved to stand next to the rubber mat.

"LaDonna didn't tell me to close early. We don't kick out paying customers."

Karen lifted the mat and took the money from under it. "LaDonna told me to bust you."

His head jerked to look over at Raynie and Harley. Raynie smiled and waved an index finger at him. Karen reached down to get his backpack from the bottom shelf. As her hand closed around one of the straps, Little Joe sprang across the narrow space to her, his pony tail flying, and pushed her roughly away with his tattooed forearm. He grabbed the backpack from her and slung it over his shoulder. Karen had nearly lost her balance. She pulled herself up to see Raynie and Harley standing at the bar.

"Don't touch her again," Harley said.

Little Joe shrugged. "She keeps her hands off my private property."

"Give her the backpack."

Karen, annoyed that the conversation excluded her, waved Harley off. "Put the money on the bar, Little Joe, and walk away."

He smirked at her. "Call the cops."

"I can do that. LaDonna will go for full restitution if I do."

"Oh, yeah? Well, I can see a lot of problems with that. Begin with the cops actually showing up. Then prove it. I hear the courts are all jammed up. You think anybody's gonna give a shit? You read the paper? The murder rate's skyrocketing."

"I read the paper. Did you see the guy who was in parish prison for nine months, just got released, arrested last September, a few days after the storm, for looting a grocery store? He walked out with a couple of loaves of bread and a jar of peanut butter. Never even got arraigned. Said the smell of piss and shit can't begin to cover the smell of death over there. Want to take your chances?"

They stared at each other. Little Joe broke first. "What are you going to do if I just walk out of here?"

"That isn't going to happen."

"You think he can stop me?" He lifted his chin toward Harley. Karen nodded. "With a little help, sure."

"With or without," Harley said.

Little Joe paid him no attention. "Who's the help, your boyfriend Luc?"

"And his friend Buddha." Karen held out her hand.

"You're so important you have your own henchmen now? I guess henchmen are the new accessory." But Little Joe's face had lost the raised eyebrow and cocky smile. Buddha, a six foot seven bald man, with the build of a Sumo wrestler and very small ears, had a bad habit of sitting on people. In spite of his name, he worshipped LaDonna, who hired him for odd jobs and called him La Costa Brava's official bouncer. Little Joe handed over the backpack.

"Not all of it's yours," he said as Karen shook the money out of yet another bag of stolen money.

"None of it's mine."

"I brought money in here with me."

Karen sliced him a look. "You're getting the backpack. Show some gratitude and," she said tossing it to him, "run."

He walked out slowly, hanging on to some attitude. When he opened the door he saw Luc and Buddha half a block away and took off like one of those kids who grabbed women's purses over on Bourbon Street. Luc said later it was impressive for a sixty-something.

Karen had both her old jobs back, but that didn't mean La Costa Brava as she knew it would survive. LaDonna got stranger by the day. She'd left two nights ago, just before the second show at eleven, telling Karen to keep the place running. Karen asked her when she'd be back.

"I don't know, Honeycutt," LaDonna had said. "Sometime. I'll call."

But it was almost three days now and she hadn't. She wasn't answering calls either. Karen had been trying to figure out when to start worrying.

ELEVEN

The next morning when Karen opened the door to the office, LaDonna was sitting at the desk, shuffling papers with her old-time lightning speed.

"Honeycutt?" She said it so loud Karen jumped. "Have you been to the Lower 9 since you got back to town?"

"No."

LaDonna slapped some invoices on the desk. "What kind of fucking citizen are you? Come on. I'm taking you on the Misery Tour."

—⁓—

The roof of LaDonna's Lower Ninth Ward house stood on one end, leaning against the house next door, which looked as though it had started toppling under the weight until some invisible super-hand had stopped its fall and held it in its precarious position. The rest of the house had been reduced to an eight-foot high stack of pick-up-sticks from the force of the water breaking through the levee. The ground had a crusty look, and when LaDonna rolled down her window, there was an unpleasant smell, something toxic underlying the stench of organic decay. LaDonna rolled up her window.

The landscape was eerily deserted. All over town FEMA trailers stood in front of houses that the residents were rebuilding or intending to rebuild. But not here. The devastation was too complete. The houses left standing were too unstable to cover with a blue tarp. Nine months after the storm and still there was no electricity, no gas, and worse, no potable drinking water. The city couldn't say when the services would be restored.

LaDonna had driven Karen past the place where a barge had broken through the levee at the Industrial Canal. She zig-zagged through the debris-littered streets, Karen hoping they wouldn't end up with a flat tire, or two, or four. She seemed to be looking for something, maybe signs of life, but the only people they'd seen had been over on St. Claude Avenue, a church group with their van in the parking lot of a former auto parts store, eating an early lunch around a camp stove—a whiff of meat cooking that made Karen feel a little sick as they drove past—and a Humvee with four National Guardsmen dressed in camouflage, driving the wrong way on St. Roch. LaDonna said the church group was probably gutting houses in the Holy Cross neighborhood closest to the river where the damage hadn't been so severe and people were fighting to return. Fighting, she said, because the city wasn't making it easy for them, and there had been rumors of developers wanting to take over the land near the river.

LaDonna stared out the driver's window at what was left of her house. Karen wanted to ask her where she'd been the past three days, but now didn't feel like the right time to bring it up.

"It's supposed to be removed tomorrow," she said, and then she laughed. "Mother Nature took care of the demolition."

"What are you going to do?"

LaDonna turned to Karen so fast that the beads at the end of her braids hit the glass, clicking against it.

"What am I go-ing to do?"

Karen looked at her. She must have just said the stupidest or most insensitive thing she could have said to LaDonna.

"There is nothing I can do. I let the flood insurance lapse a couple of years ago, for which I beat myself up on a daily basis. The government is supposed to help us out, but we don't live in a foreign country, so that don't look like it's gonna happen. There is nothing to do. And let me tell you, if I had any choices, I wouldn't know what to do. Just keep on keepin' on, I guess, but isn't that what we do in New Orleans? All the time?" She shifted in her seat and turned away from Karen. She said quietly, alarming because of the anger Karen thought she heard raging underneath the quiet, "I don't even know if I want to be here any more."

For the first time Karen understood that what had happened to LaDonna lay far beyond her imagination. When she was leaving town with Jack, LaDonna had said, "Why would anyone want to be anywhere but New Orleans? Don't do it, girl. You'll regret it." No doubt this wouldn't be a good time to throw LaDonna's words back at her. Karen looked out at the street.

LaDonna said, "I'm so fucked up I don't even know if I want to be with Ramon. Here I been grieving over that man all this time, and he finally comes back groveling, and I can't decide if I'm in or out." She turned from the destroyed house toward Karen. "You know me, girl. I've hardly experienced an indecisive moment in my life. I feel fuckin' insane."

"So that's where you've been. With Ramon."

"Three solid days, and I still don't know what I want."

"Why should you want to get back with him, LaDonna? His behavior has been shocking, leaving you at what had to be the worst moment in your life. I think you should boot him right back to California."

LaDonna laughed. "You are righteous, Honeycutt, you know that? But if you want to talk about shocking behavior, you should've seen what people were doing after the storm. Forget looting for food; the bunch of us down here were looting for booze. We waded barefoot into the Robért's grocery that had five inches of putrid water in it, in the pitch black, all the way to the back and discovered no one had found the wine yet. Shelves of it. And we didn't have nothin' to carry it in. We broke as many bottles as we finally took out of there. Everyone was drinking as much as they could, and then they started fucking all the people they know they should never fuck. Nobody gave a shit. We were all insane. Yeah, girl, don't look at me that way. I balled Little Joe. You believe that?"

"For Christ sake, LaDonna, I hope you got tested."

"You know how long that little son-of-a-bitch has worked for me? Over two years, something like that. He came on right after you left. So one crazy night, both of us drunk, Ramon hadn't been home for two days, and I let the asshole bust a nut. One time. Never came up again, and he starts stealing from me, like I owe him something 'cause I got laid. Just goes to prove not all whores are women."

"So you knew he was stealing and you let him get away with it."

"I sort of knew. Look, by that time my emotions felt like they were in one of those daiquiri blenders, maybe my brain fell in too. Not that I'm so different than anyone else in this city. Nobody knows what they're doing, what they want to do, if they're coming or going. It's like mass insanity. Even the people sitting in their high and dry houses, they don't know what to do. One day they put their house on the market, the next day they take it off. They're acting just as nuts as anybody."

"That must be annoying."

"No, that's not annoying. That's a post-Katrina fact of life. Hell, most of those people were displaced too, but they feel guilty their house is okay, their life is easy compared to all the homeless people. They've got survivor's guilt so bad they can hardly feel lucky."

Karen was shaking her head. "I know I don't understand, LaDonna. I don't understand why you think you want to go. What would you do with La Costa? Why would you leave your friends? I know you lost your home, but the city's still home.

Why would you leave it?"

LaDonna looked away from Karen, pursing her lips. "Maybe so I don't have to look at it everyday. Maybe because my heart got broken twice, right in a row, and believe me, the city was the bigger loss."

Karen could see that she was fighting tears, but LaDonna turned toward her with something like ferocity. "I can see why you're confused. You're glad to be home, and you came back with certain expectations that life would be more or less the same, even when you know it can't be. It's nine months later and maybe you don't get it why people are acting the way they are. It's like, let's get a move on, right? But this thing is far from over, I mean really far. The system is fucked up, the mayor seems to be spending a lot of time in Dallas, people like me are waiting for money it's going to take months maybe years to get, the levees aren't fixed and hurricane season just started. Everyone's scared shitless. If the thing touched you at all, even on a bureaucratic level—I can't wait to see how bad all that gets—you are fucking insane. You can't grasp it 'cause it didn't touch you. You weren't here. You are confused, girl, but understand me, you are not insane."

"You don't think coming back after the fact makes me eligible? Look, I get it, LaDonna. I don't think everyone should just *get a move on*. And it isn't my fault I wasn't here."

"Don't you go get pissed now, you hear me? I got enough piss and vinegar for the both of us."

"Well, let it rip. And, by the way, I caught Little Joe stashing the money and I fired him."

"Yeah? Gonna be real hard for the poor son-of-a-bitch to find another job."

"What, now you feel sorry for him?"

LaDonna shrugged her face. "I wouldn't go that far. He could go uptown. I hear they're scrounging for help on Magazine Street.

But he won't. That one is a true Quarter rat. He won't ever live any place but downtown. The thing is, he's getting old, he'll never make as much money as he made at La Costa—before and after the storm—and if he ever steals again he might not be so lucky to stick it to someone who'll keep their mouth shut. Little Joe's getting poorer by the day and the city's getting more expensive. In the brave new world, Little Joe is an endangered species. New Orleans gonna be a place for rich people. And Little Joe could end up homeless while he waits to go extinct."

"You really think the city's going to get too expensive to live in?"

"Don't panic, Honeycutt. You'll be all right. Anyway, what do I know? I already told you I don't know shit from shit."

LaDonna put her face in her hands. Her shoulders shook and Karen thought she was crying. When she took her hands away she let out a shriek of laughter. "You want to hear some shit, girl? Here's what Ramon wants me to do. Since the first reality show didn't quite pan out, now he wants to do a documentary— and don't go call this no reality show…New Orleans after the storm, follow a woman, me, who lost everything, and see what happens to her."

"That could be pretty good. I mean, you lost your house and you're trying to keep one of the landmark nightclubs running."

"I really shook you up with all that talk, didn't I? But that's okay, you'll start thinking straight again."

"I'm thinking straight. Look, LaDonna, whether you admit it or not, you're going to let Ramon back in. Whenever a woman's in doubt about a man the way you are, she always lets him come back. If you weren't going to, you would have known it three weeks after he left, and you wouldn't have been on the phone with him for the last six months. Look at you. You're totally upset. You say you don't know what to do, where you want to be, and you don't want to look at it everyday, but what you ought to do is look at it up close, every single day. You can sound off, you can be heartbroken, you can let it all out. Then you'll know."

LaDonna looked hard at Karen. "You're smart, Honeycutt—you know that?—for someone your age. We're starting tomorrow, coming out here with the camera while they take away this pile of splinters." She put on what Karen called her cat smile. "Ramon says I am eloquent when I'm upset. He says he's through being a jackass. He says this time we're going to L.A.—him and me."

Karen thought about the musician who went to New York without LaDonna, then Ramon takes off for L.A. Always being left behind. Maybe that had more than a little something to do with LaDonna not knowing where she wanted to be. It didn't feel too good to be second in line.

The cat smile turned into something else. Maybe a smirk. "You know what else he says? He says I'm gonna be a star."

But with her twice broken heart, LaDonna look tired. More than tired, world-weary, and, right now, old, as though she no longer had the energy to believe in any kind of future, much less a star-studded one.

TWELVE

"Has Johnpier asked you out yet?"

Karen and Raynie were on the I-10 in LaDonna's Prius on their way to Judy Honeycutt's money club meeting. Raynie had tried to escape what she figured would be a two-hour struggle to stay awake with the lame excuse that she was tired. Karen said no way, the word fuck hadn't left her mouth for a solid week, not even at work, and Raynie was going.

"Johnpier's a puzzle," Raynie said. "He comes to the restaurant every night, hangs out with me on his way in then again on his way out, but that's as far as he goes. He doesn't even seem tempted to see me without that counter between us."

"What does he talk about?"

"He likes to tell stories or maybe it's more that he tells little episodes, things he overheard at a party, something he saw when he was walking on Magazine Street. They're usually funny in some weird sort of way. He likes to talk."

"Give me an example."

Raynie turned to look out the window at the suburbs and strip malls they sped past. She started off slowly. "He told me he was at this charity ball, everybody dressed to the teeth, out at the Museum."

Karen interrupted. "Recently? Since the flood? What kind of charity?"

Raynie looked at her. "Do you want to hear the story? He

didn't say when it was or what kind of charity. That wasn't the point. Anyway, he sat at a table that was mostly women, a couple of other single or widowed men. He said he thought the organizers might have been trying some matchmaking to liven things up. So this older woman asks a younger woman…Jimmy said the younger woman wasn't in her circle of filthy rich house-and-garden matrons…what she did. The younger woman says she's a lawyer and returns the question. The older woman looked flummoxed, as Jimmy says, one of his favorite words, then she turns to her friend who's sitting next to her and says, 'Weezie, what do I do?' Weezie goes, 'Well, you're sick a lot.' And the woman says to the lawyer, "That's right. I'm sick a lot.'"

"That's pretty funny," Karen said but without laughing.

"It was, the way he told it, only I thought it was sad too. It reminded me of my mother. Finally, all she did was get sick a lot. Then she died."

"Is that why you left Rayne?"

"Yep, it sure is. I didn't want to get that depressed and then die."

"Did you tell Johnpier that?"

"God no. He was trying to be entertaining, and anyway, I don't know him well enough."

"But mostly because he was telling what he thought was a funny story."

"For pity's sake, Karen. I might have told him if I knew him well enough."

"Why is it I get the feeling you will?"

"The only thing I can think? You want me to."

—⁂—

Six women sat around Judy Honeycutt's glass coffee table, three on the sofa, Karen, Raynie and the gray-haired woman who looked the oldest on large floor pillows. Judy poured an orange-hued concoction of herbal teas and honey from a large pitcher. Across the room covered casserole dishes were lined up on the counter.

"We don't drink wine or eat until business is finished," she told Karen and Raynie, and took her seat in the sole wing chair. Her throne, Karen thought. Still holding court with a bunch of women at her feet. "Which just goes to show you how serious we are about what we do here."

There were murmurs of assent. Judy, barefoot, her hair blonder than the last time Karen had seen her, looked slim and youthful in her Capri pants…She settled in her chair, pulled her legs up and crossed them in a half Lotus, perfect posture.

"The whole thing started when Joan—" she gestured toward the woman sitting next to Raynie "—and I were talking one night and I was bitching about money, as usual. Tell them what you told me, Joan."

"I said that women were afraid to talk about money. Oh, they would bitch about it, but no one would talk about what they really wanted. They'd joke about being rich, but they never thought that was an idea they should take seriously because it wasn't realistic. I'm talking about women in my age group; you younger women might be more open about it. For us, anything about money was taboo. We were secretive. It wasn't polite to talk about money. That's what men did. I told Judy I'd just read a fascinating book called *Think and Grow Rich!* by Napoleon Hill. I said she ought to read it."

"So I did," Judy said, "and I did everything he said to do. I made my affirmation, decided how much money I was going to make, and I waited for my plan to reveal itself. And after the flood or because it, it did. I had decided I was going to get rich, and I knew how to do it."

Karen managed not to say for fucksake. She'd heard all this

affirmation crap before. She remembered her mother and other women making affirmations on scraps of paper, mostly about men, and putting them under lit candles in tall jars with saints painted on them. Karen once told her mother their house looked and smelled like a Catholic church. A lot of times the little pieces of paper had to do with men and getting them back, but sometimes they were about jobs, getting better ones. She didn't remember anyone ever saying they wanted to get rich. She suspected that in the New Age of finding one's higher self, a desire to get rich would have been considered base and crass, a request unworthy of the Magnanimous Universe that would only entertain loftier goals. Of course, if the money came...

"I told Joan that what we needed was a Napoleon Hill Master Mind group. And here we all are!"

One of the younger women started speaking. "I was brought up to believe it was impolite to talk about money, but that's not the worst of it. My mother thought you should only associate with people in your own economic class or you'd be jealous of what others had, like if you weren't born with money, you couldn't have it. If I said anything to her about self-made millionaires, she'd say they were geniuses and she didn't see any geniuses around our house."

In unison the women yelled, *"Positive mental attitude always trumps genius!"*

What was this, some kind of show for the newbies? Karen shot a look at Raynie who was smiling and seemed like she was getting off on all of it.

Judy broke into the laughter and raised voices. She looked at Raynie as she spoke. "It's that kind of negativity that Shelly and a lot of us grew up with that makes women anxious and depressed about money. We don't think we can have it, but we feel guilty or resentful if we don't. So what happens is we get emotional about money. What this group is all about is getting past our emotions, getting rid of the feelings of inferiority and lack of self-esteem, and getting in touch with our true feelings about money, understanding what we want and what's stopping us, and then going after it with confidence!"

That did it for Karen. A three decade-long echo, all the catchwords—self-esteem and confidence, especially the low varieties, anxiety, guilt, depression, inferiority—the words Judy had once used to describe the after-effects of a man gone bad, only now she was using them to talk about all the evils money could cure.

The women, though, seemed close to delirium. The woman on the sofa nearest Karen raised her hand. Everyone got quiet.

"I'm a fairly new member of this group." She shifted on the sofa so she could speak directly to Karen. "I met your mom when she and Kirk did some work on my house. Don't look so surprised—your mom helped Kirk gut the house. I have terrible allergies and couldn't get anywhere near all that mold. The whole first floor was flooded, which made me lucky, I know, because I had a second floor to live in, but I've never felt as down and out as I did then." Her eyes filled. "I'm not going to get emotional," she said with exasperation. "This group is the best thing that ever happened to me." One eye spilled and she looked around at the group. "Really, you guys, without all of you...I don't know what would have happened to me after the flood." And she broke down.

"That's okay, honey." Her friend next to her put her arm over Cheryl's shoulder.

"What I'm trying to tell you," Cheryl said, her voice wavering, "is that I have a dream now, and nothing's going to get in the way of it. I'm not afraid of money any more. I've got a new job and a goal and I feel positive about myself." She sniffled. "And I've saved over a thousand dollars since January. Before I spend money on anything, I ask myself if it's putting me any closer to my dream. If it's not, I put it in my savings."

Judy said, "Let's hear it!"

Together they all yelled:

If it's on your ass, it's not an asset!

If it's in your mouth, it's going south!

If it's in your car, you won't go far!

Money left over, you're sitting in clover!!

Karen leaned over to Raynie as the women laughed and clapped. "Do you fucking *believe* this?"

"You just said fuck, Karen."

"Right. That means we can go now."

"That would be totally impolite."

Karen could feel Judy's eyes on her. If there wasn't a man around to distract her, Judy could read Karen's mind—or her lips. Her mother somehow knew she'd just told Raynie she was ready to leave.

Judy raised her hand. Everyone got quiet again. Like a fucking school room.

Judy said, "Karen, Raynie, this club exists to bring people of like minds together. We're the people we turn to if we want to talk about anything, anything at all, though we've all come to the same conclusion: money, our own money, money that we make, can make our lives better and easier. We're not talking about obsession with money, like it's the only thing we think about, and we're against greed and hoarding money. Every one of us has learned through life experience that when you share your wealth, you create more wealth. Most of us give away part of what we earn."

Cheryl, recovered after the cheering, said, "I didn't have much money to share for a long time so I gave my time—cooking for people who were rebuilding their houses, keeping their kids..."

Judy nodded vigorously. " 'People first, then money, then things.' That's what Suze Orman says. The time Cheryl gave saved those people money so they could replace their things."

A key turning in the front door lock interrupted her. When the door opened everyone called out, "Hi, Kirk."

"Ladies," he said strolling into the room.

He reminded Karen of an Elmore Leonard character, a guy closing in fast on forty, who's been down on his luck, maybe done some time, but things are changing now. Kirk had a slightly seedy look about him, his lank hair too long, and he had on a worn, faded blue work shirt, but freshly laundered and tucked neatly into pressed khaki pants. He moved with confidence—that's how you could tell things had changed for the better—straight to Judy. He sat on the arm of her chair, his back to the group, one hand grasping the wing of the chair, and when he bent down to whisper in her ear, his other hand found the side of her neck with a touch Karen felt down deep.

Judy listened then gave a soft kitten-like cry and hugged Kirk around his slim middle. He got up and said, "See you later, ladies," and let his hand skim over Judy's clavicles as he moved away. He crossed the den and the kitchen, and went down to where the hallway turned toward the guest bedroom. A door closed.

Joan broke the silence that had heat waves coming from it. "Well?" she said to Judy.

"Girls, Kirk and I just got a big renovation job. My million dollar goal is coming faster and faster all the time."

Karen tuned out, her mind flipping around, all around Jack. She felt his touch, what it used to do to her when she was still in love with him, the way feeling it was the most important thing in the world, what she lived for. Then she saw the money in her hands, lying with it at the bed and breakfast the way she'd lie with a lover. Tainted money, except she wasn't so sure that she wanted to give it up now. The trouble was, she always felt the Miami greaseball and his Bullmastiff breathing down her neck. She had the money, but it couldn't buy her what money was supposed to buy—freedom. What was it her mother had said, "Take freedom over material gain?" That meant she had to give it up, just like that?

One thing you had to say about Mom, she called the shots now. It may have taken her half a century, but she had her life together. Karen had to admit, Judy had changed, and yeah, it was real.

For Christ sake, was she jealous of her own mother?

—⁓—

They were quiet as they started the drive back to the Marigny. Karen was going to say something flip, that they'd just experienced a new kind of twelve-step program: instead of keeping you sober, this one showed you how to get high—on money. But she didn't say it; she didn't want to slam her mother. Not yet.

"I knew I shouldn't have gone," Raynie said. "Now I'm depressed. It's like I lost my virginity and it wasn't supposed to happen this way."

"Exactly what I've thought ever since I lost mine, but I don't have the vaguest idea what you're talking about."

"I was innocent, you know? When I walked in there. Didn't have a care in the world. I like my life, I like my job. I'm a happy person. I get in there, the bubble bursts. I spend every dime I make. Rent, food...I only have three outfits for work. That woman who saved a thousand dollars since January? I couldn't save a thousand dollars in six months if I starved. It took me two years to save two thousand so I could leave Rayne, and I didn't have to pay rent then. At this rate I'll never be able to have a place of my own. And a car? Forget it."

"Give it a year," Karen said. "You'll be manager of Le Tripot."

"I don't think Pascal would trust anyone but himself to manage Le Tripot. He has floor managers because he doesn't seem to like to come downstairs much when the restaurant's open, but I don't think they make that much money."

"Then another restaurant. . ."

Who was she kidding? She had close to ten years on Raynie and she still couldn't afford a place of her own or a car.

She almost passed the Esplanade exit and turned hard to make it. Most of the street lights that had been taken out by the flood hadn't been replaced. When Karen came off the ramp it was dark, pitch in the shadows of the overpass. No traffic lights at the intersection either. She gave a quick look left and ran the dinky stop sign on the tripod at the corner, turning onto Esplanade.

"The truth is," she said, "no one makes big money in the service industry except the owners."

"What's big money?"

"Pick your figure."

"I think your mother's going to make herself a million."

"She just might. I hope she does and saves a lot. Makes more big bucks on investments."

"I sort of like what they're doing, Karen. It's smart."

Karen nodded. "Maybe you should join the club."

"What about you?"

"No, not me. It wouldn't be a good idea for me to join any club my mother belongs to. I'll wait for my inheritance and hope she doesn't give it all to Kirk first."

THIRTEEN

Raynie said all this talk about money—she needed a drink. Karen said she needed to walk off her aggravation, and no, she didn't know why she was aggravated. Raynie said she'd drop the car off at the lot where LaDonna kept it and bring the keys to La Costa Brava. Karen let herself off at Esplanade and Dauphine.

All Karen could think as she walked, she wanted to get back to her place and sit there in the peace and quiet, alone.

Her cell phone rang. It was Luc.

"I thought you were coming in for a drink, maybe we'd go out for a while after."

"Raynie's there?"

"And Ramon, and LaDonna's around somewhere. Come on over. LaDonna can close tonight. She's gonna have to let Ramon talk himself out. His brain's downloading movie ideas. It was fun for a while..."

"I'll bet." Karen stopped on the sidewalk, a block from St. Philip, only a couple of blocks from home. The back of the French Quarter, mostly residential, was quiet. She hadn't seen a soul on the street; only a few cars had passed. She turned back toward Esplanade and the Marigny, took a few steps, then retraced them and walked toward home again. "I'm just too drained from going to my mother's," she told Luc. "Let's hold this thought. We're working together tomorrow night, right?"

The connection sounded open but the music had gotten dimmer. "Luc?"

"I'm here. I got Ramon another beer and I'm in the storeroom." He grunted as he moved a box from under one of the shelves. Karen could hear it scrape on the gritty concrete floor. "Karen? Shit. I can't believe I'm sitting in this storeroom on a box of Rolling Rock…going nowhere. Look, I like you. I'd like to see you sometime when we're not at work. When we're not in this barroom."

"Me too."

"Me too," he said, repeating it in her same monotone. "What does that mean? You'd like to see you sometime, not in this barroom?"

She laughed. "And you too."

He waited. "Just tell me, are you, um, otherwise engaged… with someone else…"

"No. Luc…" She could see him in the small room lined with shelves, crammed floor to ceiling, sitting with his elbows on his knees, one hand in his hair, holding the cell phone, and the sleeves of the plain black tee he liked to tend bar in rolled up over his biceps, which were big enough but not too big, and no tattoos to hide the lift and line of muscles working over bone… "I need to be alone, while Raynie's over there. I'll call you back."

"How 'bout I call you when she leaves?"

"Fine."

Karen stood at her gate. She closed the cell and fumbled for her key. The phone rang before she found it. Raynie.

"He's here, Karen. The cowboy, only he's not dressed like a cowboy and when he asked for a beer, he didn't sound like one either."

"Has he seen you yet?"

"What? You're breaking up."

"I said *has he seen you yet?*"

"No, I was coming from the bathroom. I ducked back in."

"Where is he sitting at the bar?"

"The short end. Get this, he's wearing a Hawaiian shirt and a lei. The guy likes to dress up."

"Wait there. I'm calling Luc."

Luc answered saying, "That was too quick. Don't call it off."

"What? No, I'm not. The guy at the end of the bar, in a Hawaiian shirt—that's the cowboy, the one who spiked Raynie's drink."

"I know him." The music faded as Luc moved into the storeroom. "Avery Legendre. Brother of Pascal who owns Le Tripot—where's Raynie?"

"Hiding in the bathroom."

"Tell her to come on out, act like she's never seen him before. She's never seen him at the restaurant? I thought he ate over there all the time."

"Maybe not, not if he saw her first. Luc, walk home with her, will you?"

"As soon as I can get LaDonna down here again. She got tired of listening to Ramon a couple of hours ago. If he's going to hang out like this, she needs to give him a job. Let him work off his nerves."

—∞—

Karen closed the gate behind her and stopped. The French doors to the living room were open and the TV was on. Karen and Raynie didn't watch TV and they never left the doors open when they weren't there. Unlocked most of the time but not open.

"Who're you talking to out there, baby?"

Karen stood at one of the doors. "Jesus, Jack, do you want me to stroke out? How did you get in here?" She turned off the TV.

He lounged on the sofa, bare feet crossed at the ankles, giving her that lopsided smile of his.

"Oh, right," she said, "breaking and entering—another of your many trades." She walked into the living room, over to the kitchen and opened the refrigerator. "Who told you where I live?" She poured some orange juice into a glass.

"What?" Jack grunted as he sat up on the sofa. He saw her in the small hallway off the bedroom, fooling with the thermostat. She turned off the air conditioning. "Christ, Karen, the place was a fucking inferno when I walked in."

"Broke in. The choice here is open doors and ceiling fan—" she pointed above him "—or closed doors and air conditioning."

"Shit, then. I'll close the doors."

"I didn't say *your* choice." She walked toward him, stopping at the counter that separated the kitchen from the living room.

He did that thing with his hands, patting the air, which meant for her to calm down.

"I am calm, Jack."

"But you don't seem very glad to see me. Of course, I can understand that." When she raised her eyebrows, Jack said, "The money. My money. That you ran off with."

"Solo's money, but you can have the money back. What's left of it."

"I don't get it. Why did you take the money and leave? What did I do?"

"Think about where you were at three o'clock in the morning."

Jack's face showed the strain of thinking then it lit with understanding. "What are you saying? You took it because you were jealous of that little girl at the bar?"

When she didn't say anything he said, "I won five grand at her table. We were having a celebratory drink."

"Silly me. I thought she was going to jack you off right there, maybe take you out for a sunrise screw on the beach. I said, let him have his fun after all that hard work, stealing all that money, the psychological stress of knowing Solo would try to hunt you down and kill you. Then I said, wait a minute. You can't really steal money that's already been stolen, right?"

"It's just pissing money, baby. Chump change. It's all right. You can have it."

"That's generous of you, Jack, but if it's just pissing money, how come we had to run for our lives? Am I missing something?"

"Look, it's a long story. Solo let a guy walk out of a game with it. He wouldn't of if he thought it was a lot of money. He could afford to lose it."

Karen scratched her nose with the side of her index finger. "It's the kind of answer I expect from you. Here's the thing, though. Solo's honor and reputation have been compromised. His manhood is threatened. You know, *quién es más macho*. The answer always has to be Solo. See, he caught up with me, and he said if I don't call him the second you show up in New Orleans, his young thug Ernesto will be allowed to show off with his knife. So you can have the money, Jack."

"Aw, sweets."

Karen cringed and Jack said, "What?" Then looking confused— "Wait, so you went back to Miami?" He looked around. His eyes lit on the commode, the library table. He looked down at the sofa.

"I did. And, really, Solo couldn't have been nicer. He let me keep the cash I had for the mover."

"He knows you have the money?"

"No, he knows you have it." Jack stared at her, his mouth open. Struck dumb, she thought. "That's what I'm saying; you can have the money. There's better than fifty left."

Jack got up from the sofa and took his time walking over to her where she leaned against the counter. Karen felt an involuntary straightening of her posture, the edge of the counter cutting deeper into the small of her back, as though she was trying to back away from him.

He stopped about ten inches from her and put his hands on her shoulders. "I don't want the money, baby, I want you." He moved his hands to her neck, up under her hair, and his body leaned toward her, crotch first. Karen closed her eyes and tipped her head back. He kissed her neck. That smell, that musky, dark, mysterious odor that at one time would have been the only reason she needed to give in to him. If she wasn't careful, she was going to whimper.

He lifted his head and moved in for the kill. Karen opened her eyes, looked into his. She clutched his forearms and he released her neck, his hands beginning to travel south. Karen slid to the side.

"Back off, Jack."

"Come on, sugarplum," he said reaching for her, "You can't stay mad at me forever, you know you can't."

She stood in one of the French doorways, one foot in the courtyard, her arms folded.

"Here's the thing," Jack said. He sat on the arm of the sofa, keeping his distance. "Everything's just fallen into place as nice as can be. I went up to Hot Springs and made a big pop. That's why I don't need the money. I come to town and just like that—" he snapped his fingers "—I got some heavy action set up. Baby, it's going to be a large payday." He rubbed his hands together fast, the sound grating on Karen's ears.

"I thought you had enemies here. That's why we left, remember?"

"Sure, but things change." His face lit up. "The floods came along and washed all those old bad guys away."

"Lucky you. But don't forget about Solo. He didn't get washed away."

"I can see Solo salivating. He's like a cartoon character, you know? Can't you picture it? In his shiny suit with all those little nubby things all over it? All hunched up like a gorilla, drool down to his knees? He'll get his money back plus some, the chump."

"Chump? Solo?"

"He's been taken a couple of times. The guy I took the money from that night? He wouldn't of been back to play double or nothing."

"Why's that?"

"I think he was wise to the game. But it doesn't matter. He died. Heart attack. So you see? It's a good thing I took the money."

"How do you know he died?"

"Solo told me."

"You've talked to him?"

"I have. He's on his way."

A wave of anxiety rushed through Karen. "So, the new bad guys are coming."

Without skipping a beat, Jack said, "I tell you, baby, I'm glad to be back. I went over to La Costa looking for you, and I got a damn buzz just being in the place. We had some good times there, didn't we? Saw a couple of people I knew—oh, and I met LaDonna's latest boy toy. Ramon." He rolled the R. "Says he's going to make *the* definitive Katrina movie, says he and LaDonna have already started. He was talking a bunch of shit about film tax credits and investors. They get all this money back if the movie doesn't earn out. I don't know, it didn't make a damn bit of sense to me. He must've said a hundred times, a *movie industry incentives program*, trying to sound hot shit, like he's Steven Spielberg or something. You get all these tax credits, but you can't take them, then somebody else not even connected to the movie pays you for them. *Creative accounting*. He liked saying that too. I always thought that was just another way of talking about fraud. I sure hope LaDonna knows what she's doing, cuz the guy is really full of it. Man, I'm gonna sell it to *HBfuckingO*....Oh, sugarpie, look, that reminds me—you gotta get cable in here. I mean, no ESPN. The screen's so full of snow you can hardly see through it."

"But you were watching anyway. Jack, who told you where I live?"

He laughed, sat on the sofa and slid horizontal. "Oh no. I can tell by that tone of voice my source would never hear the end of it. That wouldn't be fair." He settled into the cushions, one arm behind his head.

"Don't get comfortable. You're just leaving." She motioned him to follow her through the French doors.

He didn't budge. "Come on, Karen, let me stay tonight. We can talk things out in the morning, get everything straight, pick up where we left off…"

What amazed Karen was how much she didn't want to talk. She didn't want to explain anything, or try to reason with him, or get angry, emotional…she didn't want to put any energy whatsoever into Jack.

"You can't stay here. I don't want you to, and I have a roommate."

"You know I love you, baby. I'm never gonna love anyone the way I love you."

Karen was thinking about the money. She didn't want to let it go, but her conscience decided she had to try one more time to give it back. She stepped back inside.

"Take the money, Jack, settle things with Solo. If you really won money in Hot Springs, then you're that much ahead."

He sat up. "You doubt me? Of course I won money in Hot Springs. That's what I do. I gamble. I want you to have the money, the 50K, whatever's left. We get back together, we don't get back together—it's still your money. Okay? I'm going to tell you something, Karen, and it's the gospel truth. When you make money doing things that are…" he rocked a hand, trying to find the right way to say it "…well, not quite the traditional way of making a living, it's all pissing money. It's easy come, easy go. You always figure there's more where it came from. When you work for it, that's different. You watch it, you save it, you don't feel so, uh, free with it, if you know what I mean."

"I'm not sure I do," she said.

She was spared any other insights from the criminal mind by Raynie's laughter coming over the brick wall and the gate swinging open. She and Luc sort of spilled into the dark courtyard. Luc was holding the key.

Jack's forehead creased. "The roommate?" He looked again. "The bartender."

Raynie stopped laughing when she saw Jack.

Luc said, "You were in the bar earlier, talking to Ramon and Avery. Jack, right?"

Raynie gave Karen a nervous glance.

"Yeah, Jack O'Leary." He looked from Luc to Raynie, then to Karen. "Which one's the roommate?"

—∞—

It took almost forty-five minutes but Karen finally got Jack to the gate. She unlocked it.

"Why are you kicking me out? Come on, babycakes sugarpie, let me stay with you. Just tonight. I'll make other arrangements in the morning, if you still want me to. Come on, Karen."

"I hate it when you whine."

"You haven't gone lesbian on me, have you, sweetface?"

"Stop it, Jack. Stop calling me all that shit. I don't know what you're up to, but there's already a smell coming from it. That guy Avery—he's the one? He's the action?"

"You see, you can't stay away from me. I'm the action." He moved on her again.

She pushed him away with one hand and the gate open with

the other. "Don't break in any more. Call me on the cell phone. You remember the number?"

"You know me. I never forget a number."

She watched him go down the street, a swagger in his walk, Mr. Happy-Go-Lucky. She wondered what he would do if he ever caught her with another man, if he walked in and found her in bed with someone. He'd probably go over to the guy's side, stick out his hand and introduce himself, ask him if he wanted a beer or something.

—∞—

Raynie and Luc told Karen how the cowboy, a.k.a. the Hawaiian, tried to act cool, like he wasn't in a hurry, then nearly overturned his bar chair trying to get out of the place. They told it a couple of times, adding more details, before Raynie said, "So now I know who he is, what can I do about it?"

"Maybe you should talk to Pascal," Luc said.

"I think I'd be too embarrassed, but what if I did tell him? What can he do?"

Luc reached across the sofa and gave her shoulder a squeeze.

"Probably nothing," Karen said. "But we can do something. Let me think about it."

She told them she had to make a phone call. She closed the door to the bedroom, and after rummaging through a dresser drawer she found Solo's card under a short stack of camisoles.

He answered the phone with a curt, "*Sí.*"

"It's Karen Honeycutt."

"Ah, Karen, how nice to hear from you."

"Thanks. Jack said he already talked to you and you know he's here, but since you can never tell what truth Jack has pulled out to fit the occasion, I'm calling like I said I would."

"Yes, you are interested in keeping your money and maybe

other things of importance to you."

"Jack also said your, um, player died. That must take some heat off."

"That is of no importance, Karen."

"Really? It might be to the, uh, player's loved ones. Oh, I see what you mean. You still want your money. Jack said it was a good thing he took the money after all or it would be gone for good."

"You don' want to make me angry, Karen. I know you stole the money. I hope you have kept it safe."

"*I* stole the money? Jack told you that?"

"He did, and I believe him. I understand women, Karen. You needed your revenge. I have no hard feelings. You keep the five thousand dollars, give me back the rest of the money, and we forget any of this happen."

Karen felt the flush of anger hit her face. "You think you've got everybody's number, huh, Solo? Well, let me tell you something else Jack said. He said money he gets from—let's call it what it is—criminal activities, it's all easy come, easy go, because there's always more where it came from. He told me that just tonight. After he broke into my house, waiting for me when I got home. Told me he hadn't been in town any time at all and already he's got some big action—you're both going to be rich and happy. Looks like you and Jack are best friends again, like he never left Miami with the money to begin with. Tell me any of this makes sense. Tell me when Jack ever made any sense. Tell me I broke into a hotel safe and stole a dead guy's money."

Solo waited. When he spoke his voice was calm and quiet. "I am on my way to the Miami airport with 'Nesto. We take the red-eye to New Orleans. When I get there, I will deal with this matter. I can assure you, Karen."

Karen closed her cell phone. She could have gotten out of the way of danger, she was pretty sure, if she'd just agreed to give

Solo the money back. Instead she'd stepped right into the heart of it. So what did that make her? Some kind of player?

FOURTEEN

Karen and Luc sat in the dark courtyard at a rusty round iron table off Karen's bedroom. A stand of banana plants next to them rustled now and again with the light breeze, their leaves making a swishing sound that Karen had found was good for falling asleep.

She and Luc and Raynie had sat in the living room, Luc and Raynie on the sofa, Karen in the big chair, until awkwardness had settled on them after Jack left and Raynie got tired of being on— showing off for Luc was the way Karen put it to herself. When Raynie said she had to work a double the next day and went off to the bathroom, Luc and Karen went to sit in the courtyard. He asked her if she wanted to go out for a while, but she didn't. She got drinks for them then closed the doors to the living room and turned on the air conditioner. She came out to the courtyard through her bedroom door, the room dark behind her.

Luc sat so that the light from the living room lit one side of his face, leaving the other in shadow, mysterious. If Karen had still been into romance, she would have thought he looked dangerous. That alone would have sparked her interest. It didn't now; if anything, it put her off, though in the light, the setting, he was better looking than he'd been the first time she saw him. The only reason that didn't put her off was that except when he was behind the bar, performing, he didn't seem to be eaten up by his own looks.

She put a drink in front of him and sat, turning the chair so she faced him more directly. "Tell me about Avery Legendre."

"Pretty much a nut case, given what he did to Raynie."

"And before that?"

"A whack job no matter how you look at him. I never thought he'd do anything like that, though. He seemed pretty harmless, likes to dress up, came in the bar one night in an old Confederate uniform jacket he found on Royal Street. He's got to be loaded. He and Pascal own the building Le Tripot's in, and I think there's other property too. He lives in the Quarter and he hangs around. That's about it."

"What about Pascal?"

"Never met him, never even seen him. He doesn't hang around. He's all about business from what I've heard. The restaurant was a huge success before the storm and one of the first places to open after. Raynie says it's full almost every night. The talk is he's thinking about another theme place downtown. He's one of the guys we should all be afraid is going to turn the French Quarter into Disneyland."

Karen twirled the ice in her Ginger Ale. "Raynie likes him. He gives her responsibility, lets her work the best shifts. Since she's never seen Avery there, he must not have much to do with the restaurant." The finger in her drink stopped. "Maybe Pascal doesn't want Avery around."

"So…what?"

"I don't know. I'm just thinking."

"You want to get him, don't you?"

"Yes."

"How?"

"I'm getting an idea. Don't have the details yet. How often does he come to La Costa?"

"Irregular. Maybe three times a week, then I might not see him for a couple of weeks. He says he goes to Vegas a lot."

"So he doesn't work?"

Luc shrugged. "Never says anything about work."

"For Christ sake," Karen said, "the guy's that rich, why doesn't he pay for it?"

"Maybe he craves the excitement."

"Excitement? Anyone who gives a woman drugs? They're like fucking necrophiliacs." She uncrossed her legs, crossed them the other way. "You know anyone who can get those drugs?"

"Is that what you're going to do? Dope his drink?"

"That's just the beginning. Do you know anyone?"

"Little Joe would've been the one to ask, but I don't guess he'd help me out after I chased him down the street the other night."

"He might if there's a few bucks in it for him, but I'll ask Jack. It used to be he could get anything he wanted around here."

"It might not be so easy since he hasn't been around. Times have changed."

"But Jack hasn't. He connects to the sub-strata by instinct."

Luc moved his chair closer, the metal legs scraping on the bricks, so his knees were almost touching Karen's. "Tell me more about Jack."

"What do you want to know that isn't fairly obvious? How I could have fallen in love with him?"

Luc leaned back, put one ankle over the other knee. Karen noticed that whenever she fired a question at him or took a certain tone, he moved to put distance between them.

"Who can explain love?" he said. "I guess the worst part is falling for someone then realizing they're not who you thought they were."

"That's not what happened with Jack. I knew who he was, and if I didn't LaDonna was there to tell me. I decided not to pay attention. I let his looks and his age be more important than what he was doing with his life."

"Were you looking for daddy?"

Karen lowered her eyebrows. "If you want to talk psychobabble, I'll introduce you to my mother. She's much better at it than I am."

He held up a hand, similar to Jack's "calm down" gesture, but he said, "Okay, I'll lay off. What was he doing with his life?"

"Gambling, drinking, drugs—the same thing he's always done and what he's going to do till…whenever."

"You stayed a long time. You said something—remember?—about it being like jail."

His eyes were steady on her, interested. Jack had once looked at her like that, but she'd realized too late that he had very little interest in her. He either wanted her to do something he knew she wouldn't want to do or he wanted to do something he knew she wouldn't want him to do.

"It was fun at first, all the big parties, Miami heavies, plenty of beautiful people, lots of drugs, but cocaine made my heart race, pot put me to sleep, and too much to drink gave me a two-day hangover. I liked watching for a while." She shrugged with her lips. "It got boring."

"Why didn't you leave?"

"I wanted to…" She had to think about it. "I thought if I left I might miss something."

"Something…" Luc rolled his hand.

"I don't know what. It was the first time I'd been away from home, the first place I'd ever had that wasn't a dump. I didn't like to think about where the money for it all came from, so I decided not to think about it. I wanted to leave Jack, but I didn't want to leave my things and I couldn't afford to move them." She stopped and he waited. She flipped a hand. "You know how that is. Lack of money almost never stops anyone from doing what they really want to do. Maybe I thought I'd miss my things."

Luc stuck out his lower lip, considering what she said. Her insides jumped when she had a thought to bite it.

"Maybe," Luc said, "you thought you'd miss something... exciting. The lifestyle sounds pretty risky. Maybe you liked that." He surprised her, saying that.

"Maybe. I think back, it seems like I was a lot younger. Living in Miami—it was really different. I had this thing, I don't know, like I'd come up in the world, that I was more sophisticated than I was living here, that I was better than I had been because I hadn't gotten stuck in my home town."

She was talking too much, telling too much. She said, "Have you ever lived away from here?"

"I was a ski bum for a few years. Aspen, Park City, Sun Valley. It was outdoors, healthier—a lot colder—but in some fundamental way it wasn't all that different from here. I waited tables, tended bar, and didn't have an ambition in the world except getting out on the next slope."

"What do you do when there's no slope?"

"Follow the action. The music, the next party, the next festival." He moved his crossed foot to the bricks and put his elbows on his knees. Then he softly tapped the back of her hand that rested on the chair arm. "You know what? I think I'm getting bored."

He picked up her hand and she laced her fingers through his. She saw Raynie cross in front of the French doors.

She brought her eyes back to his. "Boredom's dangerous," she said. "It either makes people do crazy things or it makes them think they want to grow up."

"Does that mean not wanting to live in a dump, wanting nice things?"

"That might be part of it."

"Or maybe wanting a woman who wants all that."

"You think? I've never known a man who grew up because of a woman."

"It's been known to happen, though." He pointed to the living room with his chin. "Are those your things from Miami?" She nodded. "So how did you get them here?"

She looked down at their intertwined hands, moving them back and forth. The light went out in the living room. Raynie going to bed. She heard something rustle in the banana leaves that wasn't the breeze, probably one of the real Quarter rats, and she leaned forward, away from it, closer to Luc. "I stole money from Jack."

He shook his head, not getting it. "To move? He wouldn't give it to you because he didn't want you to leave?"

"It was money he'd stolen from...this is where it gets complicated. Let's just say he stole the money from a gangster in Little Havana..."

So she told him about it, leaving out a few things, like the man who had the heart attack, the blonde, her fingernails...

"He came here to get the money back?"

"He says he doesn't want the money back."

She could see the breath leave him. "No problem, then," he said.

"Not quite. The gangster wants it back. He's on his way as we speak."

"How much money did you steal?"

The question made her uncomfortable. She was going to lie to him and it didn't seem right after giving him what to her was a close look inside. "Five thousand dollars."

"That's all? I mean, it would be a lot to me, but to guys like that..."

"Just pissing money as Jack says. There's something between him and Solo Fontova. They'll get it straight, run a few gambling scams while Solo's here in town, and be best friends again."

"You're talking real lowlife here, aren't you?"

"Does it bother you?"

She waited for him to take his hand back, but he leaned closer, his face an inch away. He shook his head, bumping her nose with his. "Is it going to get scary?"

"I don't think so...you can let me know."

"I will..."

He kissed her and she got into it, a deep, good kiss, no holding back. When they broke from it she had a second's worth of misgiving, that she was going back on her promise to herself to be alone long enough to know what it was like, and not to get involved with any more immature men.

Then Luc said, "Let's go to bed, Karen."

She glanced at the darkened living room before she led him through the door behind them. She forgot any second thoughts soon enough. He was a careful lover, unzipping her dress, pushing it first to her waist then to her feet, keeping her back to him as he managed to hit every erogenous zone from her shoulders to the back of her knees, inventing new electric places as he went. He put on a condom—it pleased her that she didn't have to ask—and lay with her, finding her eyes in the dark, stroking her hair, whatever he could reach as she explored him. Once they got into it, there were no first-time hesitations, no awkwardness. Karen lost herself in it, unaware of anything around them until Luc lifted himself and fell beside her, and she heard sounds in the hallway, water running, Raynie awake and prowling, and she wondered how loud they'd been at the end.

Raynie slouched behind the counter at the restaurant. The end of her double shift was near; it couldn't happen soon enough. The restaurant had only one lag during the late afternoon, which had made Raynie more tired than all the running earlier. Pascal came down before the dinner rush and said this was probably— how had he put it?— "the last gasp" before things started to slack off during the slow summer season.

It had alarmed her when he talked about the tourists dropping off. They had a good local following, but the tourists fattened everyone's take-home. She was afraid he'd give her fewer shifts, that her tips would drop off too.

That was only part of it, though. Last night—it was like a week had happened last night. The money club, Jack O'Leary knowing Avery Legendre, all her flirting with Luc, her shame at realizing he had no interest in her. It had all left her drained. How could it be that yesterday, before it all started, her life had seemed so good? Now it was lacking in both the work and love departments.

How could she have missed all the signals between Luc and Karen? At the bar she thought he'd been interested in her, not Karen. She searched her memory for anything she'd done that gave her away. She was too tired to remember, tossing and turning in the daybed after she'd heard the chairs scraping on the patio and sat up to see Karen leading Luc to her bedroom. A little later she'd gone to the bathroom. Just in time for the finale. Damn it, she thought. How could she live there if Luc was going to be around all the time, if she was going to hear that every night? She was fairly certain it had been the first time, and if it had been good...

She mentally slapped herself. One foot in front of the other. *Too busy thinkin', cain't hear oppo'tunity ringin'.* That was one of Uncle Dudley's ditties, as Raymond called them...then she was thinking of Raymond, Daniel, her father, Peewee, and most of all Bernie. What she wouldn't give to talk to Bernie...

And now, look, here came Jimmy Johnpier.

"Hi, Jimmy. You're a little late tonight. Want me to call Chef? Pascal?"

"No, dear. I just ducked in to say hello. I'm coming from K-Paul's. Dined with the competition tonight. Don't tell Pascal."

"Between you and me, Jimmy."

He took up his position, elbow on counter, one foot crossed over the other and on point. "What's this? Not your usual lively self tonight, Raynie."

"Beast of a double today. I'm tired."

"And last night? A little too much on your night off?" He mimicked drinking, hand to mouth a couple of times.

"That's not usually my problem."

She wished he'd go. She'd been deliberately abrupt, hoping he'd get the message, but he stood looking down at her with that crooked smile that gave his bone-ugly face a lift, and resistance faded. She sighed and put both elbows on the counter, holding her chin in her palms. "No, Jimmy, it wasn't a night for partying. It turned out to be a night of revelation."

"Uh-oh, that sounds dire indeed."

She stood up straight. "No, I'm just tired. A good night's sleep and all will be well."

Johnpier switched his crossed feet and pivoted so he faced her. "Now, now, you know that kind of talk won't get Uncle Jimmy to go on home."

One of the last parties, a group of eight, left one behind the other, all of them laughing boisterously. Raynie didn't bother telling them goodbye. Behind the wall she heard Harley singing "Happy Trails." He looked around the corner, saw Johnpier, called out hello to him and disappeared.

Jimmy watched until the door closed behind the last one and turned back to Raynie with a question on his face.

"They wouldn't have heard me," she said. "They've been so loud they've given me a headache. I promise I'll be better tomorrow." Glasses and silverware clinked and clanked with a near echo effect in the large dining room. Raynie put a hand to her temple.

"Not the old headache excuse. I want revelation."

He wasn't going to go away unless she said something. She started to just say it, that she had no future here. She'd almost forgotten he owned part of this restaurant.

"I was just thinking..."

"Yes? Thinking's good."

"Not according to my Uncle Dudley, but that's another story."

"A real uncle? I guess there is a family somewhere. I'd like to hear that story."

"I was thinking about the future, wondering if going back to school would somehow make me more useful to Pascal."

"I understand what you're saying, Raynie. You don't want to be behind this counter forever, and a girl with your looks and smarts—you shouldn't be. You know, I might have some ideas. Why don't I take you to the famed Commander's Palace for dinner—you need to see the competition too—and we can talk. Have you ever been there?"

She shook her head.

"Work the day shift tomorrow. We'll go tomorrow night."

"But Pascal..."

"Pascal can do without you tomorrow night. It's early in the week. He mostly does what I tell him to do, about the important things, anyway."

Earlier that day Ramon set up the lights for a shoot inside the nightclub. "No, no, LaDonna, turn it this way."

LaDonna had called Karen and Luc, their phones vibrating one after the other on Karen's bedside table, leaving them both messages to get to La Costa Brava pronto, Ramon wanted them for a scene before they opened for lunch.

"This way?" LaDonna had the light turned toward the bar.

"No. Jesus. Put it on him, directly on him." He meant Luc.

"It is on him."

"No it isn't." He walked over to her, snatched the pole out of her hand and said, "This is on him. This—" he turned the light back where she'd had it "—is on the liquor. Do we fucking care about the liquor, LaDonna?"

"Okay, that's it. I've had enough. Find yourself another star, Ramon. You are an asshole."

She stalked off toward the stairway. He ran after her.

"Please, LaDonna, *bambina*, I beg you, come back. I'll try to be more patient, really, I'll try. I know, I know. I am an asshole."

She'd been slouched, weight on one foot, arms folded, looking anywhere but at him. Now she stood up and tried to get in his face, which was difficult. Ramon was a tall man, six one or two, and LaDonna seemed to be speaking into the big gold medallion around his neck. "Ramon, honey, I'm going to give it another go, okay? But if you ever speak to me like I'm your goddamn lackey again, I'll quit on the spot and you go find yourself another fucking movie—because Buddha will sit on you if you ever step foot on this set again."

"Okay, okay," he said and went back to getting the light on Luc.

She moved off muttering something about fucking killing him.

Karen sat at one of the tables on the sidelines. Ramon had decided he didn't need her after all. She and Luc looked at each other, smiles playing at their lips, but they knew they better not let LaDonna catch them at it. She'd turn her desire to kill Ramon on them.

LaDonna sat at the bar, Luc in the background shining wine glasses with a towel for the scene.

Ramon adjusted the tripod and got behind the camera. "Okay, LaDonna, whenever you're ready, chiquita."

Ramon liked to spice up his vocabulary with Spanish words and endearments, some of which Karen thought he made up, when he was behind the camera, but his name was about what was left of any Spanish ancestry. He was a New Orleans-born, light-skinned black man, good looking with his stubble goatee, huge brown eyes, and major bling in his ears—about five carats of what Karen assumed was cubic zirconia. He'd gone to the University of New Orleans in Film Arts. His major achievement had been to get an intern position on the movie *Ray*.

LaDonna had on the peplum dress Ramon had bought her. She'd made up her eyes with a little gold at the corners. She gathered her braids then shook them out, sat up straight, shoulders back, and looked directly at the camera.

"The evacuation after the flood was hard. I'm just lucky I stayed at the club that night and wasn't at my house when the levees broke. One of my neighbors stayed 'cause she had a son with cerebral palsy, a grown man who was so crippled he was bedridden. When she got out of bed, the water was at her ankles. Her husband managed to get her and their son to the attic, then to the roof of the house. By that time the water was filling the attic fast. He tried to get her mother to the roof. She said the water came so fast that the last words she heard her mother say was, 'I can't breathe,' then she watched the two of them drown in the attic—right through the hole he kicked in the roof."

She stopped, waved her hand at Ramon as she looked down and wiped below her eyes. He got her saying, "I can't tell that story," before he turned off the camera.

"Don't tell it, *bebé*." He went to her and put his arms around her. "You were gonna tell about the evacuation. Go back to that."

LaDonna composed herself. She talked about the evacuation, and this time Karen felt the mud between her toes from LaDonna's cousin's house in Erath after they ran into the second storm, Rita.

She told her story to the point that they arrived back in the Marigny, how they had to talk their way into the city because it was sealed off, no one allowed in, except LaDonna told them she was a restaurant owner, so they made an exception.

"Strange is what it was. I mean, that's the best word to use. It all looked the same, no flood mess, no roofs on the street or anything, but still it was strange. The club had been broken into, all the liquor stolen, but I guess I expected that."

She rambled on for a while, not sounding feisty, not able to gather her thoughts. She talked about going to the two bars that were open, Molly's and Johnny White's, people wanting to be around each other. "Like we just wanted to make sure we were all there. 'Cause none of us knew what was going to happen. We had the news people around some of the time, the Guard, but they were, like, surreal. What was real was us. The people who still lived here, who weren't going anywhere. Sometimes I thought of us as a tribe of people who lived in this ancient, crumbling urban jungle. We had to go out and search for food. We cooked together, ate together. Every once in a while someone would go home and disappear for a day, and we'd all go pound on their door to make sure they were okay. We didn't have any plans. It was like being free, but it was a bizarre freedom. We were free from the future. No future existed."

La Donna got up, paced a few steps one way, then the other, then she stood in front of the camera. Luc had stopped wiping the glasses; Karen leaned forward on the table, holding her breath.

"We got up every day because it was the beginning of another day. What we had to do—just go out on the street and see what was happ'nen in our territory, see if anyone had found food, if anyone new was around. We didn't do this with a whole lot of purpose. We were very lethargic. We had the resolve to keep on going, but we didn't know where and we still don't know where. We have resolve but we lose our focus. We don't concentrate too well. Our memories seem to be impaired except for what happened after the floods. Here we are at the beginning of another hurricane season, and we still drink too much and sleep around too much. You know, that really bothered me at first, all the sleeping around that was goin' on. Then I realized it was an affirmation of life, that's all it was, sayin', "Here I am, I'm alive!" Except it complicated lives that were already complicated, not by having anything to do or too much to do, but because we were all living so close to each other and because of the uncertainty of it all. People don't realize how much they depend on planning the future, even if it's just the next day, to fill up their lives, to make them meaningful. But we've kinda lost our—what is it?—our desire to plan? The need to plan? You can't plan for an uncertain future. I don't know what it is." Her eyes moved around the room, looking for something but it wasn't there. "What it is," she said at last to the camera, "it's the Katrina effect."

She sat in the nearest bar chair, told Luc she needed a glass of water. The camera, on its tripod, rolled on, but Ramon came out from behind it, his eyes closed, one hand clutching his chest. He took a step then he fell toward LaDonna.

"Oh my God," he said.

LaDonna swiveled the bar chair to him. "What?"

"Oh my God." His voice sounded strangled. He leaned on the bar. He looked as though he could be sick.

"Ramon, baby, what is it? What's wrong?"

LaDonna pushed the bar chair back so hard it fell. Luc ducked under the counter, Karen got up from the table.

"Ramon, are you having a heart attack? Talk to me." She took his upper arm in both hands and gave him a gentle shake. "Ramon! Are you stroking out? Jesus, what's happening?" She turned toward Karen then Luc.

Ramon opened his eyes, he took her hands. "Ssh," he told her. "That was a beautiful moment, LaDonna. Beautiful."

"Oh, for Christ sake." She grabbed her hands away from him. "You're a goddamn freak, you know that?"

"What?" He sounded hurt. "I can't be moved? That was moving, LaDonna. This gonna be a great piece of work. And besides, you gave me the name of it—The Katrina Effect."

"The only piece of work around here..." She saw the camera light on. "Ramon, go turn the fucking camera off. There ain't gonna be no piece of work if we run out of money."

"It's a tape, LaDonna, costs nine bucks."

"Yeah? Like nine bucks is nothin'? Nine bucks buys a tape. Isn't that what you just said? So turn the fucking camera off."

"*Mujer*, you killin' me, you know that? Fuckin killin' me."

"You're both killing me," Karen said, and she picked up her purse and started for the dining room to get things ready for the lunch shift. When she reached the foyer, Jack, Solo and the Bullmastiff were standing at the front door.

Where the hell was Buddha?

FIFTEEN

Karen unlocked one side of the double glass door. "Solo," she said, "welcome to La Costa Brava."

"Thank you, Karen."

He had on a cream-colored raw silk suit with a blood red shirt and the requisite matching handkerchief. His outfit lit up the foyer. The gold cross was still around his neck to accent his silky smooth chest.

Jack followed him in, said, "Sweetums," and planted a big one on Karen's lips. She broke away, aggravated. Outside Ernesto gave her what she thought was an evil look, though maybe he simply couldn't help the way he looked, and moved so he stood like a sentry to the side of the door closest to the restaurant window. Karen closed the door and locked it. La Costa didn't open until 11:30, another hour.

Solo heard the commotion in the bar and walked through the foyer toward it. LaDonna and Ramon were still bickering. Karen slid to Solo's side, calling, "LaDonna, Ramon." Once she had their attention she said, "This is Solo Fontova, from Miami. Solo, LaDonna Johnson, Ramon Thomas—" she gestured toward the bar "—Luc Celestin."

Solo, not big on shaking hands with men, acknowledged Ramon with a slight nod and didn't look at Luc at all. He seemed mesmerized by LaDonna. He took her hand in both of his, as he had taken Karen's so many times, and said, "The pleasure is all mine." He grazed the walls and ceiling with his eyes, and in his formal, accented English he said, "You have a very appealing establishment, LaDonna. I would like to see the rest of it."

"Come on, then, I'll show it to you." LaDonna shoved the tripod she'd just folded at Ramon and led Solo into the music room.

Ramon said to Jack, "I see you found her," meaning Karen. "Hey, man, the movie is going good. I can show you some footage, see if you still interested in investing."

Karen stared at Jack as she said to Ramon, "Jack loves to gamble. I'm sure you can count him in for a sizable chunk."

"My man." Ramon and Jack bumped fists.

"And Ramon?" She turned toward him. "Don't ever tell anyone where I live again."

He bunched his fingers together and put them on his sternum. "But, girl, you know I never been to your house."

"That's lame, Ramon. Don't do it again."

He dropped his hand. "Aiight." He went back to packing up the equipment.

Karen took Jack to the restaurant side. "I don't know what you're up to, Jack, but I know I'd prefer it not to be under my nose."

"I never told him I'd invest. I told him I might know someone interested."

"Like Solo?"

Jack shrugged. "You never know." He gave her his best smile.

"In that case, give the fifty to Solo and let him become a movie mogul."

"You give it to him, sugar. That way, maybe he'll be satisfied with fifty. He already upped the ante on me to seventy-five."

LaDonna and Solo wandered into the dining area. LaDonna was saying, "There's nothing much to show you upstairs, a messy office, a storeroom, and a room with a mattress on the floor. Where I live at the moment."

"Your house…"

LaDonna nodded. "My family home. Destroyed. That's what the movie's about, the flood and what happened afterwards."

Solo closed his eyes briefly. "Your family home—that is a terrible thing. I am deeply sorry."

"No doubt you've heard plenty of this in Miami but here we didn't have a natural disaster, I'm sure you know. This was a major failing of the government, the Corps of Engineers." LaDonna was beginning to sound like the movie all the time. She caught herself. "But don't let me get started. I save the rage for the movie."

Ramon entered on the word "movie," just as Solo said to LaDonna, "Perhaps you will let me take you to lunch today, tell me more about what has happened to you, about your movie."

Karen would have sworn LaDonna was about to accept, but Ramon put his arm over her shoulders and said, "That would be great, but can we take you up on that maybe tomorrow, the next day? We're shooting down in the Lower 9 this afternoon. Come on down, take it in, you want to."

Solo turned to Ramon, his face stiff. "Thank you," he said, always polite but not his usual gracious self. "Perhaps another time. I have business appointments this afternoon." He took LaDonna's hand again and raised it to his bloated lips. "We will talk again soon." As he let his hand drift down with hers still in it, his eyes cut to Ramon, then back. Ramon's grip on LaDonna tightened; his whole body got tight.

Well, look at that, Karen thought. She waited for a reaction from LaDonna, but LaDonna was being her cat self.

—⚊—

As Karen, Jack and Solo took a table in the dining room, Solo said, "Your employer LaDonna, she is a very accomplished woman."

"She is. Too bad you missed the scene Ramon shot just before you arrived. Impressive."

"I'm sure." Solo adjusted himself in the chair. "I will make it my business to see it."

Luc brought three mimosas in tulip glasses to the table. "Anything else?"

Karen shook her head. She waited until Luc was out of hearing range and said to Solo, "Is there anything you'd like to know about Ramon?"

Jack made a sound that was a grunt covered by throat clearing and slid his chair back so he could stretch out his legs. Both Karen and Solo ignored him. He slurped down a quarter of his mimosa.

"I know everything I need to know about Ramon, thank you, Karen."

"Just thought I'd ask." She caught a movement in her peripheral vision and turned toward it—Ernesto in the big window, checking on the boss. She turned back to Solo. "What about Ernesto? Do you think he'd like to come in?"

"No. He is fine where he is."

"It's pretty hot out there, Solo. Maybe he could use something to drink. Luc could bring him something."

"He needs nothing. 'Nesto is like a camel of the desert. He drinks long but infrequently. He will wait for his *cerveza* this evening."

"So he's old enough to drink?"

"Karen, you try my patience and you waste my time. I am here to talk about my money. I suggest that one of you—" he shifted his eyes from Karen to Jack "—produce it quickly. Today."

Jack laughed, his mouth at his glass. "Don't look at me, Solo. I don't have it."

Solo's eyes went to Karen.

Karen said, "Believe whoever you want to believe, Solo. You know both of us. Take your best guess."

"Look, Solo," Jack said, his humor excellent, "she offered it to me while you were chatting up LaDonna. I told her if I gave it to you, it had to be seventy-five. You'd accept fifty from her, wouldn't you?"

"You're calling me a liar, Jack? Right here in front of Solo?"

"One of us is a liar, sugarbuns."

"I don't believe Solo has ever known me to lie or steal money from one of his games. Or leave town with it." She said to Solo, "How do you justify Jack running out on you, leaving Miami in the middle of the night?"

Solo slapped the table, a rare show of anger, and Karen jumped to catch his mimosa before it turned over. "This," he said with quiet fury, looking from Karen to Jack, "is nothing but a fucking cheap Mexican standoff. Excuse me, Karen." Polite but flavored with viciousness. "I hate Mexicans."

He paused a moment to pull down his suit jacket, and when he spoke, he was Solo the businessman once again. "No more talk. You do not tell the truth. Whatever the two of you are up to, it will stop now. For the trouble you are causing, I will expect a hundred. I will keep raising my price until you think your life isn't worth that much." His eyelids dropped and Karen thought he'd never looked more like an iguana or one of those reptiles of the desert. "This action you have promised, Jack. It had better be worth my time."

"It will be, Solo, I'm telling you. We'll get this done then we'll work on the hundred, promise."

Solo held up one hand. With utmost deliberation, he got up from the table and walked out the front door. He looked straight ahead as he and Ernesto passed the front window, but 'Nesto, of course, could not resist one more tough, threatening look.

Karen and Jack sat, watching until they were out of sight. Jack tilted his head, a lopsided grin on his face. "We're pretty good, aren't we?"

"At what? Getting our lives threatened?"

"I don't get it, Karen. The way you've been acting. Trying to give me the money back, like you can't wait to get rid of it. Why don't you just give it to Solo?"

At that moment, Karen realized that she would give the money to anyone but Solo. If Jack wanted to take it and give it to him, fine, but she wouldn't do it. She also realized the bind she'd put herself in: How could she give away tainted money without passing on bad karma? For fucksake, that karma crap had popped into her head as naturally as if it was coming right out of her mother's mouth.

"What money?" she said.

Jack threw his head back and laughed.

Then she said, "Jack, I need you to get me some drugs."

"Sure, baby. Tell daddy what you need."

—⁂—

Late that night Pascal Legendre and Jimmy Johnpier sat in the office above the dark Le Tripot, nursing at one of Pascal's expensive portos.

"Okay," Pascal said, "you got her to go to dinner with you. Impressive. I owe you a big one on that. I hope you saw a fair number of people you knew at Commander's."

"A fair enough number, thank you. But quality, not quantity is the issue. That blowhard Chapman Fitzhenry was there. Chappy thinks he's quite the ladies' man. His eyes were popping and he was dying to make a play, but, alas, Mrs. Chappy was with him, which means most of uptown will be flapping their yaps tomorrow."

"Jimsy, I don't know why you give a great goddamn, but congratulations."

"It's the game, Pascal. If you've got a lot of money and you live uptown, you get to play. You qualify on both counts, but you don't indulge. I realize, of course, that you stay down here much of the time." He tilted his head in the direction of the bedroom down the hall from the office.

"I prefer it down here. It's too quiet uptown. I like the action, everyone coming and going. Well, almost everyone...I might sell the house."

"The only thing I've ever regretted was every piece of property I ever sold. It's the Garden District, Pascal. Hang on to it. One day maybe you'll want to play in that yard, indulge in *the game*. Maybe us swells, we're a dying breed, but I would have bet my soul it's just plain ole human nature. Of course, I've never considered you quite human."

"Maybe you'll tell me how to take that."

"With dignity. You are who you are, and I consider myself lucky to be your friend and business partner. You are an enigma, though, young as you are, anti-social as you are, yet successful as you are."

"Thank you, Jims, and I have picked up a few tips from you over the past few years, so I'm not a total loss."

"Ah, but where's the woman?"

"What woman?"

"*Cherchez la femme*, Pascal. Look for the woman. You're lonely. That's why you choose to live up here, *above* the action. I hope I live long enough to see the woman who thaws your heart. She will have to be an amazing creature."

"Hm. But we were talking about you, James. Perhaps you avoid the real question—did she tell you her name?"

Jimmy's smile, always playing with his lips, broadened enough for face-lift effect. He reared back slightly on the leather sofa, making it creak comfortably, then sat forward to snip and light the cigar he'd been fondling. The smoke trailed from one side of his mouth, drifted toward the ceiling and left its quality cubano fragrance in the air.

"I know I will tax the outer limits of your credulity by saying this, but it's the gospel. It's the first thing she told me after we got to the table and had a drink in front of us."

"You're right. I'm taxed here. She what?—and why?"

Jimmy rolled his port around the glass, took a sip, put it on the table. He tapped his temple with his forefinger. "You weren't thinking, my friend. She's too sharp not to have inquired as to why I hang around here a lot and take my liberties coming upstairs. We sat down, she said she knew I was your business partner, and from that she deduced that I most likely already knew her real name. She wanted it out on the table, so to speak."

"Well, I'll be damned."

Jimmy put two fingers up in the air, wiggled them, then pointed at the coffee table. Pascal shook his head and lifted his hips to get to his wallet. He put several bills on the table in front of him, got up, unlocked a desk drawer, counted out another several, came back to his club chair and lightly tossed the wad to Jimmy's side. It disappeared into the inside pocket of Jimmy's jacket.

"Where do you want to go from here?" Jimmy wanted to know.

Pascal crossed his ankle over his knee and the motor in his foot began to run. "There is nowhere to go. I assume—" he tapped his temple "—that she'll go out with you any time you ask now. After all, you're the boss."

"Oh, come on, Pascal, use your imagination. This is too much fun. Where do we go from here?"

The foot stopped and Pascal took a couple of sips of port before he answered. "You really want to do this? Okay, I'll bet my gold Eldorado you can't get her to marry you."

"That old piece of shit?"

"That's my favorite *antique* car. Well, almost. Next to the Spider."

"Bah, antique. All right, I'll take it, but even if you like it, it doesn't wave my flag. How about LaDonna Johnson's note and the Cadillac? I'll throw in the Silver Shadow."

"You're bluffing. No way that girl's going to marry you."

Jimmy shrugged. "Are you in or out?"

Pascal's foot started going. He drained his glass. "Fuck it. I'm in."

Raynie sat on the sofa at Karen's apartment. Jimmy had dropped her off an hour earlier. She knew he wanted her to ask him in, but she wanted to be alone. No, not alone—she didn't want to be with him any longer. It wasn't anything he'd done; he'd been charming and sympathetic when she'd told him about her family and Daniel and how she couldn't be the wife of a rice farmer, help in the fields at crunch time, keep house, haul kids to school in a truck for nine months of the year, look after them and cook frogs all summer. He'd told her he could see she was made from different stuff than that. He said nothing to put life in the fields down, and for that she gave him credit.

Talking about it all had left Raynie homesick, the worst since she'd left Mamou. She didn't want to go back, but she missed her friends and her father. She missed Daniel, being in love. She didn't miss Raymond though, with his pinching and loud, curse-filled abuse. Talking to Jimmy, she'd said she missed the people, not the place, and he'd said he was sure they missed her too. It was what anyone would have said and never should have said, and no one should have said it the way he did—looking at her, his face without its usual amusement playing with it, but battered and soft, his words quiet and kind, as though he knew just how badly she felt about what she'd done, leaving the way she had, yet understanding it was the only way she could get out. He understood too that she had to do something about it before too long, let them know she was still alive, anyway, but he hadn't said anything about that, hadn't tried to give her advice.

If Karen had been home, Raynie would have told her everything, but Karen would probably spend the night at Luc's again, like last night. If this kept up, Raynie would feel as though she had her own apartment. If it kept up too long, Raynie would likely end up without an apartment. Everything seemed to be changing too fast, although as she sat there in the living room, only the silence crowding her, she realized she was resisting anything changing, and if she did that, she was bound to be unhappy. Whatever happened, she had to go along with it, consider it another chapter in her new adventure. She would control what she could, which meant all she had to do was make the right decision when a choice presented itself. She hoped she could do that.

She picked up the TV remote, held it a moment, then put it on the sofa seat next to her. The picture was too bad to try to watch anything. She was tired but not tired enough to go to sleep. She could listen to music or read one of Karen's thrillers, but the music wasn't going to stop her from thinking and the books required too much effort.

She got out her phone. Sometimes during the week some of the aspiring musicians would have jam sessions at Savoy's in Eunice. If one was happening tonight, Peewee would be there.

The phone rang then stopped, and she said, "Hello?" into a lot of white noise. She said it again and started to close the phone, a little relieved, when Peewee said, "Earlene? Jesus Christ, is that you?"

Such a dork. Her eyes filled with tears. "Hey, Peewee, how you doin'?"

"Jesus Christ, Earlene, I thought you'd never call. I'm coming down there. Just wait till I tell you…"

Raynie sat up straight. "You're what? No, Peewee, don't come."

"I have to, Earlene. I waited for you to call, but I finally gave notice here at work. I'm packed up and I'm leaving tomorrow after I close the store. Tell me where you live. God, I can't believe you called tonight."

"Peewee, you can't stay here, you can't…"

"Don't worry, Earlene, I won't bother you or anything. I just gotta get out of here."

"Why? What's wrong?"

"I went and knocked up Alice Roy, that's what."

"You…Alice Roy Pendergast?"

"Anyone else named Alice Roy around here?"

"But how could you knock her up that fast…you mean, since I've been gone?"

"No, she's, like, almost 3 months. I mean, we were foolin' around, but I, uh, you know, uh, pulled out…"

"Spare me the details, Peewee. How can you run off and leave her? That girl's life won't be worth living."

"What about mine? I need to think, Earlene, and I can't do it around here. All this bitching and yelling, I can't take it. I've locked myself up here in Savoy's. I'm afraid to walk too close to a church. If her parents don't push me in, mine will, and Father Crotty will hold me hostage until Alice Roy can find a dress and hire a limo."

Raynie smiled. "She wants to marry you, Peewee?"

"Well, yeah, but, I mean, I'm not sure…I'm not sure about a lot of things."

"You need some help thinking?"

"I really do, Earlene. Please let me come see you."

"Okay, but don't you dare tell anyone where you're going. I'm not ready yet."

"Don't worry. I told 'em I'm going fishing out of Venice. And, listen, Earlene, when I get there? Do you think you could call me Peter?"

Raynie laughed at that. When she got off, she was wide awake and thinking her problems weren't so bad. Poor Peewee. He could run, but he'd never be able to run away. And what was she going to be able to tell him?

She was agitated. She picked up the remote, put it down, picked it up and flicked on the TV. The picture was as bright and clear as...she noticed what she'd been too distracted to see before, the black box on the shelf under the TV. Karen hadn't told her she'd decided to put in cable. They really couldn't afford it.

Raynie surfed the guide. "Friends" was on, three in a row, reruns, but that didn't matter. She'd seen them all more than once. She got the pillow from her bed and settled in, not a care in the world for the next hour and a half.

—∽∽—

"That was pretty good," Karen said. She pulled the light blanket up, feeling a little chilled in the air conditioning with her bare shoulders exposed.

"Just pretty good?"

"No, really good."

"Let me show you this other move."

"Okay." She plumped the pillows and lay back on them.

Luc stood naked at her side of the bed so she could see him do the yo-yo tricks. He walked the dog, and now he was doing something that looked complex with the string, circling the yo-yo around, and all the while his balls and penis bounced and swung as he moved. If he thought that Karen could watch a yo-yo with that show going on...she was getting a little stirred up again. He was adorable, a word that didn't occur to her much to describe men, with his hair messed and falling over his forehead, his smooth skin and his nearly hairless chest, which she found quite appealing. He was good in bed; she might be saying great in bed in another week or two. He was sweet too, without being a sap, and smart. He liked to talk after they made love. She assumed it wouldn't be long before he fell asleep the moment the act was over, but for now, it was from start to finish a pleasurable experience. But here was the downside, right in front of her. He liked to play and he wasn't too concerned about anything else in life. He was, maybe, a little too easy going for her. And he liked to drink more than she did.

So what? It wasn't forever. She didn't want anything forever, remember? Not even for very long. Enjoy the moment. Her mother liked to say *carpe diem*, seize the day. Yeah, yeah, all that crap. Yet, there she lay, telling him he was a genius with a yo-yo while wishing for a little more—what would you call it? Fire? She pulled the covers closer, and he jumped over her and under them in one fluid movement. He wrapped his arms around her then pulled away.

"What?" she said.

He reached way down, near their feet, and came up with a Nerf ball. He threw it into a little goal hanging on the wall across from the bed. A perfect 3-pointer. Then he started kissing her, his mouth and hands always where she wanted them to be. She felt weak until he got inside her. Here was the fire. It turned her wild, trying to keep things under control...until she couldn't. She went first. He raised himself on his hands and smiled at her. "Ready?" Talk about moves. She came again and still he waited, then they came together. She'd never come at the same time as her partner. Who needed a week? He was great. What had she been thinking earlier, complaining because he liked to play with yo-yos and Nerf balls.

—ɯɯ—

Avery Legendre broke out in a sweat. His zebra-print shirt was sticking to him. He needed some fresh air, but that was in short supply here. They were in one of the old corrugated steel boathouses out by the lake on S. Roadway, only a string of them left standing after the storm. This one was under repair. Upstairs, where they were playing, the wall that should be doors to a balcony overlooking the owner's boat and the marina was boarded up. The rest of the place smelled as though it had been finished moments before they walked through the door—the noxious smell of new carpet and paint, a vague odor of sawdust. The eight bodies in the room had begun to reek of dirty animal, and three of them were heavy smokers, but nothing cut the underlying stink of mold. Four hours in the place and he hadn't gotten used to it. He was feeling sick to his stomach and headachy.

He couldn't get up from the table either. It was what he liked to call the truth-or-dare moment, though his nerves wouldn't stand for any joking around. He signaled to the dim-wit spic who stood by the door. The guy could get a job at Buckingham Palace he stood so still. But he caught Avery's look right away and came over, bending his head down, asking, "*Sí*," and adding the stench of refried beans into the diseased air. Avery asked him for ice water with a twist of lime.

He hadn't liked the setup to begin with, the isolated boathouse and all of them spics except Jack O'Leary. "Cubano," the one named Solo—stupid fucking fake name—told him. Cubano, whatever, they were all spics to him. He'd let O'Leary drive, a mistake he'd never make again. The rest of them, four other players and the dealer, spoke Spanish to each other before the game, but as soon as they started playing, it was all English, unless they were begging mercy from God after a bad hand, thanking the Almighty for a good one, or cursing, all of which he understood. If they'd kept up with the spic talk, he'd have made O'Leary take him home. He had his little gun strapped to his ankle just in case, about the only thing making him feel good at the moment.

The game was Texas Hold 'Em, last game of the night, ten-twenty stakes, two thousand ante. Avery stood to lose better than forty grand if he lost this hand. He'd have to hold up Pascal again if that happened. But if he won, he walked out with close to eighty, not a bad night's earnings. He held a jack and king, which gave him two pairs with the three-card flop the house had showing. O'Leary and the spic on the other side of the dealer had folded, but the player next to him had bumped to twenty so Avery thought he had something, a possible straight, or absolutely nothing but a bluff. The other two guys had stayed in but hadn't raised. It went to Avery now, ten large to stay. He put it in and checked.

Here came the little mirror with the coke. He knew he shouldn't do another line, but he thought maybe one more and the ice water the rancid spic was putting in front of him might clear his head.

He tooted up and looked to the dealer. The turn was a deuce, no help at all for anyone. It was back to Avery now.

So Avery sat there sweating, bathed in sweat. He kept wiping his forehead to keep it out of his eyes. The other three guys were sweating too. He kept looking at the player next to him, the one he thought most likely to have something, but the spic's eyes seemed glued to the table. Everyone else, though, was staring at Avery. Coke juice roared around his arteries. He took a gulp of water. The cold hit him in his chest and head. His left arm felt heavy, maybe going numb. Judas Priest. His throat was closing. Avery thought he was having a fucking heart attack.

SIXTEEN

Karen and Luc managed to get their hands off each other and around cups of coffee. The only thing that had gotten them out of bed was a huge hunger that seemed to hit both of them at the same time. They were getting dressed to go to Coffea around the corner from Luc's in the Bywater.

Luc showered then toweled off as he walked into the small cluttered living room where Karen sat. He was laughing.

Karen stopped turning the pages of the latest issue of *offBeat*. "What?"

"LaDonna and the gangster. Do women often have that effect on...what's his name?"

"Solo Fontova."

"As in, I'm going solo?"

"His mother almost died in childbirth and his father named him Solo because he was going to be the only child. As he tells it."

"Sort of sad."

"Hm." Karen went back to the magazine.

"Anyway, he's got the hots for LaDonna and he's got Ramon pissed. Serious pissed. Said the Cuban dissed him and that wasn't gonna be the end of it."

"Nothing much will come of it. Solo probably won't be in town much longer."

Luc tossed the towel over his shoulder. "That's good. Maybe he'll take Jack back to Miami with him."

Karen closed the magazine and smiled up at him. "That would be convenient, although Jack manages, without ever thinking about it, never to do anything convenient. He'll take risk over convenience any day. Now Solo, that's a different story. Solo hates inconvenience. He'll always take risk over inconvenience. It's part of his machismo thing."

"I think you lost me somewhere."

Karen pulled her legs up on the ratty couch, tucking them under her. "It's easy, really. It's why they've made such good partners. No matter what the circumstances, one or the other of them has a feel for the risk involved, so they're usually pretty successful at whatever scam they've decided to run."

Luc ran both hands through his wet hair, pushing it back. "Does that mean they both might go back to Miami?"

"It only means they'll do whatever they find either convenient or inconvenient to do."

Luc looked exasperated. "Mumbo-jumbo."

"Or another way," Karen said, "they'll go wherever the smell of money and danger is the strongest."

"That I get. I vote for Miami. We're small potatoes here."

"Yeah, maybe, but Jack's still got his connections and that's what counts. When he came by the bar last night he brought me two roofies."

Luc came over to the couch and sat next to Karen. "You're really going to do this, whatever it is you're going to do to Avery?"

"Definitely. He gets a taste of his own medicine, right? You don't think he deserves it?"

"I don't have a doubt in the world he deserves it. But I have a lot of doubt about pulling it off. So you knock him out with a roofie. Then what do you do with him?"

"You'll see. I've got a few things to line up first. Like a public place that's private for a few hours. And a car. I need a car on no notice since we have no idea when he'll show up. And not LaDonna's car. And Buddha. I need Buddha."

"The public place, I don't know about that. But the car— Buddha has a car."

"He does? I can't imagine Buddha driving a car, can't imagine him fitting in a car. What's he got, a Hummer?"

"No, a Hyundai."

"A Hyundai...I don't know. All that weight—looks like he could crack an axle."

Luc looked at her, biting at the inside of his plump lower lip. "Two things, Karen. I'm not giving Avery the roofie, and I want to know if Jack's going to be involved."

"I'm not asking you to give Avery the roofie. And, no, Jack's not involved. I wouldn't tell him what I wanted the roofie for."

"And it drove him crazy, didn't it?"

Karen moved so she was farther away from Luc. "What's your thing with Jack?"

"Mine? Karen, think how it looks from my point of view. You say you're not with the guy any more, but he hangs around your place, and you act like..."

"Like what?"

"Like you're friends? I don't know."

She put her hand on his bare leg. "It's better to be friends with Jack than not friends. He'll get bored. He'll go quicker if I don't fight it."

"I think the way you're acting makes him more interested."

"Maybe for a while, but Jack can't stay still very long. I take that back. He can if there's football on TV." She smiled and ran her finger along Luc's leg. "I want to tell you—I never had sex like..." she pointed at herself then at him "...with Jack O'Leary."

"I wasn't worried about that." He leaned in to kiss her.

She put her hand over his mouth. "Celestin, you have to feed a girl once in a while."

—∞—

Karen found Raynie at work. "You're racking up a lot of doubles lately," she said.

A couple came in, stragglers. The lunch rush was nearing its end, though the first floor was still full. Karen waited for Raynie to bring the couple upstairs. She watched the glass elevator disappear.

"Karen."

She looked toward the dining room. Harley Sands stood at the wall, just inside the big room. He had on the wait staff uniform, black pants, white shirt, sleeve garter, long white apron.

"Have any more cases for us?"

"Maybe. Yeah, I just might."

"Stick around. I got a three-martini lunch going on over here." He was gone.

A minute later Raynie came from the same direction and eased back behind the counter. "I'm working today because I've got a friend from home coming to visit. He's getting in late tonight. I'm hoping Pascal can give me tomorrow night off."

Karen said, "Daniel?" and startled Raynie.

She frowned. "No. His name is Peter Meeker. Look, if you're staying at Luc's tonight, would you mind if he stayed at the apartment?"

"It doesn't matter if I'm at Luc's or not. That daybed, there's a bed underneath. It's a trundle. If I do stay with Luc, you're welcome to use my bed. Just, uh, change the sheets."

"It's not like that. He's an old friend, from childhood."

"You never know when it will get *like that*."

"Not Pee—Peter. You'll see when you meet him." She tilted her head and smiled. "So things are pretty hot with Luc, huh?"

"Yes and no. He's such a…little boy. But what I came to tell you—Jack got the drugs."

Karen couldn't tell if that scared Raynie or excited her. A group of men entered the foyer and Raynie put on a smile Karen wasn't sure she'd ever seen before. "Thanks for lunching with us, gentlemen. Come back soon."

One of them leered at her and started to say something, but his friend steered him through the door. Could have been Harley's martini lunchers.

Raynie said, "Yuk," then to Karen, "So, what's next?"

"We wait. When he comes into La Costa one night, I give it to him. Buddha's got a car. He'll get him out."

Raynie made a face. "Buddha's got to be in on this?"

"Raynie, who else can carry that much dead weight?"

"True."

"What do you have against Buddha?"

"He's scary."

"Only until he opens his mouth. Have you ever talked to him? He has a sort of high-pitched voice. It ruins the effect. LaDonna tells him try not to talk when customers are around. He's dumb and doting. He'll do whatever we need done."

"Okay."

"The other thing we need is a public place that's private for a few hours."

Raynie said, "Like where?"

"I don't know." Karen drummed her fingers on the counter. "Harley. Maybe he'll know."

"Does Harley need to be involved? This is beginning to freak me out."

"Harley doesn't know?"

Raynie nodded. "I told him about it one night. He asked me how I met you."

"So what's the problem? Having some men around is a good

thing."

"Luc?"

"Luc too."

"Not Jack."

"No one wants Jack around."

"But he got the drugs."

"But he doesn't know why he got the drugs. He'd love to know, but he's busy with other things at the moment."

Raynie stepped around the wall. She motioned to Harley.

"What's up?" he said.

Raynie told him.

He thought a moment. "How about a place that's private all night? That's locked up, no one in or out, until morning?"

"Shit," Karen said, "you know a place like that?"

"I do. The rooftop pool at the Royal O. And I know a guy who can let us in and out."

Karen looked at Raynie and made a "you see" gesture. "Brilliant. Just let me know your days off and can you find out when the guy will be there?"

They agreed that if Avery came into La Costa Brava, they'd check with Harley before anything happened.

"Gotta go," Harley said, glancing over at the bar. A tall man, well-dressed Karen could tell, even from the back, without a suit jacket, was talking to the bartender.

"Pascal," Raynie said. "Maybe he's gonna tell me if I can have tomorrow night off."

He might have heard her the way he turned and started walking toward them.

"Mr. Legendre," Raynie said. "This is my roommate, Karen Honeycutt."

Karen put her hand in the one he offered. "Pascal," he said, "and Raynie, you're clear tomorrow night. Elaine's on."

"Great," she said, watching him. His eyes hadn't left Karen, and Karen was staring at him, not saying anything.

Karen found herself looking up—the man was tall—at the GQ type who had been sitting at the table with LaDonna and the other man, the ugly one, with all the papers.

They were the lenders. Or the loan sharks—she didn't know. And the ugly one, he would be Jimmy Johnpier, who had an eye for Raynie.

"Nice to see you," Karen said. Then, "Again."

He opened his mouth, but Karen told Raynie she'd see her at home. As soon as she pulled, he released her hand, and she was through the door so fast, Raynie almost said, "What the hell?"

Raynie never said, "What the hell?"

—⁓—

Karen needed to shower and change before she went to work. She was thinking she should pack a few things, in case she decided to stay at Luc's that night. She was interested in Raynie's friend from home, and not only that, she'd hardly been able to walk when she got out of bed that morning. They could probably use a night off. But you never knew.

The wood gate hadn't been pushed hard enough to engage the lock. Karen slowly opened it. When she stepped into the courtyard, she could see Jack reclined on the sofa through the French doors. He looked as though he might be sleeping.

She burst through the doors, making as much noise as possible. "Jack, you're not supposed to be here. You're not supposed to break in. You could at least close the gate."

She knew she'd waked him the moment she walked in, but he opened his eyes slowly. "Hi, baby," he said sleepily. "How's it going?"

Karen threw her purse on the big chair. The TV was on; Jack was watching reruns of football games. She turned toward it.

The picture was clear; she could see the ESPN logo on the screen. She bent her head and saw the box.

Jack sat up. "See, I got cable for you." He put one foot up on the coffee table and began feeling between his toes for toe jam.

"You are disgusting," Karen told him. She crossed her arms. "I don't want cable, Jack. I'm going to cancel it."

He gave her the full set of his white-white teeth. "You can't. It's in my name."

"You don't even live here."

"They don't care. I called from here, gave them my social, and the Cox guy was over the next day."

"Why can't you watch TV wherever it is you're staying?"

Jack smoothed his hair down, pulled his pony tail so the band was tighter and starting twining it. "I wanted to talk to you about that. I'm not really staying anywhere." Another big grin. "I'm just sleeping around, you know?"

"Cute. Why don't you rent something and put cable in your own place?"

"Oh, sugarbabes, why would I do that? It feels like home here. All our stuff is here."

"My stuff."

"I don't know how long I'm going to be in town."

"That's what hotels are for."

"Come on, honey bunny, that's expensive. Just let me stay here until I figure out what I'm doing."

"Jack, if one thing has become clear to me over the past three years, it's that you will never figure out what you're doing because you do whatever happens to come along to do. I've noticed how difficult it is for you to make plans. You don't like to commit to a plan."

"Yeah, you're right."

"I'm glad you see that. The other thing, I have a roommate. I'm not going to toss her out so you can live here. That's sounds right too, doesn't it?"

"Sure, but she doesn't have to go anywhere. I'm not gonna be here much at night anyway."

"She pays rent. She has a say in who lives here."

"That's easy. I'll pay all the rent. Everyone will be happy with that."

"You're so full of shit. I could ask how you can afford to pay the rent on this place when you think a hotel is expensive, but I don't want to hear it."

"Hear what?"

She dropped her folded arms. "Christ." She leaned over close to his face. "Your fucking logic, that's what. It's fucked!" She walked into the kitchen.

"I'm not gonna argue about that just because you're wrong."

"Jesus."

Behind her the game was interrupted by a voice saying the National Hurricane Center was predicting thirteen to sixteen named storms, eight to ten hurricanes, four to six of them major, category three or above. Dr. Gray confirmed an above average season with seventeen named storms, five major status. People should familiarize themselves with evacuation routes, know their destinations, make plans for their families and pets. Karen saw the remote on the floor. She picked it up, turned off the TV and went to the kitchen.

Jack got up and followed her. "I mean, I'm not logical in the same way most people are. I have my own logic, you know? But what do we care who's right, huh, baby?"

He moved up behind her. She slipped to the side and flung the refrigerator door open in his face. "Whoa," he said and caught it. Karen got out a bottle of water and closed the refrigerator.

"I'll pay the rent and all the bills. How's that?"

Karen, taking a deep drink from the bottle, shook her head slowly.

Jack took advantage of her mouth being full. "Baby, you should see the fish we got." He rubbed his hands together. "You know, we put it out there—" he went through the motion of casting a line into the water "—we got him to take the bait—" he jerked the line "—we set the hook."

Karen put the bottle on the counter, walked to the other side and sat on a chrome stool so she was facing Jack. "You don't fish, Jack."

He did his deep growling laugh, mouth closed, that she used to love for no good reason, then said, wagging a finger at her. "You don't know everything about me, sugar. Fished when I was a kid. City Park lagoon. But those were leetle fish." He held up his thumb and forefinger the length of a bait fish. "This is a big fish." He held his arms wide then did a little drum roll on the counter.

Karen slid off the stool. "I'm so happy for you and Solo, too bad you have to leave…"

"Solo! This guy gave Solo arrhythmia. He got his best dealer in, brought in three primo Cuban card sharks. I mean, he *invested* in this show. And they fuckin acted for him. The guy was sweating so bad they had to Lysol the place after he left. Right before he made his last bet, he looked like he was gonna puke on the table. When everyone folded, I thought he'd faint from relief. Guy walked with close to eighty, a little rich for Solo's blood, but he's coming back tomorrow night, and once we gut him and filet him—" more play-acting, slitting the fish open with a knife "—Solo's blood pressure will stabilize. Maybe we'll hold the performance over next week."

"Too many metaphors."

"What?"

Karen sat back on the stool and propped herself on one elbow.. "Jack, how am I going to get rid of you?"

He hitched his shoulders to his ears, slapped the counter and said, "You could shoot me. Which reminds me, can you give me the gun you took? The city's dangerous right now."

Karen knew she would never need the gun. She knew it shouldn't be there in the apartment. She hated guns, so she couldn't understand why she let her eyes go dead, the lids at half mast, why she said, "What gun?"

Good-natured ass that he could be, Jack laughed. "Sugarbabes, shoot me or not, you still kill me."

—⁓—

When Karen got to La Costa Brava later in the afternoon, she found Buddha sitting on his usual perch, a reinforced steel stool at the door, its joints creaking under his weight, the sides of his rear end hanging over the seat.

"What are you doing here, Buddha? There's almost no one—" she looked into bar "—there isn't anyone here."

"Nothin else to do," he said.

"Don't you want to sit somewhere more comfortable?"

"Unh-uh. They fightin upstairs. Cain't hear 'um from here."

"LaDonna and Ramon?"

Buddha nodded. Karen started to move on, but he stopped her. "Look, Karen, got me a new tatt." He yanked up his T-shirt to expose his huge shelf of a stomach and showed her a whirlpool of bright blue ink with a large red Gothic K in the center. "For Katrina. I'm gettin tatts so I remember all the big shit in my life."

"Good idea, Buddha. I wouldn't want to forget Katrina either. You know, if I'd been through it."

She walked into the interior. Something large hit the floor upstairs. "For Christ sake," she said.

Zachary came out of the storeroom. "I hope she didn't just throw the computer at him."

Karen bolted for the stairs. Midway up she heard LaDonna say,

"Oh, so what's good for the goose ain't good for the gander? Is that it, Ramon? You can go fuck anybody looks like a good fuck but I can't go to lunch with a man who might throw some money at this so-called film of yours? What? Because he's got one of those things?"

"I never should of done what I did, LaDonna. I tole you that a million times. I tole you I'm sorry a million times. I don't know what else I can do."

A little more groveling apparently. Ramon said, "I don't like the Cuban. I don't trust him."

Maybe Ramon had more sense than Karen had credited him with. She yelled, "I'm coming in."

She opened the door, saw the coffee table on its side, all the papers on it all over the floor, as LaDonna said, "This fool thinks I wanna fuck that butt-ugly friend of Jack's. Just 'cause I did lunch with him." She turned to Ramon. "He's a businessman, Ramon. He has money. He's turned on by the idea of a movie, investing in it. Is there anyone upstairs, Ramon?" She knocked on his head with her knuckles. Hard.

Ramon winced and edged away from her. "Fuckin stop that shit, LaDonna. He wants to fuck you, that's all he wants. He has to invest in the movie to do it he will. You don't get that?"

"No, I don't get nothin like that 'cause I ain't gonna fuck the motherfucker. You don't get *that*?" She looked at Karen. "What you think? This dumb ass reads all those crap magazines. He thinks everybody got to fuck their way into the movies."

What Karen thought was that LaDonna needed to know that Solo wasn't just any ordinary businessman. Karen would have to set her straight, but she knew better than to do it in front of Ramon.

"You know what, Ramon?" LaDonna said. "You think Hollywood's just a regular fuck fest. You know what else? I'm done with fuck fests." She kicked the front of the coffee table.

"Listen up, woman. You told me you thought the man's attractive."

"She did?" Karen looked from Ramon to LaDonna. "You did?"

"I said that men can be ugly and good-lookin at the same time. I didn't mean nothin by it, Ramon. Look at Yves Montand, Roscoe Lee Browne…"

"Who the fuck you talkin about?"

"You see?" LaDonna said. "He's so young he don't know nothin I know. How 'bout Humphrey Bogart? You remember him?"

"This asshole ain't no Humphrey Bogart, LaDonna."

"Christ A-mighty, Ramon, that's not the fucking point." She turned, her braids flying behind her, and walked around the table, across the office. She turned again braids following a second later. "Listen, Ramon," she said, trying for calm, "the guy's an opportunist, just like all these fuckin opportunists runnin around New Orleans right now. Thinks there's a buck to be made, sees a glamorous way to do it. None of this working in old moldy houses for him. He likes Hollywood South, keep his sharkskin business suit clean, the high shine on his shoes. You with me so far?"

"Uh, no."

"Look, a city in a country is devastated. The gov'ment decides to write it off. They lie, they don't send aid, the people don't believe they competent to help anyhow. Next thing, we got people runnin through the streets with guns, looting, like it's everybody for themselves. So they send the military in and they ride through the streets in Humvees, guns at the ready, while the citizens sleep out in the streets because they got nowhere else to go, they got no clean drinking water, no food. What's this sound like? Some third world country? Some place where there's a war? Hell, yeah, that's what it sounds like, only it isn't. It's America, and the city in question is the only place like it in the whole country. You still with me?"

Ramon nodded.

"Okay, so all this shit happened, nobody's fixin it, so these other people start comin to town, 'cause now we the land of op-po'-tun-it-y. You can't make a buck in this town, they say, you must be lazy. I say we make damn sure the opportunists don't make a buck without leaving a footprint. I say we make damn sure they give us some bang for the buck. Because this here is the fuckin U-nited States of America, and we got a guy on the line who's trying to give us money. You hear that, Ramon? Oh yeah, he's here to make money, no doubt about that, pushing that security business of his. He wants to give us that money back for your movie, you gonna refuse?"

Ramon took her by the upper arms. "Jesus, baby, that was beautiful. The way you talk, get into it, you..." He closed his eyes tight, his face screwed up, shaking his head.

"Ramon, you too damn emotional. Makes me crazy, you know?"

"No, no, no." He let his face loose. "You gonna talk like that you got to tell me, mujer. The fuckin camera wasn't running."

"For Christ sake." She twisted away from him. "I can do that again. I can do it better. I been working on it."

Ramon went and sort of threw himself in her office chair, rubbing at his chin stubble. "But it's a documentary, LaDonna. It's not supposed to be rehearsed."

"Ramon, you get that camera on, I'll make it look like spontaneous combustion. Okay? Forget that, this here's what we got to talk about—we need more people in this movie, more people from the Lower 9, from Lakeview, New Orleans East, Broadmoor, Gentilly, all the neighborhoods. I can't carry this thing all by myself."

This was set to go on for another few hours. Karen said, "Yeah, well look, I'm gonna bounce, okay?"

Neither one of them so much as glanced at her. She went downstairs to relieve Zachary.

—⚏—

As soon as Luc and Karen walked into his apartment, Luc turned on the TV. Karen tossed her bag toward the bedroom door and slumped into the sofa. A loose spring poked her in the butt. She watched as Luc surfed the channels. The TV sat on a cardboard box, the rug had a hole in it, and dirty dishes surrounded the sofa. The place looked like a frat house.

"So the honeymoon's over," she said. Luc stopped surfing to look at her. "The TV goes on, the honeymoon's over."

"Nah." He crowded up next to her, one arm around her, his lips on her cheek, his thumb paging, one eye on the screen.

"I'd rather watch you do yo-yo tricks."

"In the morning. Let's watch a movie. I'll throw some popcorn in the microwave." He put the remote on a piece of wood atop two cinder blocks—the coffee table—and went into the small gallery-like kitchen.

He'd stopped on *The African Queen*. Hepburn furious, trying to read on the deck of the boat, Bogart trying his best to ignore her but eyeing her with resentment, interested too.

Karen took a big breath and let it out slowly. She heard ice going into glasses, she started to smell the popcorn, she stretched her legs out to the coffee table, careful not to upset its balance. Ah, too bad—the movie was on a channel with commercials. She zoned, eyes closed, until a voice, a notch louder than the commercial, said, "Are you ready?" She opened her eyes. The words were writ large in bold black against a sea-blue background.

"The National Hurricane Center and Dr. Gray of Colorado State University have made their predictions, an above-average hurricane season with as many as seventeen named storms, up to ten hurricanes, four to six with major status, which means category three or above. In the event of a hurricane: Do you have a disaster survival plan? Do you know the evacuation routes? Do you have a destination? Are your important papers…"

"For fucksake." Karen reached for the remote, muted the sound, and moved to Luc's side of the sofa where the springs were not so aggressive. She closed her eyes again and inched further down into the sofa. She tried to relax.

SEVENTEEN

Peewee Meeker sat at the bar at LeTripot and ate like he hadn't had a decent meal in weeks, which was pretty much the case he'd told Raynie. He arrived after the kitchen had closed, but Chef liked Raynie and he put on a steak and home fries for her friend.

Peewee sat with his back to her. She looked at his thin frame, boyish shoulders, his dark brown hair a little long in the back, hanging up on his shirt collar. She'd noticed that his face had cleared up some; he looked different, better, and she embarrassed herself by wondering if it had to do with getting regular sex. The thought of Peewee having sex...

Peter—she needed to remember to call him Peter. What about Peter having sex? No, didn't help much.

Jimmy Johnpier came from the dining room and assumed his position at the counter. "Has your friend arrived yet?"

Raynie nodded toward the bar. "The skinny one, white short sleeved shirt, with his back to us."

"Has he brought news?"

"Big news, but we haven't had much of a chance to talk yet. He knocked up one of the local girls. Nice girl, but he's freaked out about it. He's run away."

"Has he considered this might be the best thing that's ever happened to him?"

"Hardly. He thinks his life is ruined."

"And you—do you think his life is ruined?"

Raynie had been talking, her eyes on Peter. She turned to Jimmy. "I don't know. I'm having trouble imagining him not living in Mamou, but I suppose plenty of people would have thought that about me."

"And you—would you have thought your life was ruined?"

"Oh yes, oh most definitely yes."

Jimmy laughed. "And for you, precious, it would have been. You were too smart to let that happen."

"I don't know. I feel sorry for him. It could happen to anyone."

"Oh bullshit," Jimmy said. "You made up your mind that you were going to live a different life and you made it happen. Your friend there let life happen to him. World of difference."

"Well, life *does* happen." Raynie let herself slouch on the counter.

"Forget about that. Let's make exactly what we want happen. What's the next night you're off?"

"Tomorrow, but I'm taking Peter out on the town."

"Why don't you start the evening by meeting me for dinner at Tujague's. Early, then you two can go your merry way well fed."

Raynie considered this. "It might be awkward…"

"I won't persist if you'd rather not. Or you can call me tomorrow."

Before she could decide, Peewee pushed himself away from the bar. She introduced him to Jimmy as Peter, and Jimmy asked if he'd like to go to dinner the next night, and the way he reacted, Raynie realized why she would never be able to think of him as anyone other than Peewee Meeker. His eyes darted from Jimmy to her and back and he shrugged in the way that only people with skinny flexible shoulders can, all the way to his ears. "Sure," he said sounding dubious.

—⁓—

Back at the apartment, Peewee said for about the fourth time, "I *mean*, that is the *ug*liest man I've ever seen, Earlene—Raynie. I mean *weird* ugly."

He was sprawled on the sofa, experiencing what appeared to be some kind of euphoria, which could have been from the steak and potatoes, since all he'd eaten during the two weeks he'd locked himself in Savoy's after hours was Taco Bell. Or it could have been from the wine he and Raynie were drinking. Or the escape from Mamou. Raynie had put on George Porter and Peewee was drumming his fingers to the music on his stomach.

Raynie closed her eyes and leaned her head back in the big chair. "Okay, yes, he is weird looking, but can you get off that? He's being a good friend, and he's the only person in this city who knows my whole story. And he's cool about it. Not even Karen—the woman I live with here?—not even she knows. Can you remember that, Peter? Can you remember not to call me Earlene in front of her?" She opened her eyes and looked hard at him.

"Don't get bent. I'll remember." He sat up some on the sofa, one foot on the floor. "This Karen, when will she be here? Is she good looking?"

He put on what Raynie figured he thought was a cool-stud look. "For pity's sake," she said. "Are you serious?"

Cool-stud was gone. Little Peewee Meeker was back. "Why not?"

"For one thing, she's almost ten years older than you. For another, she's probably not coming home because she and the hot bartender at La Costa are having a *thing*. And then there's Alice Roy." Peewee whimpered. Only Peewee would whimper. Raynie reached for the wine bottle. "I can't believe you didn't tell me you were going with Alice Roy."

Peewee held out his glass. "Do we have to talk about this now?"

Raynie poured. "Yeah, yeah we do. That's what you came here for, isn't it?"

"I don't know. Maybe I came here to stay. Like you."

Raynie drank some wine, quiet for a minute. "Is Alice Roy excited about the baby?"

One of Peewee's shoulders jerked up to his ear. "I guess so."

"Maybe it's hard for her to be excited if you aren't."

He wouldn't look at her. "No, she's excited."

"She's a nice girl, Peewee. I think y'all could be happy together. Think about it, you're going to have a beautiful little baby."

"I don't know if I even want a baby."

Raynie gasped. "Peewee, you didn't...did you?"

"What?"

"You know."

"Tell her to get an abortion? Jesus Christ, Earlene, you think I'd be alive?" He looked upset. "I wouldn't do that. No one does that in Mamou. We'd go straight to hell."

"Like you won't go straight to hell if you don't marry Alice Roy?"

He ran a hand through his hair. The gesture, the depth of his misery...for the first time Raynie thought he looked grown up.

"I don't know if I want to get married. I would support the baby..."

Peewee closed his eyes tight. They were both quiet until he got a grip on himself. "See, the thing is, I don't know if I want to get married, but I don't know that I don't either."

Raynie got up and turned off the music. She sat at the end of the sofa, making Peewee move, sit up all the way, both feet on the floor.

"What's the problem, Peewee? Don't you love her?"

Peewee got fidgety, the way he did when he was excited or nervous. He put his glass on the coffee table, picked it up, put it back. "You don't get it, do you, Earlene? How can you not get it? The problem...is *you*. You know I've been in love with you all my life."

"But not like *that*."

"Why not like *that*? Why, because I'm not hot enough? 'Cause I'm just Peewee, stupid Peewee Meeker?" He shut his eyes again.

Raynie moved closer to him. "Come on, Peewee, you know I don't mean it that way. We're friends. Old, old friends. Of course we love each other." She put her hand on his forearm.

Without opening his eyes, he covered her hand with his. When he could finally look at her, he had to blink several times. "I just had to see you one more time, Earlene. I had to make sure it was impossible. I mean, I know it is…shit." A tear escaped one eye.

She moved so she could put her arms around him. When she held on, he put his around her. They sat like that for a while, rocking each other ever so gently.

—∿—

The apartment dark save the light that got past the trees in the courtyard, they were in bed, Peewee in the trundle, Raynie in the day bed. Several minutes had gone by since they'd said good-night. They had their backs to each other. Without turning Peewee said, "Do you think we could sleep together tonight?"

Raynie turned, then he did. She propped herself on an elbow. He did too.

She could see his face in the semi-dark. He looked so different to her now. "Peter," she said and he nodded. "I haven't slept with anyone since Daniel."

"Is he the only person you ever slept with?"

She nodded.

"Maybe this isn't right, but I don't want Alice Roy to be the only person I ever sleep with. Do you think that's wrong?"

"No, I don't think that's wrong." He waited. She said, "Do you know how Daniel is?"

"He's okay. Well, he doesn't look so good. Everyone's pretty worried about you."

"Is Daniel seeing anyone?"

"I don't think so. When are you going to let them know?"

Raynie shook her head. "I'm just not ready yet."

"I understand."

They sat propped in bed, looking at each other.

Raynie said, "I don't want Daniel to be the only person I ever sleep with either." She flipped the covers back.

—⚏—

Raynie spent the next day at work in a fog of longing, not for Peter Meeker, who had surprised her with his agility, but for Daniel, the big love of her life. For the first time since she'd left Mamou, she let her mind go to the pain she must have caused him and stay there. What she'd done, not telling them all she was leaving, going to live the life she thought she was supposed to live, had been weak and cowardly, not strong, as she'd convinced herself. It would have taken real strength to leave with Daniel, Bernie and her dad all trying to convince her that her real life was in Mamou, life anywhere else was a fantasy. If she wanted to go back, they might never forgive her. Daniel, with his easy way in the world and his sweetness, was slow to anger, but once the fire caught, he didn't let go. She'd seen it before, how he held a grudge.

Peewee had more strength than she did. He'd left saying he needed to go away, spend some time alone, think. And now, what had she done, sleeping with Peewee? He wouldn't want to go home and marry Alice Roy. All day it was hard for Raynie to smile at the customers, be friendly, tell them to come back soon. She wished Harley Sands was there to make her laugh, but he came on as she got off.

Peewee knew something was wrong the minute she got back

to the apartment.

He met her at the gate, a sleepy smile on his face, and when he saw her, he said, "Oh God no, you're sorry you slept with me." His hand raked his hair.

She assured him she wasn't sorry.

She didn't say so, but she was sorry she'd agreed to go to dinner with Jimmy Johnpier. Her guilt and remorse had turned into anger. She got dressed, thinking that Johnpier always acted like he didn't want to be pushy, but he always got her to agree to do whatever he wanted her to do, mostly go to dinner or lunch or for a drink. She'd gone out with him a few times after work, enough that Harley had started making fun of her new boyfriend.

But the dinner turned into fun. There were lots of downtown locals Jimmy knew at the restaurant, and he gave Raynie and Peter the lowdown on them all—the gallery owner who hardly ever left the Quarter, stood on his corner of Dumaine where he traded local gossip the way some people traded drugs and said fuck the hurricanes, they'd have to take him out in a body bag; the chanteuse who'd stood out in the middle of Royal street in front of a huge tourist bus, in protest of the buses on the narrow Quarter streets, and had been picked up like a mannequin and removed by the police (the buses were no longer allowed); the painter known internationally for his large nudes, who lived in one of the oldest houses in the Quarter, full of priceless antiques—a living museum, Johnpier called it—who was also known for his forty-year feud with his neighbor, a restaurant he called the Court of Two Shysters.

He got Raynie and Peter to talk about the characters in Mamou. Once they started telling stories, Raynie lost her regret and homesickness. She knew where she belonged, in her new life, with all its new characters. She'd left all those old stories and old characters far behind. She hugged Jimmy when they left, grateful to him for bringing her back.

"Okay," Peewee said as they crossed Decatur, "I see why you like him. It doesn't hurt that he's rich as shit, either."

"Peewee," Raynie said and gave him a look.

"Well, does it?"

—⁂—

Avery Legendre was feeling good. He felt so good he put on James Brown and sang along, "*I fee-eel good, nah-na-nah-na-nah-na-nah....*" He bent down over his air-mike, pivoted smartly on one foot, got down in a squat, jumped up to hit the high notes. He had on his feel-good rayon Hawaiian shirt with the yellow hibiscus flowers, a pair of expensive buff-colored linen slacks and his Panama hat. He liked watching the little tassels on his Gucci loafers bounce when he kicked and turned.

Avery felt good because he had eighty thousand cash in a brushed-aluminum briefcase, but he wasn't so sure he wanted to go to the card game at the boathouse. It had occurred to him the morning after the first one that all that cursing and calling on God in spic-talk was some kind of code. And the way they rolled their eyes to heaven, that too. They'd been talking to each other the whole game. He was supposed to win. Tonight he would lose.

On the other hand, there would be lots of good dope and booze, and it was the only action in town, insofar as he knew. If he only took forty large with him and he lost it, he was even. Maybe he was wrong—he did have a size triple X hangover when he had all these thoughts—and Lady Luck would shine on him once again. Or maybe he would hit a couple of bars tonight and take a plane to Vegas first thing in the morning.

The night was young yet. He could decide what he wanted to do over a drink. He took seven thousand in hundreds, a little mad money in case he ran across some unexpected action, and slid the briefcase under the bed. A couple of lines of coke, one more whoop and holler with the Hardest Working Man in Show Business, and Avery packed five grand in his custom-made money belt with the silver alligator buckle, folded two into his pocket, strapped on his ankle holster, and started walking over to La Costa Brava.

———

Five men sat around at the boathouse. One was at the poker table; two others, along with Jack and Solo lounged on a large purple semi-circular sectional, a new addition to the décor. Ernesto stood at the door.

Jack closed his cell phone. "Not answering."

"Leave a message," Solo said.

"I left three messages."

"We are all ready. Where is my player, Jack? Your job was to pick him up and get him here."

"He didn't want me to pick him up. Wouldn't let me."

"You are supposed to be more persuasive. You pick him up by the hair of his balls if you have to."

Jack laughed. "That's funny, Solo. I'm dealing with a whack job—I'm supposed to twist his arm? He'll shoot me with that little gun on his ankle."

"You might prefer him to shoot you."

"He's a gambler, Solo. This is an occasion. He's probably coking up. He'll show after he gets his jets fired. Needs some heat to gamble."

The other men began complaining. They stopped when Solo stood and looked down at Jack.

"Call him again, Jack. Hope that he answers."

Jack opened the cell and used his thumbs on the pad. "Voice mail," he said.

"Forget the message. Go find him."

—◊—

Cell phones rang all around downtown.

Avery checked his, saw Jack's number and turned off the phone.

Karen called Raynie as she and Peewee sat out on the Moon Walk. "Operation Longhorn in countdown," she told Raynie and Raynie said, "I'm a few blocks from the Royal O. Where do you want me?"

"Where are we going?" Peewee wanted to know.

"To the garage at the Royal Orleans."

Raynie called Harley Sands. "He's at La Costa Brava."

Harley called the guy at the Royal O. "We're on tonight."

The guy confirmed for eleven o'clock on. Harley told the rest of his wait team that he had to leave—an emergency.

Luc called Buddha who was sitting in the foyer of La Costa. "We need the car. Then get back in here."

Buddha got up, lumbered down the street toward the parking lot.

Luc called Zachary, told him to come in. Zachary didn't want to. Luc shook his head at Karen. Karen took Luc's cell. "Zachary, it's important...Two hundred, over and above...Okay, make it three, but that's it...didn't I just say that? Yes, over and above tips and everything."

Karen called LaDonna upstairs. "Change of schedule. Zachary's coming in. Luc and I are going out."

"Oh yeah? Where you going? We're bored."

Karen closed the phone. "Jesus," she said to Luc, "LaDonna and Ramon want to come."

"Tell them no," Luc said.

The cowboy in the Hawaiian shirt with his Panama hat pushed

back on his head sat at the end of the bar next to the lift top, a draft beer in front of him, oblivious. He finished his beer, stood up, and reached into his pocket. "Oh no," Karen said. Luc froze. Avery took out a wad of folded bills, pulled a couple to put on the bar. He checked his watch. Do or die time. He looked up as Karen, the woman bartender, looked away. Was she giving him the eye? He sat down again. "Another of these," he called.

Luc unfroze. He nodded at Avery and finished the drink he was mixing. Avery watched Karen go partway into the storeroom at the other end of the bar and bend over to get something from a lower shelf. Fine ass, he thought. Over the juke box he could hear jazz leaking from the back room every now and again. His fingers drummed the bar. He needed a bump. He got up and went to the bathroom. When he came back, he pulled the fresh draft to him, and as he put half his rear end on the bar chair, he took a gulp. He sat back and grooved to Robert Plant and Alison Krauss. Karen looked at him, held his eyes this time. That was the decision maker for Avery: fuck the card game.

The bar was noisy, all tables occupied, most of the bar chairs taken. People stood behind them, talking over the music and drinking. Above their heads he saw Jack O'Leary come in and grin when he spotted Avery. Avery swilled the last of his beer and thought about a quick exit through the dining room while Jack made his way through the crowd, but he put a foot on the floor and the room gave a short spin.

Jack squeezed in next to him, put his cell phone on the bar and said, "Hey, man, you forget we had a game up tonight?"

EIGHTEEN

"I thought Jack wasn't going to be involved in this," Luc said.

Karen didn't like his tone. "I can't predict or control when he's going to walk in here." She watched the cowboy almost miss the seat of his chair. Jack steadied him, his hand on Avery's arm. "The man's timing is always impeccably inappropriate," Karen told Luc.

Luc didn't answer. Someone called, "Bartender," and he moved off to take the order.

"Man," Jack said to Avery, "you look like you could use something to toot."

"Yeah," said Avery. He shook his head like a wet dog. His panama hat came off and drifted to the floor. He looked down at it, thought he was falling, rocked sideways and fell into Jack.

"Hey hey, my man," Jack said, "you gonna make it to the bathroom?"

"Hat," Avery said.

"I'll get it. Come on." Jack grabbed Avery's arm to help him up.

Karen called out to Jack and put down the drink she was mixing for one of the waitresses. "Luc, get her, will you?" She was already moving to the other end of the bar.

She motioned to Jack to lean over the bar, closer to her. "Buddha's going to take him home," she said.

"He's going anywhere, he's going with me."

"Your sucker, huh? He's in no condition to play cards, Jack."

"Couple of toots, I'll have him fixed up in no time."

"No you won't."

Jack did a swift turn to Avery whose eyes were fluttering, then a slow smile back to Karen. "The roofies?"

She nodded.

"Fuck, Karen, you've gone and messed up a big production."

"Yeah, yeah, yeah," she said, "all those actors with their fishing poles. Like I give a shit."

"You should. Solo's gonna go ballistic on us."

"Your problem."

"Not just mine."

Avery opened his eyes enough to see Karen shaking her head at Jack. The last coherent thought he had was, the woman bartender—she doesn't want me to go. He slumped down, the front of the bar stopping his slide.

Buddha was coming from the foyer. LaDonna and Ramon were coming from the other direction.

LaDonna looked back, laughing at something Ramon said. He put his hands on her hips, as though guiding her to the bar. "What's up?" she said to Karen before fully taking in Avery, his head on his chest, Jack next to him, his elbow in Avery's armpit, pinning him to the chair. "What's with them?"

"Hello to you too, LaDonna."

"Jack." She stepped on something, looked down and saw the Panama hat. She kicked it out of the way of the lift top.

Buddha, dressed in huge, loose sweats and a muscle-man U-shirt stretched to within its last gasp of spandex, stepped up to Avery. He glanced at Jack and Jack moved his arm and got out of the way. Buddha grasped Avery under the arms and lifted him as though lifting a child.

LaDonna said, "You got a cab for him?"

Avery was up on his feet. What was left of his consciousness was trying to make his legs work. Buddha, man of few words with LaDonna said, "My car. Royal O."

"He's staying there?"

"Yes," Karen said.

"No he's not, LaDonna," Jack said. He gave her his madman grin. "I think he's going to a little party."

"What party?" LaDonna said to Karen.

Ramon danced with LaDonna's hips, singing, "Goin' to a party, party…"

LaDonna elbowed him. "Stop it, Ramon. What the fuck is going on?"

Avery's legs stopped working. With one graceful move Buddha swept him up into his massive, powerful arms. All around them people stopped talking and stared. Buddha shifted Avery's weight then effortlessly slung him over one of his enormous shoulders. He held Avery there with one huge hand on his rump. The crowd parted like the Red Sea as he took Avery out through the dining room. The noise in the back part of the bar started up slowly then reached a new pitch. From the front station at the bar the waitress yelled at Luc, "I need drinks *now*."

Zachary arrived in the midst of all this. He saw LaDonna and said, "Whoa—I hope nobody thinks I'm working this crowd alone."

LaDonna's eyes left Buddha's back. "You'll be fine," she said to Zachary. "Come on, Karen, let's go."

With that, LaDonna ran to catch up with Buddha, her braids swinging. Ramon was on her heels, "LaDonna, shouldn't I go get the camera?"

"Don't yell in my ear, Ramon."

With a quick glance at Karen, Jack followed them.

"For fucksake," Karen said to Luc. "We better go."

"I'm out," Luc said.

Zachary ducked under the lift top, Avery's Panama in hand. "Are y'all going to leave me here alone?"

"Can a guy get a beer here?" someone called.

Karen started reaching toward Luc, but her hand ended up on her forehead. "But this was our deal," she said.

"No Karen, this was your deal. Maybe Raynie's. I don't know."

"Goddmanit," the waitress yelled from the front station of the bar. "I don't have all night, Luc."

He reached for the glass Karen had left with the beginnings of a drink in it. "What's this?"

"A cosmo," she said. "Shit, Luc."

"Just go," he said.

Zachary, drawing a beer, said, "So I'm not alone, right?"

"Right," Luc said.

His brows drew together and his expression turned dark. Was he about to have a temper tantrum? Was he in a jealous snit? Maybe he was just a wuss. Karen went outside and scrunched herself in the back of Buddha's Tucson with LaDonna and Ramon.

LaDonna shifted her butt back toward the rear seat. "Now," she said to Karen, her face alight. "What are we doing?"

—⟋⟍—

The guy at the Royal Orleans got jumpy the minute they all unloaded from the Tucson. "Shit, man," he said to Harley, "you didn't tell me you were talking cast of thousands."

One of the garage attendants looked a little too interested. Harley moved up the ramp to the hotel and stepped closer to the guy. "Look, what, there only five, six of us."

"Not by my count. I see eight and that's not counting the corpse."

"Jesus, it isn't a corpse."

"Yeah, but you know what I mean."

"Why don't you just grab a wheelchair and get us out of here?"

Karen could see him shaking his head. Everyone had gotten

out of the SUV except Jack. They all stood looking toward Harley and the guy.

Karen said, "Wait a minute," and left them to go up the ramp.

"What's going on?" Peewee said to Raynie.

"Who's he?" LaDonna meant Peewee.

Ramon said to Raynie, "Yeah, who's he?"

Karen asked the guy if there was a problem. He told her yeah, there was, and he didn't think any of whatever they were up to was a good idea any more.

Karen reached into her purse. "Would this change your mind?" She held out two bills folded in half.

He didn't even look at it. "No. You think jobs are easy to get these days?"

She went back into her purse. "Five hundred. Gotta be more than you're making tonight."

He held up his hands. "Yeah, maybe, but I got a bad feeling and Julio over there can't peel his eyes off the body."

"I'm counting on you, man," Harley said.

"Sorry to let you down on this. I owe you one." He gave Harley dap then couldn't get through the hotel door fast enough.

Karen put up the money. She took a deep breath, let it out, and said to Harley, "Plan B." They went down the ramp. "Okay, everybody, it's Woldenberg Park."

Raynie looked worried. "Out in the open? Karen…"

"Don't worry, it's okay. I'll walk over with you and Peter. Harley, will you ride with them? Try to keep everyone under control?"

"Thanks," he said. He was carrying a brown paper bag. He rolled the top tighter.

"What's that?"

"Slime," he said.

"You brought your own? We should have gone to one of the City Park lagoons to begin with."

Karen walked over to the passenger side of the Tucson. "What are you doing, Jack, looting the body?"

He was putting Avery's belt on above his. "Never let a body go unlooted. I learned that from a cop." He hooked it in place. "Love this alligator."

"For Christ sake."

—⚉—

Woldenberg Park was upriver from the Aquarium of the Americas, an easy walk along St. Louis Street to the Mississippi. Karen hadn't met Raynie's friend yet. She saw what Raynie meant about him not being a friend you might sleep with. He was skinny, kid-like. She felt she towered over him, though he was a little taller than Raynie. His hair was gelled back, his black polo shirt sleeves rolled up, and he was puffing on a cigarette. No attempt at cool could make him look any less ready to jump out of his skin.

"So, what are you, uh, going to do to him?" He tried to be casual about it, but his voice inched upward at the end of his question. He cleared his throat.

"We're going to undress him and leave him in the park."

"Oh." He laughed in that way that you knew he wasn't really laughing. "Kind of, uh, risky, isn't it? I mean, outside and all."

Karen smiled at him. "Half the fun." He didn't seem to have a clue to what she was talking about. "The risk."

His shoulders jumped. "Yeah, sure, I mean, yeah. Sure."

Raynie spoke for the first time since they'd started walking. "What's the matter, Peter? Don't you think he deserves it?"

"Yeah. I mean, you know…"

"What do you mean? We're just doing to him what he did to me. Only he didn't mean just to dope me up and take my clothes off. I mean, you know, Peter? He was going to, uh, rape me? You know?"

Peter seemed stricken. "No, Er-uh, no, Raynie. He deserves to die. It's just, I mean, if we get caught, then the scumbag can really put the screws to you."

Karen laughed. Peter had no idea why she was laughing. "That's good, Peter. Put the screws…listen, just take it easy. Think about if we don't get caught."

—◇—

Karen, Raynie and Peter walked up as LaDonna said, "This is Pascal Legendre's little brother?" She leaned over him, scrutinizing his face. She pinched his Hawaiian shirt and rubbed it between her thumb and forefinger. "Doesn't look a thing like his brother. Sure doesn't dress like him."

Buddha had found a dark place in the park behind some bushes where he'd laid Avery down like a baby. He stood sentry, his arms folded, his back to the group and the river, which was just a few feet away.

Karen took a deep breath. River smell. Nothing like it—fresh yet loaded with odors, whiffs of the river traffic swirling through the cool night air, ships and machinery, and foreign smells that rode her imagination and made their way to the docks. She watched the lights of the city dancing on the water. She could stare at it all night.

But back to business. She looked down at Avery Legendre. "Let's do it."

After a slight group hesitation, Jack bent down and Karen heard a zipper. LaDonna began unbuttoning the Hawaiian shirt.

"Man," said Ramon, "I should have brought the camera."

LaDonna said, "Think about that, Ramon. Think about all the reasons it wouldn't be a good idea to video this."

Ramon lifted his hands and backed away. He went over to Buddha. "That woman can't get behind a goof no how."

Buddha looked straight ahead. Ramon walked a few feet away from him, folded his arms, and stood sentry too.

LaDonna shrieked, everyone except Buddha shushed her, and Ramon ran over. "What?"

Raynie had squatted down next to LaDonna. Jack had Avery's pants to his knees.

"You see why this asshole needs to drug women?" LaDonna pointed at his shriveled penis. Raynie laughed.

"What you sayin, it's small?" Ramon said

"Yeah, just a little ole thing." LaDonna muffled her mouth against her upper arm to keep from shrieking again.

"It's not that little," Ramon said. "The man's been drugged and..." he reached down, put his hand on Avery's bare chest "... his skin's cool to the touch. That's what they do; they shrivel."

"Ramon, you will argue with me about anything."

Karen and Harley were standing off to the side. "For Christ sake," she said under her breath.

Peter stood off from them, the loner. He did a little rubber-necking around Jack to see what the fuss was about, then he resumed twitching. That was the only word for it, Karen thought.

Jack had taken Avery's shoes off. He lifted his right leg and said, "Well, well, what do we have here?" He ripped the Velcro strap and held Avery's Smith and Wesson .38. His hand was like a mitt around it.

"You missed that the first time around?"

"I sure did, doll face. It's either these loose pants—" with a grunt he pulled them off Avery "—or I'm losing my noodles." He looked up at Karen and grinned. "What do you think?"

Karen said out of the side of her mouth to Harley. "He only ever had one noodle."

The laugh exploded against Harley's soft palate and sounded like a strangled snort.

The Good Humor man said, "Now you all stop laughing at old

Jack." He stood up, finished with Avery.

Raynie said, "I brought a marker with me."

Harley went around and kneeled opposite her. "I brought something better." He took a jar and a small paintbrush out of the brown paper bag he'd been carrying all night. "It's net dip." Raynie furrowed her brow. "The fishermen coat their nets with it. Strong stuff. It sticks. And I got them to make it extra thick."

He unscrewed the top and handed it to Raynie. The stuff was green, viscous when she stuck the paint brush in it. "It looks like, like..."

"Slime," Harley said. He gave an evil, horror-movie laugh.

Everyone had gathered around. Even Buddha couldn't help looking over his shoulder.

"Hold it." Harley reached into his shirt pocket and took out a disposable razor. He held it up for everyone to see before he bent over Avery and shaved off his eyebrows, dry. LaDonna picked up the hair and held it tight in her fist. Harley said, "Okay, Raynie, slime him."

She dipped the brush, wiped it along the rim of the jar, and began to paint with a delicate touch. The goop wasn't easy to work with; she had to keep going over and over her strokes to make them solid. For the first time, Karen began to feel nervous.

"Beautiful," LaDonna said when she finished. "May I?"

"Do with him whatever you will," Raynie said and handed her the jar.

"Wrap this up, LaDonna," Karen said.

"I feel you, Honeycutt, but we outta here in five seconds."

She dribbled the green goo down Avery's hairy chest. It pooled at his sternum and ran off the sides of his belly. When she got to his pubes, she said, "And something special for the little prick." She dumped the rest of the net dip.

—m—

197

It had taken less than an hour. They piled into Buddha's Tucson and went back to La Costa. They were all as rowdy as if they'd been drinking since sunset. Except for Raynie's friend Peter. He wasn't being rowdy. He sat squeezed in the middle of the back seat but, still, he was the odd man out.

Karen went over to Buddha's window before he took off to park the car. "We couldn't have done that without you, Buddha. Thanks." She handed him the same two hundred dollar bills she'd tried to give the guy at the Royal O.

Buddha looked at the money. "I can't take your money, Karen. I don't do nothin less I wanna."

"Sure, Buddha, I know, but still, you took your time to help, your car…"

"We all help each other. LaDonna pays me." He drove off.

What was this? Some kind of post-hurricane mentality? Karen put the money in a pocket in her purse and went inside the club.

The crowd had thinned because Charmaine Neville's second show had started in the back room. Luc was drawing a beer as Karen ducked under the lift. He seemed to be deliberately not looking at her.

She said to Zachary. "You can leave if you want." She rummaged in her purse, adding another hundred to the two folded bills. She handed them to Zachary.

"You're paying me yourself?" He wasn't reaching for them.

"Thanks for helping out. I appreciate it." She stood holding the money out to him, beginning to feel ridiculous. She liked it when money changed hands quickly.

"You weren't gone very long," Zachary said. "I don't want to take your money. You helped me out plenty of times."

For Christ sake, she couldn't give any of this money away. She'd gone to the safe deposit box earlier in the week and taken a thousand of it to spread around to the people who helped. The tainted money. What—could people smell it?

"No, go on, take it. That was the deal. I'll square up with the receipts later."

Zachary, who looked more like a California surfer than a New Orleans night prowler, smiled and shook his head. "Unh, uh, LaDonna isn't paying me three hundred bills for, what, forty-five minutes. That woman's too cheap. Look, Karen, the tips are really good tonight. I'll take my cut and regular pay and put it down you'll give me a night when I need one." He took a giant step under the lift top. "Hot date waiting," he said when he popped up on the other side, and with that he was out of there.

Once again, Karen put the money away.

"He wouldn't take it, huh?" Luc was behind her, spraying soda into scotch or bourbon.

"No, and neither would Buddha. What's with these guys? Doesn't anybody like money any more?"

"You must have laid it on the guy at the Royal O."

Karen heard something in his voice that made her wary. "If you're interested, we ended up at Woldenberg Park."

"What happened?"

She hesitated before she said, "I don't know why I didn't think about the park to begin with."

She turned away from him to put ice in a glass, pour in some Coke.

"Too many people, huh?"

Karen took a long slow drink.

Luc said, "Do you feel better now, since you got revenge?"

She looked at him over the top of the glass.

Luc said, "I mean, did it feel like revenge for what happened all those years ago?"

He was looking at her intently, ignoring a man behind him who was demanding another Rock.

The music was pounding; it seemed to be all bass and she felt every vibration. The people around the bar sounded loud, a raucous laugh on one side, somebody yelling, "Fuck *that*," in another part of the room. Any other night she didn't hear sounds so separately unless there was trouble—booze-fueled tempers blowing, spilled drinks, a woman crying. Any other night it was white noise.

She pulled a Rolling Rock out of the cooler and popped it open. She reached around Luc to hand it to the man. She asked him if he wanted a glass, but he was already moving away, his head back and the bottle tipped up to the ceiling. She picked up the five he left.

She said to Luc, "I don't know."

"That's why you wanted to do it, right?"

She couldn't pin it on him, it was all in the tone, the look, but she felt he was making a judgment against her. "Why does it matter?" She finished her Coke and put the glass in the sink, the five on the cash register. "I'm tired," she said. "If you can handle this, I'm gonna cash it in early tonight."

"Sure." He started to reach out to her, but she moved away too quickly. He watched as she hitched her purse a little higher on her shoulder and walked out like a person who had energy to burn.

Raynie was watching too from where she and Peewee sat at the front of the bar. Some kind of trouble brewing there, and guilt washed over her as she recognized something like satisfaction trying to get hold of her. But she watched as Luc chatted up the women around the bar, and when he got to the front of the bar, chatted her up the same way. Maybe Luc was one of those womanizers. What was the word her mother used? Philanderer. She would never be able to tolerate that kind of hurt but she couldn't take her eyes off him. He fascinated her, and part of it was that his sophistication out-distanced hers so significantly that it would take years for her to catch up, if she ever could. She let out the breath she was holding, and with her elbow on the bar, rested her head on her hand. She took in her miserable friend, Peter Meeker. No getting around it—he'd been a drag tonight. And now with Karen gone, the moment of triumph was gone too.

"Earlene," Peewee said, "could we go back to the apartment? Do you mind? I can go alone if you want to stay."

"No, let's go."

They walked back without saying much. Raynie wanted him to go, but she wasn't sure how to tell him. If he was going to stay in New Orleans, he needed to start looking for a place. And a job.

When they got to the apartment, she asked him if he wanted a drink. He said bourbon, as though he thought that's what a world-weary person would want. She went over to the commode where Karen had set up the bar and poured him one. She put some ice in it and got herself a glass of water.

She sat with him on the sofa.

"We need to talk." They'd said it in unison and laughed, but not long and not convincingly.

"You first," Peewee said.

"No, you. I need to know what your plans are."

He wouldn't look at her. He ran a finger around the rim of the glass, then he swirled the ice. He took a sip. "I don't think I can stay here." He looked up at her.

"Do you mean here at the apartment or here in the city?"

He looked meeker and more miserable than he had all night. "Look, Ear…"

"Shh." Raynie pointed toward Karen's room. She didn't know if Karen was there or not.

Peewee lowered his voice. "I had to come, but now I have to go."

"I understand. Do you miss Alice Roy?"

He nodded slowly. "I didn't think I would, but I do. But it isn't just that. I don't belong here. This place is too...it's too fast for me."

When he said that, something jumped inside of Raynie. It took her a second to recognize it—excitement. Some fear too but that was part of the excitement. The place was fast, considering Mamou. She had to run to keep up but that made it worth it.

"I know," she said.

His body got wired and he turned more to her and dropped his voice further. "You do? I mean, will you come back home with me, Earlene? It's where we both belong."

"It's where you belong, Peewee, not me. This place has something for me. I need to stick around and see what it is. But, Peewee, what are you going to do when you get there? You gave up your job!"

"Mr. Pendergast owns a printing company. He asked me to come work for him."

"Oh, that's good." She gave a short laugh. "They've really got you, Peewee, every which-a-way."

"They do." He looked confused for a moment then said, "But it's good, you know? The future is sort of all laid out."

A few seconds later, when she didn't answer, Peewee said, "You know I didn't mean you should come back *with* me."

"I know." She reached over and took his hand. "I'm glad you came, though. You did the right thing, to go off so you could see what you want, how good your life is."

He squeezed her hand and nodded. "But, Earlene, you can't ever, ever tell anyone I was here, okay? I mean, Alice Roy...and especially that we..."

"Stop, Peewee. I'm never going to tell, and neither are you, right? You're not going to tell Raymond or Daniel or anyone where I am."

His head bobbed around happily. "Never." He made a cross

over his heart. "But when are *you* going to tell, Earlene? You got to tell them sometime."

"I told you I would—when I'm ready."

"Do you think you'll be ready in time for the wedding?"

"I don't know. That depends on when it's happening."

Peewee twisted his mouth. He looked goofy. He said, sounding more like himself than ever, "Quick. Hell, Earlene, they'd have had it without me if they could've."

NINETEEN

On his way to the Quarter, Jack listened to the three messages Solo had left on his cell phone. The first short, to the point, "Call me." The second said they were leaving the boathouse, meet him at the Chateau Sonesta, the hotel where he was staying. The third was angry: "I think when I see you Jack, I first have Ernesto use his blade to cut off each of your fingers before I kill you. Then I will send your fingers to Karen. They will have special meaning to her, I'm sure." Jack turned off the phone.

At Avery's place on the corner of Bourbon and Barracks, he used the keys he'd found on Avery to open the outside gate and the door to the building. He walked up to the third floor as he patted the roll of money in his pocket, and hoped when he opened the door to the condo, an alarm didn't go off. He turned the bolt lock and gently cracked the door. Nothing happened.

With all the time in the world, the first thing he did was take off the silver alligator belt, make himself comfortable on the sofa, and unzip it. He pulled the hundreds out and counted them. He put them back and stuffed the two large from Avery's pocket in with them. Standing again, he took off his own belt, threw it on the sofa, and put on the alligator. It was a little snug, stuffed to the max, but it looked okay. He rocked it into the most comfortable position and stood absolutely still, deciding where to start searching the apartment.

He hoped the little dickhead hadn't done something intelligent like put the money in a safe deposit box. If it was in a safe in the condo…well, hell, maybe he'd just blow it up. But he decided to assume that the dickhead was as dumb as he acted most of the time. So the first thing he did was look under the bed. He saw the aluminum case Avery had with him at the poker game, slid it out and opened it up. Then he sat back against the nearest wall and nearly laughed himself sick. When he finished he flipped open his phone.

"Solo," he said, "don't say a word. I'm headed over to the hotel with the easiest money we ever made ."

Solo didn't say a word. He hung up while Jack laughed into a dead connection.

—⚏—

Dawn was breaking over the Mississippi River when Avery started coming around. His eyelids fluttered. Slowly, his senses began to wake up. The soft light hurt his eyes, and they were dry. His mouth tasted like stale beer; he made smacking sounds. He felt cold; he reached for covers and realized he wasn't in bed; whatever was under his hand wasn't a sheet. His arms, his back, the backs of his legs began to itch. He could smell something… the river. Judas Priest, he was outside and he didn't have any clothes on. He tried to sit up but between his legs something pulled at his balls, at the hair on his legs. He lifted himself on his elbows and looked down. High pitched noises came from him, a series of raccoon-like squeaks and squeals. He scuttled his butt backwards on the grass, trying to wipe off the green stuff. Puke green. It didn't come off. He lay back. His breath was labored, irregular. Carefully he touched his chest. The shit was like tar—it didn't come off on his hand but it was soft, like if you put your finger down in it, you'd hit goo.

He looked at the brightening sky. His thinking was clearing, his breath getting more regular. His head hurt. He lay quietly so he could figure out if anything else hurt. He didn't think so. He reached down to feel his penis. He couldn't. His heart beat accelerated. He pushed into the shit, ladled on down here, and still couldn't feel it. He squeezed. Ah, there it was.

"Fuck." He whimpered, lying back in the grass. "Fuck me."

He needed to get out of here. He sat up, wincing at all the hair getting pulled and looked around. They'd taken his fucking clothes. He spotted a piece of paper near his feet, stuck down in the grass, something written on it. He picked it up and squinted: HERE YO EYEBROWS.

What the shit? He looked over on the grass. It looked like a wad of spit. He looked closer.

"Holy crap!" Avery's scream was up in the range of a eunuch, and his hand flew to where the wad on the ground used to be on his face. His fingers touched gunk on his forehead; he ran his hands down his cheekbones, felt his nose—it was all over his face. Then he put his hands on his head and ran them through his hair, pitiful with relief.

He got up, taking small steps on his toes. Hunched over in an attempt to hide himself, he twinkle-toed over to the nearest trash barrel. Nothing but go-cups. He scurried several yards to the next can and was rewarded with a beer-soaked newspaper. He tried to lift it and the corner tore away. He got it up, managed to separate it, and fashioned a fragile loin cloth. He got very tired doing this on his toes. Holding the paper front and back, he started toward the park entrance, realizing halfway there that his hair pulled the same whether he was on his toes or flat footed.

In the parking lot that ran along Decatur he tried to squat so the parked cars, a surprising number at dawn, would hide him, and he quietly roared with pain while his rear end nearly destroyed his cover. Back in a hunch, the well-built naked man with green ooze from his face to his groin lurched from car to car. At Decatur he took a deep breath and ran across the street. A few cars passed, but none slowed for gawkers. For some reason that even Avery couldn't fathom, this pissed him off. He held his breath all the way to the side entrance of the restaurant.

St. Louis was clear—no moving cars or people, too late for the all-nighters, too early for a lazy Sunday. He went for the doorbell to the left of the iron gate and the front newspaper fell to the flagstones. He left it there and stood with his back to the street and leaned into the button until it felt as though his finger would be permanently bent backwards.

At last he heard the intercom open. Hard to believe he would ever be glad to hear Pascal's voice, especially his annoyed voice. "What?"

"Thank Christ! Let me in. It's an emergency."

Pascal did not respond with the buzzer. He held for a pause then said, "I believe, Avery, you have a key."

"You don't think I'd use it if I had it, you flaming asshole?"

"Why don't you come back later, Avery."

"Pascal." It was a massive effort at self-control. "I'm standing in front of your restaurant naked."

The buzzer was still going as Avery's baby-white ass disappeared down the alley.

—⚏—

"If you laugh..." Avery said.

But Pascal was frowning. "Go clean yourself up. The razor's out, new blades in the top drawer."

"Is anyone here?" Avery nodded toward the bedroom.

"No. I'll get you some clothes."

Avery went to the bathroom. He saw the razor, found the blades, turned on the shower, took out a couple of towels, and only then did he look at himself in the mirror. He expected to be horrified—no eyebrows and green shit all over his face—but along with horror was humiliation and rage. Written across his forehead, and from cheek, over his nose, to cheek was:

RAPIST
PIG

He wanted to break the mirror but figured Pascal would throw him back on the street. He looked around for an outlet for his rage that didn't include destroying the bathroom. Finally, he took one of the towels between his teeth and bit as hard as he could, until the fire in his brain cooled. He stepped into the shower, turned the water as hot as he could stand it, and began the tedious and painful attempt to shave off the green paint, or whatever it was. When he finished, his balls, inside his thighs and his chest burned and were spotted with blood red and green. He couldn't deal with his penis, but at least it was separated from his balls. He got out of the shower. After he dried off and ruined one of Pascal's expensive towels, he rummaged through the drawers and cabinets until he found a cooling talc. He dusted himself, then with his legs spread and braced, he stood in front of the mirror to shave his face.

He scraped at it until he couldn't stand it any longer. Little green specks were embedded in his pores. His nose was the worst. He looked raw, and without his eyebrows, insane. He put on a pair of Pascal's boxers, loose-fitting gym pants and a t-shirt, and went into the office.

Pascal handed him a mug of coffee. "Sit down, Avery."

"Don't give me any shit, Pascal."

"Not my intention."

Avery sat carefully on the sofa. "All this goddamn leather," he said. "I could use a down pillow."

Pascal got up, went to the bedroom and returned with a pillow.

"Thanks." Avery got adjusted. "Excuse me for being suspicious, but you're being nice to me."

"I can see you're in trouble." With his index finger he tapped his own face.

"You think I'd do that?" Avery shifted around as though he was thinking about getting up, storming out, but pain made sitting still an easier choice.

"Have a conversation with me, Avery. Two adults. Two brothers. To answer your question, no, it never crossed my mind that you would give anyone drugs to rape them."

Avery's forehead wrinkled in shocked outrage. "I didn't give anyone drugs."

"But someone gave you drugs. Isn't that what happened?"

Avery nodded.

"So someone's got it in for you?"

Avery's brain was in overdrive. He wasn't about to tell Pascal he'd given that bitch of a girl a roofie. It was the only roofie he'd ever given anyone; mostly he paid for it when he was in Vegas. He hadn't seen the girl last night. The last thing he remembered was Jack O'Leary standing over him at La Costa Brava, asking him if he wanted a toot. Had he gone to the bathroom? If he couldn't remember did that mean someone had doped his beer before Jack got there? It plain hurt to think.

"Yeah," he said, "but not because I did it to anyone." He drank coffee, wouldn't look at Pascal.

"Then for what?"

Avery didn't answer, kept looking in his coffee.

"Don't clam up, Avery. This looks like a prank, something a bunch of kids would think up. They really wanted to be vicious they would have super-glued your penis to your testicles. But the question is, are you safe? Was this Act I?"

"Why do you suddenly care?"

"I don't care. Drink up. Go home. Don't come back if you

need help."

Avery didn't go. He didn't like orders. "You suddenly want to help me?"

"I thought I already did." Pascal knew he wouldn't get any acknowledgment. "You want to tell me what's going on, I'll listen."

Avery smirked. "The good brother. And what do good brothers do after that?"

Pascal took a sip of coffee. "I can get in a work-out before things crank up around here." He leaned forward to put the cup on the coffee table.

Avery said, "You know Jack O'Leary?"

Pascal sat back in his club chair. "Cardsharp. I heard he was in Miami."

"He was, but he's back, and he brought Little Havana with him."

"What does that mean?"

Avery jiggled eyebrows that weren't there. The small spotlight in the ceiling above him caused his nose to glow an alien green. Pascal suppressed an urge to laugh. He reached for his coffee cup.

Avery said, "How do you know him?"

Pascal hesitated. If Avery was in deep enough to O'Leary, he might be forced to let Pascal buy him out of the building. "Johnpier and I caught him cheating at a poker game one night. Jimmy made it very attractive for him to leave town."

"How much does he owe you?"

"Nothing. We took what we came with and told him he was finished here."

Avery grinned. "Shit. I didn't know you and the Phantom went slumming."

Pascal wanted to put the worm in his proper place, but that wasn't the object here. "Hm. Slumming. I suppose we do sometimes. Jimmy likes the characters."

"Judas. That uptown swell?"

"Quirky. Like a lot of them."

"O'Leary either thinks he's done enough penance or he brought his own thugs back. I took him and his coo-bano podna the other night."

"Little Havana—that's who you mean?"

Avery nodded, smug, know-it-all. "Whole table full of coo-banos. Everyone except O'Leary."

"And you're supposed to go back?"

"For the big rip-off."

"So what was last night all about?"

"I was supposed to go back last night. I blew it off. The woman bartender looked interested. I thought I'd stick around."

Pascal let his eyes get wide. No big buy-out in sight. He needed to find another angle.

"Who knows," Avery said. "O'Leary's demented. His idea of fun maybe. Like you say, a prank."

"That sounds right. Was the Cuban with O'Leary last night?"

"No."

Pascal sat in thought. "I'd say that means it's not O'Leary you need to worry about. The one who runs the show is careful about when he appears. I think, Avery, you need to watch out for the Cuban."

"You think I don't know that? Shee-it."

TWENTY

Karen woke up at two in the morning. A lamp was burning in the living room and she could hear low muffled voices. Raynie and her friend Peter. She lay there until something uncomfortable, like regret, got the better of her.

She called Luc's cell. When she got voice mail she hung up. He would see that she'd called. An hour later, when he would have closed La Costa, he still hadn't called. She had a spell of agitation, which she talked herself into cutting short, and fell asleep around four.

She got up at eleven the next morning after being vaguely aware of movement in the apartment earlier, water running, the toilet flushing. She went out to the kitchen in a tank and men's pajama bottoms. No one was there. The suitcase Peter had left open on a chair against the far wall was gone. She assumed Raynie had gone to work.

It was Karen's day off. She brewed a cup of coffee and stretched out on the sofa with a well-worn copy of an old Henning Mankell mystery she'd picked up over at Beckham's, the grim story of a murder at an isolated farmhouse during the long Swedish winter. Four hours later she was frozen to the bone. She went out into the New Orleans heat to thaw.

She walked over to La Costa Brava to see if LaDonna wanted to get something to eat with her. Zachary told her LaDonna and Ramon were shooting in the Lower 9.

"Where's Luc?"

"He's taking the day off. Just as well. It's slow even for a Sunday."

She thought about calling him for all of three seconds. The kind of boredom she was feeling, it almost always got her in trouble.

She spied the Panama hat hanging on a hook in the storeroom. She took it with her and walked back into the French Quarter.

Where she expected to see Raynie at the counter behind the glass entrance to Le Tripot, Karen saw Pascal. His jacket was slung across the end of the counter, the sleeves of his crisp white shirt rolled back. His eyes scanned the computer screen. Karen stood still, staring, and was about to walk on when he looked up. A long couple of seconds passed then he motioned her to come in. She took a deep breath and pulled the heavy glass door.

He glanced at the Panama as she said, "I was looking for Raynie."

"Is that hers?" He nodded at the hat.

She put it on the counter. "Of course not. It's your brother's." His blue eyes had her. It was like physical labor to say, "He left it at La Costa last night."

"He probably doesn't know that." He took the Panama and put it under the counter.

The movement broke the spell. Karen cleared her throat. "Probably not. He was pretty drunk when he left. One of the bartenders found it on the floor."

"He was more than drunk."

Karen's eyebrows lifted, involuntary reflex.

"Was he with anyone?"

She shook her head slowly. "He came in alone."

"Did he hook up with anyone? Was he able to walk out by himself? Did he leave alone?"

Karen's eyelids dropped to half mast, another involuntary

reflex. "We were busy. Is Raynie coming in?"

He came out from behind the counter. "Look, everyone around here is always telling me not to bark out multiple questions like that."

He reached across her back, put his hand on her shoulder, and began to move her toward the bar. When she looked at his hand he dropped it down to his side again. "Let me get you something to drink and I'll tell you why I'm asking. Would you like a mixed drink, soft drink, beer, wine...?"

"A cappuccino, if it's not too much trouble."

"No trouble at all."

The restaurant was in that late afternoon lull. Le Tripot served from eleven thirty on, all day, every day, but if there was anyone in the place, they were upstairs. The bartender stopped shining everything to fix them cappuccinos. Pascal and Karen stood patiently, not talking. Karen could still feel his hand on her shoulder, the heat radiating through her. She risked a sideways glance. So did he. They both looked away.

He shifted his weight, looking at her now. "Raynie isn't coming back today. Jimmy Johnpier convinced me to let her go after the lunch rush."

"Oh."

"I think he's trying to steal her away."

"For what?"

"For himself."

The bartender sprinkled cinnamon on the cappuccinos and Pascal picked them up. He led Karen all the way across the large dining room to a four-top in the back and set their cups next to each other instead of opposite. She crossed her legs and bumped one of his. She started to say she was sorry but angled her legs away instead. The heat again, right around her kneecap.

She started talking, anything to keep him off the subject of his brother. "The first time I saw you, you and Johnpier were talking to LaDonna one afternoon at La Costa Brava."

"Ah, that answers *that* question." He fixed his eyes on her.

"I know the two of you bailed her out, not that she told me any of the details. I hope you're not loan-sharking."

He laughed.

"I'm serious. The hurricane, her money problems—business is slow. It would kill her to lose the club that way."

He stopped smiling. "You've been friends a long time?"

She nodded.

"Let me tell you something," he said. "I've known Jimmy Johnpier since I was twenty years old. He's one of the good guys. He wanted to do this for LaDonna, and that's okay. She didn't share her problems with us...maybe she told him another time...but unless he thought she wasn't capable of running the place any longer, he wouldn't think of taking it over. And if she couldn't run it, he'd buy it from her, minus the loan. I know him. He's got a sentimental attachment to the place, from when LaDonna's father was alive. He's attached to her too."

"And if he bought it, you would run it?"

If she thought he couldn't look at her any more piercingly, she was wrong.

"I'd probably let you run it." Straight face; nothing funny about his tone.

"I'm already running it so it isn't going to happen if I can help it. The payback amount is reasonable enough; I just want to know if there are any built-in interest hikes in the deal, like for missed payments, or if they're late."

"Did you ask her?"

"I'm asking you."

"It's not my place to divulge the terms."

Karen put her elbow on the table and rested her chin on her hand. She never took her eyes off his while she did it. "Maybe not, but I want you to tell me anyway."

He laughed, leaning toward her. "No," he said.

She sat up straight. "No, you won't tell me, or no, LaDonna's not going to get ripped?"

"Um, both."

She smiled. "I'm taking you at your word. I *will* find out."

"And I quake to think what you'd do."

Karen frowned. "Why's that?"

"I just do." He leaned away, pulling his legs out from under the table, then turning the chair more toward her, his arm draped over its back. He crossed his legs. "Let me tell you what happened to my brother last night."

—∿∿—

Pascal did not know quite everything that had happened to Avery the night before, and neither did Avery until he got back to his condo, ordered take-out from Fong's, and rubbed his face and body down with an expensive lotion he'd bought at a Las Vegas spa.

When he looked under his bed and saw that the aluminum case was gone, his brain fired off a series of images: Jack O'Leary in the Costa Brava; the keys to the condo in his buff-colored linen pants pocket; and strangest of all, a clear image of O'Leary bending over his unconscious body, removing the keys, and dangling them in the air with that goddamned look of self-satisfied amusement on his face.

He got up from the floor, his whole body flushed, luminous with the fire that was going on in his head. He punched out the mirror over his dresser. He fell back on the bed then sat up and watched his knuckles bleed all over Pascal's sweats.

He knew who had his money, all right. And he was going to get them...and that's when he thought, Fuck! His shiny little Smith and Wesson. Fuck a duck!

He pressed the back of his hand into his thigh, rocking back and forth, telling himself it was okay, he'd get the Walther PP out of the safe deposit box tomorrow and blow them to kingdom come. O'Leary and that smug son-of-a-bitchin Cuban.

But first thing, he better get over to Fifi Mahoney's as soon as they opened in the morning and see if they could fit him with a new pair of eyebrows.

—⚏—

Jimmy Johnpier said he wanted to take Raynie to his house on St. Charles Avenue where they could have a couple of drinks until the Upperline opened for dinner. He said he'd had grits and grillades and greens on his mind all day.

They passed the front of the house. She could see the tan stone mansion, not exactly a house, on palatial grounds through a black iron fence set in concrete. She noticed video cameras at each side of the wall, which enclosed almost the entire block, and at the front drive-through gates. But Jimmy drove his Mercedes around the corner and into a garage in the back and he took her in via the garden. Raynie told him it was the most beautiful, most fragrant garden she'd ever been in. Large gardenia bushes bloomed throughout the lush landscape. They flanked a screened summer house tucked into the back of the property, which was surrounded by a high concrete wall. It could have been the only inhabited property for miles—no views of other houses, no street noise, only a pervading quiet punctuated by bird and insect sounds and rustling leaves. It could have been rural except that the landscape was clearly planned not to look too planned.

When she told Jimmy gardenias were her favorite flower, he picked a large one and put it in her hair over her ear. She closed her eyes and breathed in the heady smell. Jimmy kissed her on the cheek, quick, before she could protest, then he opened the door and let them into a glassed-in den, though Raynie thought it would be called something like the garden room or the south sun room.

He took her through to a room with a bar and a large flat screen TV on a wall.

"Let's get a drink for the tour," he said.

Glasses in hand, he guided her from room to fabulous room. So many rooms. He named each of the rugs for her, fancy names like Sarouk and Tabriz, gave each antique's time period, pointed out the important art—the only name she recognized was Picasso—and showed her the issue of *Architectural Digest* that featured the house. He was proud of his house but it was more than that; he loved it and everything in it, which he had picked personally, even travelled to find.

As they went up the curving staircase Raynie said, "I'm just a girl from Mamou, Jimmy. I've never seen anything like this place." Gorgeous, all right, nearly overwhelming. All Raynie could think was if her mother could only see her now.

"I suppose it's sort of like living in a museum. I love looking at it, being surrounded by all this beauty. I don't use but maybe four or five rooms and the kitchen isn't one of them, unless there's a party."

The kitchen was huge, full of white Italian marble with large pots hanging over a chopping block island that had one of the stoves built into it. The kitchen at Le Tripot wasn't as big.

Upstairs seemed more livable. She liked the iridescent-blue leopard wallpaper in one of the bathrooms and the sitting room next to it, one of the rooms Jimmy used, with big comfortable chairs and a sofa she sunk into when she sat on it.

"And this is the master bedroom." He pushed open French doors and guided her in with his hand on the small of her back.

She resisted his pressure, turned to him and said in a mocking tone, but serious too, "This isn't some kind of seduction scene, is it, Jimmy?"

"Oh, dear Raynie, that isn't one of my better roles, though I won't say it isn't in my repertoire. But no. I'm saving the seduction for later, when we're relaxing in the summer house with a fresh drink." He put pressure on her back again. "I'm giving you the tour for a purpose."

He pointed out a piece of furniture here and there, more art, and Raynie took in the king sleigh bed that looked as though it was made up in silk. She imagined how it would feel to float into it every night.

She almost had to shake herself out of it. "Is this the end of the tour? I'm ready for that fresh drink."

"There is a third floor, but we can do that another time. Please tell me, though, that you like my house."

"Like your house? Jimmy, I *love* your house but it is simply not real to me. The way my life is right now? When I moved into Karen's apartment I thought I landed in the lap of luxury. This is not *real*, you know?"

He turned away to head out of the room but not before she caught the smile. Some kind of secret smile.

A fresh drink later they were in the summer house, well appointed, with its own bar and small kitchen, a lazy ceiling fan turning above them. It wasn't twilight yet but the light was soft because of the trees, all the dark foliage. Raynie kicked off her high-heeled sandals and fell back into a deep-cushioned rattan chair, her feet on a matching ottoman, and thought she could go to sleep, listening to Jimmy drone on about being in the oil service business and how he had to entertain a lot.

"And that's where you come in."

Raynie shimmied herself straighter in the chair. "What do you mean?"

"Well, I'm getting tired of doing it all by myself."

"Doing what?"

"Raynie, darling, have you been listening to a word I've said?"

He had his head tilted toward her. One eye seemed to be slanted down yet his smile was higher on that side. It was weird. Raynie shook her head so she'd stop seeing his face like that.

"Yes. You said something about being in business and having to entertain a lot."

He straightened himself, which put his face into the off-balance Raynie was used to.

"Indeed. The two often seem as one. Specifically, though, I'm tired of doing the entertaining by myself. And so I'm thinking that you could put your considerable skills as a hostess to work right here at my humble abode."

Raynie laughed. "Humble abode."

Jimmy looked pleased that he'd made her laugh. "You could help me host my dinners, sometimes at home, sometimes at restaurants, and the large parties I throw here every three months or so...I have to have the swells in, you know—all those rich, straight-laced kooks I tell you stories about. You've met a few. Actually, within their own little private community they can be quite entertaining with their various scandals and mismaneuvers, misalliances..."

"So what are you saying? It would be a job? I mean, would it be part time and I'd keep my job at the restaurant?"

"Sweet Raynie, you are so charming, so fresh, so unassuming, I often think that meeting you has been has been the best thing that has ever happened to me. No, darling girl, a job is not at all what I have in mind. I'm asking you to marry me, Raynie."

Raynie stared at him and he had to admire that she had kept a straight face. She did not laugh or seem shocked but rather locked into some variety of thought. He couldn't wait to hear what she would say. He lifted his eyebrows, gave a small thrust of his head toward her.

Finally, she spoke. "Jimmy, this the strangest marriage proposal

I've ever had."

"That pleases me greatly."

"I've only had one other..."

"But I'm sure you'll have at least a few more. After all, I'm old."

"I guess..."

"And rich."

"Yes you are, Jimmy. Very rich. Are you sure you just don't need a personal assistant, a highly paid personal assistant?"

He threw his head back and laughed until Raynie saw a tear roll from the corner of his left eye.

"It wasn't *that* funny. I didn't really mean it as funny..."

"Oh, but Raynie," he said, wiping at the tear, thinking how beautiful she looked in the near twilight, how perfectly she fit here in his beautiful house, "that's what I mean about your charm. However, I'm quite sure that it is a wife, not a personal assistant, I want. It's not a job, although..." he paused, considering "...you could, if it pleased you, think of it as a sort of business proposition."

"I could?"

"You could if you considered it a definite step up from working in a restaurant or a lifestyle that includes cooking frog legs every night, which you'd never even remotely have to think about doing again in your entire life. You see, I've given this a great deal of thought..."

—⚬—

Karen sat rapt as Pascal retold the story of Avery's abuse at the hands of his enemies. She never figured she would know what had happened when Avery woke up; she would have liked it better if he'd been rousted by police and arrested for being a pervert. The way Pascal told it, she didn't know if she was supposed to be amused or outraged.

She decided on blunt curiosity. "Well, did he rape somebody?"

"He says not. He says he has enemies."

"I don't guess he told you what his enemies might have against him?"

"No, but I thought he might have told you or that you might know." What he said, the way his Daniel Craig blue eyes nailed her, he won on blunt curiosity.

She put her hand up near her throat. "I—why would you think either of those might be possible?"

"You were the bartender last night, right?"

"One of them."

"The only woman."

She nodded.

"Avery said the woman bartender was interested in him."

She thought later that aghast was probably the only word that fit what her face must have looked like. "Why would he think that?"

Pascal's shoulders moved, barely suggesting a shrug. "Didn't you talk to him?"

"I don't think I did. I didn't get him his first beer. When he asked for the second, I nodded and brought it to him."

"Hm, only two beers? Didn't you wonder why he was so drunk?"

"I didn't give it a thought. He might have stopped at every bar on the block before he got to us."

"True."

She was more than uncomfortable, maybe intimidated, but the last thing she wanted to do was show him that by being angry or defensive. "What are you trying to say here?" Again, curious.

"Nothing. I'd just like to know."

Karen's cell rang. She didn't move to get it.

"Go ahead," Pascal said with his chin lifting toward her purse.

She reached for it, saw it was Luc, put it on silent and stowed it.

"Did Avery leave with Jack O'Leary?"

"Jack O'Leary…"

"You must know him. Everyone around here knows Jack. You must if you work at La Costa."

"Sure, I know him. I think he left with Avery. A few people seemed to leave with him."

"He walked out? On his own?"

"You're doing that thing again, you know, 'barking out multiple questions.' I think I'm being cross examined and I'm wondering why you're doing that."

"Because you were there."

"I was but so were a lot of people who were all crowded around the bar wanting drinks."

"So are you going to tell me if Avery walked out on his own two feet or if he had to be carried out—or what?"

She was tempted, no, itching to tell him Buddha had carried Avery out like a sack of flour, but if she did she'd laugh and besides, she'd decided not to give him much information. "Are you going to accept that I don't know?"

He sat looking at her. "I guess I have to. Maybe you'd like to know that the green stuff they put all over him? It's going to take a while for him to get it out of his pores. The whole time he was telling me about what happened his nose was glowing green."

Karen couldn't contain it any longer; she laughed. "I'm so sorry. Please tell me you meant that to be funny."

"I did. I thought you'd been having trouble keeping a straight face for a while."

"I am sorry. It was the way you told it."

They both laughed. It felt good to laugh with him, felt good to be with him even though she knew he considered her a suspect in his brother's humiliation. She wasn't sure he cared; she wouldn't bet on it either way. He was open, talking almost intimately. If she knew anything about body language he was also closed and she would bet he didn't or couldn't let anybody all the way in. For fucksake—why did that make him so attractive? More to the point, why did it make her want to get in?

He suggested they have dinner. He said he'd get one of the wait staff to cover while they were gone.

They walked around the corner to K-Paul's. Once they were settled upstairs in a booth Karen asked him what he meant about Johnpier wanting Raynie for himself.

"I mean," Pascal said holding up a crab finger, "he wants to marry her."

"Marry her!"

He looked around as though people were staring at her. "He's in love. People in love, they want to get married. So I'm told."

"Oh, not you."

"I don't know. I've never been in love for longer than..." he looked up, calculating "...six months."

"Yeah, that's one of those magic numbers. The one that shakes me up is seven years. Imagine, all that time, then you find out you can't stand each other."

He grimaced. "That's tough."

Even when he grimaced he was the best looking man she'd ever gone out with, not that they were going out exactly, not that she really wanted to think about that...

"Yeah. But getting back to Johnpier, isn't he worried about Raynie being so much younger than he is? In his shoes, I'd be worried that six months might be pushing it."

Pascal slid the meat off another crab finger. "I don't think he's worried at all."

"Why not, if he's in love? It would be safer if he just trotted around with her on his arm or..." she speared a shrimp but halted the fork on its way to her mouth "...if he just screwed her once in a while. If she'd let him."

"That's cutting to the chase. Would she?"

"I don't know. I'm not sure she's thought about him that way, but I don't know how she thinks. I haven't known her very long."

He reached for his glass of wine. "Did you advertise for a roommate?"

He had this way of asking a question that sounded as though he already knew the answer. He kept moving to the edge of everything she didn't want him to know. Karen wondered if she was being paranoid.

"Not exactly. That's another story..."

He stopped eating and turned to face her. "I get the feeling that everything's a story with you. I have to get back soon. Are you working tomorrow night?"

It fell right out of her mouth: "Not any more."

He was amused. "Don't play with me. You weren't working anyway, were you?"

TWENTY-ONE

Jack had taken the brushed-aluminum brief case full of money to Solo's hotel room, figuring that would be the last of his money problems with Solo. Maybe they'd find a little more action in New Orleans or maybe Solo would head back to Miami. Jack might go with him or he might stick around to see if he and Karen could make another go of it. He had walked through the Quarter swinging the brief case and whistling, one hand on Avery's gun, which he carried in the pocket of his sports coat. He wasn't worried; he'd sort it all out; he always did. Whatever he decided, life was his own private adventure.

The air conditioning felt good after his twelve block walk. He took the elevator to Solo's suite at the Chateau Sonesta. Ernesto opened the door.

Jack held up the silver-colored case. "Look what I have for the boss, 'Nesto."

Ernesto didn't so much as crack a smile. He held the door open. Jack was taking off his coat when Solo came through the bedroom door, wearing only pajama bottoms, his satiny chest bare except for his cross.

"Don' bother with that, Jack." Solo pointed at the coat, circling his finger. "You won' be staying long."

"Where's that famous Cuban hospitality, Solo? I just brought you a shitload of money." Jack grinned and slid the sports coat off his arm.

"I am tired, Jack. It has been a disturbing night."

"But it all worked out. Don't I always work it out, Solo? You're just a little short in the faith department, that's all. Open it up. Let's see how much we've got here."

"Surely you already know this, Jack."

Jack lifted his arms, let them fall back with a slap against his upper thighs. He said, "How about a seat, Jack? Would you like a drink?" Jack looked around the plush living room. "Nice place you got here. I wouldn't mind staying for a while." He gestured toward the brief case on the coffee table. "All I did was open it up to see if the money was in there then I called you." He got a devilish look on his face. "Wasn't that the right thing to do, Solo? Should I have taken a dip first? Come on, hombre, cut me some slack here. Avery was a pain in the ass. Anyway, what about my cut? I set the whole thing up, the boathouse, the fish..."

"Your cut? I believe you—*cómo se dice?*—ah, *forfeit* your cut when you leave Miami with my money."

"Maybe so but I figure I'm good for a finder's fee. At. The. Least."

"Why do you figure that? I believe you have already *dipped*, as you call it. When you return the rest of the money, I will consider your finder fee."

"Jesu Christo, Solo, I'm broke. I need a hotel room. What am I supposed to use, my charm and good looks? Karen's got the money. She's got it locked up in a bank box cuz I searched every nook and cranny in her place and it ain't there."

Solo shrugged. He walked around the coffee table and sat on the sofa, weary. "Perhaps you can find a way to make her give it to you, Jack. You are very imaginative, I believe. But if not, I'm sure 'Nesto can get her to tell me then I tell him to cut both your tongues out."

Jack laughed nervously. "Solo, why can't this money, much more than the other money—right?—square us up here?"

"You ask, so I will tell you why I must have this money, Jack. I am going to invest in LaDonna's movie. A quarter of a million."

"Holy shit, Solo. They need a quarter of a million to do a shitty little video of one woman talking? Man, I am in outer space here."

"I have other ideas about the movie. It will be much larger than..." he rolled his hand, searching for the name "...Ramon has envisioned. LaDonna and I have talked about it. It is what I am going to do."

Jack laughed, his conspiratorial laugh. "What, you bumped Ramon off his own movie? I always liked your style, Solo."

Solo did not answer.

Jack paced in front of the coffee table. He glanced over at Ernesto who was standing sentry near the front door, his arms folded, his eyes glued on Jack. He stopped and turned to Solo. "I see you have a plan here, hombre. That's good. I'll help you any way I can. But how 'bout a coupla thou, you know, a little mad money. I'm not kidding—I'm broke."

Solo eyed Jack, considering. "'Nesto, give him a thousand. Work on Karen, Jack. She is a source of plenty for you. And don' ask me for money again. Are we understood?"

Ernesto, watching Jack as though he might at any moment go crazy on them, slid the case off the coffee table and took it over to a small desk where he opened it and counted out a thousand dollars.

"*Buenas noches*, Jack," Solo said and went off to the bedroom.

Ernesto handed Jack the money then held the door open for him. Jack heard him hiss through his teeth as he passed.

"Up yours, you spic goon," he hissed back.

Ernesto took a step toward him and Jack put his forearm up, holding against Ernesto's big barrel chest. They stood that way, leaning into each other for a few moments then pushed off.

Jack needed a drink. He walked the block to the Monteleone Hotel fast and went into the Carousel Bar. An old girlfriend was working the bar. That's what Jack loved about this town. Everywhere you went, there was someone you knew. In no time at all Jack had a place to stay for the night. All he had to do was kill some time before the Carousel closed at midnight.

—∿∿—

As Karen walked down Royal Street after dinner with Pascal, she checked voice mail but it was clear. No text message. Nothing. She realized she'd started it, not that she'd thought about starting anything, but Luc was keeping it going. She was sick of playing games with immature men, only now she had no idea what to say to him. Pascal had kissed her at the corner of Chartres and St. Louis and it had hit her in the knees. And that with no soul in the kiss, only a brief touching of their lips, his hand around her upper arm. He was a killer, no doubt about it, and she needed to jump off for some down time. She'd see Luc at work tomorrow.

She turned the corner at St. Philip and saw the definition of the immature man leaning against her courtyard wall.

"What does it take, Jack, a grenade?"

"Look, I was calling you." He held up a phone.

"Calling ahead after you're already here. That's an improvement."

Karen got out her key. Before she could tell him to bounce he said, "Is the Cajun here?"

"The Cajun?"

"Your roommate."

"I've never thought of her as *the Cajun*."

"But she is. Is she here?"

"I don't know. I don't think so. Damn it, Jack, it doesn't matter, does it? You're not coming in."

"Got to, doll face. Something you need to know then I'm off." He checked his bare wrist. "Come on, hurry up. I'm in a time bind here."

"For Christ sake."

They went into the living room. Jack craned his head around as if he couldn't see the entire room from right where he was. "Good. Now listen. FYI. Solo says LaDonna is letting him buy into the movie, two hundred and fifty large."

"Why would she do that? Why would he do that?"

"He's got the hots for her; I don't know what her motive is. He's looking for your money to round out the figure. This may put the situation into urgent mode. I thought maybe you'd want to say something to LaDonna." He scowled, an indication that he was thinking hard. "I might want to say something to Ramon."

"What do you need to say to Ramon?"

"Sounds like he's got it in mind to get rid of Ramon."

"What do you mean, get rid of?"

Jack grinned. "Nothing sinister, babes. Let's just say he wants Ramon's woman and his movie."

"For Christ sake, what does that mean? How about you don't say anything to anyone for the time being. You don't need to manipulate every situation, you know."

"I don't know, sugarpie. Solo's still looking to me for that money. It's my neck, right? Well, it's my tongue. Yours too, by the way."

"There you go again, being disgusting."

"Me? Look I've actually seen Ernesto's special sandpaper glove, you know, to hold the tongue while he…"

"Stop!"

"Anyhoo, he's not beating it back to Miami any time soon."

"Whether they leave or not, you could leave."

"Why would I do that, sweetface, and throw you to the *perros*?" He reached up to stroke her cheek.

She moved her head to the side. His hand followed. "That's good of you, Jack. Why don't we give this some thought tonight and pick it up tomorrow? You're in a hurry, I know."

"Don't stall out too long, babykins. If you want to keep that money, you better figure something out fast, and that's the kind of figuring ole Jack is pretty good at." A few long-legged strides and he was gone.

Karen sat down on the sofa, her hand on her forehead. She'd go take a bath, that would help. No, she better call LaDonna. LaDonna should not be fooling around with Solo Fontova. He got nasty when women rejected him. She was going to reject him, wasn't she?

LaDonna yelled into her phone. "We're at the Boom Boom Room. Great band, Honeycutt, come on over...You need me, girl?... Louder!"

Three times and finally LaDonna repeated her. "Okay, tomorrow."

Karen rubbed her temples. She was on her way to draw a bath when she remembered something Jack had said that first night he was in town. She slung her purse over her shoulder and headed to La Costa Brava. Jack wasn't the only one who could manipulate a situation. She closed herself up in LaDonna's office and spent a couple of hours on the computer.

—⟋⟍⟍—

Raynie asked Jimmy Johnpier to drop her off at the apartment after dinner. He'd spent nearly three hours telling her all the reasons why marrying him was a good deal. He said he didn't mean to sound crass framing it that way but he was a realist and he knew she didn't love him the way he loved her.

When Karen got home she found Raynie sitting in the dark, staring out into the courtyard through the open French doors.

"Hey," she said, "you all right?"

She switched on a lamp. Raynie had trouble pulling herself back from wherever she'd been.

"Fine. The peace and quiet. It's nice."

Karen flopped in the big chair, one leg over its arm. "That's because there's not much of it around. Did Peter leave?"

"This morning. I think our sordid activity involving the young Mr. Legendre scared him off. He's gone back home to get married, settle down into a more predictable way of life."

"Whenever you've been hanging out with Jimmy Johnpier you start saying things like *sordid. The young Mr. Legendre.* Did he ask you to marry him yet?"

Raynie nearly jumped. "What?"

"I'll take that as a yes. Pascal told me Jimmy wants to marry you."

"Pascal? When did you see Pascal?"

"A little while ago. Actually, I had dinner with him."

"Dinner? Wait, I thought you and Luc had this hot thing going."

"We sort of did. Maybe we still do. The guy is great in bed, I mean unbelievable but there's not a lot of, um, I don't know— substance? That's not right. He's not an airhead. He just doesn't think about much other than the next party or a new yo-yo trick..."

Raynie laughed. "He's not too complicated, huh?"

"You know what? I don't know and I have a feeling I'm not going to get to know. I'm not so sure Peter was the only one scared off last night. That's why he didn't come with us. To be fair, I don't think he liked it from the beginning but when Jack showed up and put himself in the middle of everything, the way Jack does, that did it. Now Luc and I are playing Who Can Hold Out the Longest."

"I have to say, Jack isn't my favorite person either. But Pascal. How did that happen?"

"Jack goes down as my big mistake and I hope I don't make any more like that." She shook her head. "Big, big mistake. It won't be easy cleaning up after him."

"Pascal, Karen."

"Pascal." She let out a long breath. "I went to the restaurant to see you." When Raynie arched her eyebrows, she said, "Nothing important. I just felt like talking. I brought Avery's hat with me—he left it in the bar last night. I'm not sure but I think Pascal knows I drugged Avery or had something to do with it." She reconstructed as best she could what Pascal had said.

"So he's okay with it? Is that what you think?"

"Beats the hell out of me," Karen said. "He asked me to go out tomorrow night. Maybe he's going to dope me with truth serum. He kissed me when we parted ways." She closed her eyes remembering. "Now, that one. He's complicated."

Raynie was smiling at her. "You're ready to jump in."

"Hm, I don't know. He's got something about him that makes me go weak. I've learned this much: when someone's that attractive that fast, in that way, I should take off running in the opposite direction."

"So...are you?"

"I'm not sure I've learned *that* much."

Raynie laughed. "That's as helpless as I've ever seen you look." She rearranged herself on the sofa, pulling her legs up under her. "But given what you just said about running from men like that...well, I'm going to marry Jimmy."

"No way!"

"I've been sitting here thinking about it." Her eyes drifted out to the courtyard. "I don't see a down side."

Karen pulled herself out of her slouch. "You don't? Oh, fuck, this is bad. Why don't we start with this—would you marry him if he wasn't filthy rich?"

"Of course not. That's *why* I'm marrying him. And he's marrying me because I'm young."

"And beautiful. Raynie, the man's uglier than a toad." She waved away Raynie's protest. "We'll get back to that. Pascal says he's in love with you. Does he know you're marrying him for his money?"

"We talked half the day about it. He said I could look at it as a business proposal instead of a marriage proposal, if I found that more attractive. Karen, the man talks straight. As for love, my mother told me that if a man is good to you, you can grow to love him."

"Oh, boy," Karen said, "this is going to come back and bite you on the ass."

"Look, Karen, there are plenty of reasons to marry a person. Love doesn't have to be the only one. What we've just been talking about—half the time people get married based on the kind of attraction you have to Pascal, when they ought to be running away. Or because they're great in bed. Right? Don't tell me you haven't heard marriage compared to a partnership, a sort of business arrangement. My mother can't be the only mother who said stuff like that."

"I don't know. My mother said things like pure motives, pure mind."

"My motives are pure. Jimmy's lonely and I'll be happy to keep him company. I don't want to be poor the rest of my life, working in a restaurant, on my feet…"

"For Christ sake, you're, what, twenty-two years old? This isn't the rest of your life. Maybe being poor for a while is a good thing. It makes you work harder, makes you look for opportunity, provide for yourself, be independent. It's about learning experiences… shit, I sound exactly like my mother. The point is you didn't even think you were poor until we went to her fucking money club."

Raynie reached over, put her hand on Karen's forearm. "Isn't everything a learning experience? This will be too. Look at it this way—I am providing for myself and marrying Jimmy isn't the rest of my life either. He's a lot older than me."

"He could live for thirty more years. You could end up being his nurse. You're Catholic, right? I know about Catholics and divorce. Especially if he's sick. Rest of your life guilt trip. I'm telling you, Raynie, we couldn't sit here and think of the ways this could bite you on the ass."

"Fuck, Karen, life bites you on the ass all the time. Life is just one big old mouthful of sharp teeth waiting to bite."

"You just said fuck."

"Jimmy will be a good influence. He never says fuck."

"There's the best reason you've come up with so far. But what happens if you don't grow to love him, like your mother said? What if you grow to detest him? He's going to want you to sleep with him, isn't he? What if you just can't do it?"

"Jimmy's asking me to commit to three months. That's all. I'm out if I want out after that."

Karen put both hands on her head and ran them through her hair. "This is wild, I mean wild. Pre-nup?"

"No, three months and he'll give me whatever I think is fair."

"Even if fair is half of everything?"

Raynie shook her head. "I'd be fair."

"He doesn't know that. This man isn't just in love, he's crazy in love. Three months—why bother to get married?"

"He's never been married. He just wants to."

"I can't believe you're doing this. He's the luckiest son-of-a-bitch alive."

Raynie nodded. "He is. So am I. Here's the good thing, really good—we can talk about anything and we make each other laugh."

Karen got up, her hands on her hips. "I sure as shit can't argue with a laugh. Especially if it doesn't come cheap."

TWENTY-TWO

Pascal reached for the phone. He lay back in the comfortable depression his head had made in the pillow without saying hello.

"Pascal, are you there?"

"Jimmy? What the fuck?" The time projected onto the ceiling was six fifty. He'd worked until the restaurant had closed at midnight then in his office until after two.

"Chop-chop, my friend. You're going to have to replace Raynie who will be the first and only Mrs. James Willeford Johnpier at four o'clock this afternoon Vegas time. We're flying out in an hour."

"Congratulations."

"Tut-tut, Pascal, you don't sound as excited as I hoped you'd be. It's understandable, though. Raynie will be hard to replace and I realize this is very short notice. I must say, I did not expect to win this bet. Now that I have…tell me again, what color is that antique Eldo?"

"Gold."

"Mahvelous! Would you have it parked in the front drive by tomorrow evening for Mrs. Johnpier? I trust you remember the code on the gate."

"I do."

"And I'll pick up LaDonna's papers when I see you."

"You're rubbing it in."

"Maybe a little. I'll desist. After all, I'm the happiest man alive at the moment."

He still looked good to her, standing behind the bar, his dark hair long on the back of his neck, curling in the humidity. He was cutting lemons and limes and every time he made a slice, the lower half of his body moved, like a little body English into each cut. She stared at him as she stood just inside the big room. His arm slowed and he turned. She walked toward him. He moved to the middle of the long side of the bar, drying his hands on the towel hanging from his belt. With his hands on the scarred wood bar top and his arms straight, he both leaned in and stood back, the way he did.

"Hey you," she said, something she never said.

"Hey you too."

She angled in between two chairs and rested on her elbows, her midriff against the bar. She let her hand fall softly to one of his. He lifted it and threaded his long fingers through hers.

"Are we avoiding each other, trying to make it look like we're not?" she asked.

"You tell me."

"Maybe. I'm not sure."

La Costa Brava was having a few moments of morning quiet before opening its doors for lunch. Luc hadn't put on music yet; no sounds came from upstairs. Only the floor creaked as she shifted her weight. Until someone in the kitchen dropped what could have been a whole stack of plates and LaDonna came flying from the top of the stairs yelling, "What the fuck is going on down here?"

Luc and Karen pulled their hands away.

"You think you two could *move*?"

"No point now, is there," Karen said and LaDonna gave her an evil look as she breezed through the room.

Luc took her hand again. "You're the only person I know that can get away with talking to LaDonna like that."

"Just stating the obvious."

He smiled. "Somehow that's not what it sounds like."

They could hear someone sweeping up broken dishes as LaDonna gave them the business, loud.

"What does it sound like?"

Luc said, "I'm not sure. It's not like you're giving it back to her. It's pretty matter-of-fact but...I don't know what it sounds like 'cause I don't think I ever heard it before."

"LaDonna and I have known each other a long time. That's all it is."

"No it's not. You use it on other people too."

"And you don't much like it, do you."

"See, there it is."

Their hands were still together but only touching now, no charge between them.

"I don't know what I can do about it," Karen said.

"It's just you." He squeezed her hand, friendly. "You remember that first night, we were sitting out in your courtyard? I asked you if it was going to get scary?"

Karen drew her eyebrows together. "If what was going to get scary?"

Luc shrugged. "We were talking about Jack and Solo Fontova."

LaDonna came from the dining room, her feet pounding on the floor. "Upstairs, Honeycutt."

"In a minute."

LaDonna kept going. Karen waited until she went through the door at the top of the stairs.

"Why does Jack bother you, Luc? I have nothing for him any more, no feelings. He aggravates me."

"I know and I'm not talking about him. I'm talking about you. You got scary the other night."

Karen took her hand from him, traced the bottom of her

lower lip with her index finger then folded her arms together on the edge of the bar.

"I couldn't let it go, Luc, not once we knew it was Avery."

"What you did was dangerous."

"Because we could have overdosed Avery? Because we might have been caught? That wasn't going to happen, not if I could help it, and if we didn't do something, nothing was going to happen to Avery. That was worth a certain amount of risk."

"The thing is, you might not have been able to stop something going wrong." She looked at him hard but said nothing. He said, "I told you I'd let you know if it got too scary. It got too scary."

Their eyes held a moment longer.

"Fair enough," Karen said and headed for the stairs. No guts, no glory, she thought.

—⚋—

"Where's Ramon?" Karen dropped her purse on the floor and flopped onto one end of the sofa.

"Shooting in the 9."

"Good. We need to talk."

"What's going on with you and hot-shit down there?"

"Nothing. That's not what we need to talk about." Karen massaged her forehead just above her eyebrows, her eyes closed.

LaDonna had been about to sit behind the desk. She walked over and sat on the other end of the sofa. "What's bothering you, Honeycutt?"

"In order of importance—you, Solo Fontova and Jack."

"All right, in order of importance, why am I bothering you?"

Karen let her hands fall into her lap and turned to LaDonna. "Jack told me Solo's investing in the film because he has the hots for you. Jack's words."

"Don't let that bother you. Ramon and I are out of money. My belief is ask and you shall receive. I told Ramon we needed an investor and *voilá*, Solo shows up."

"LaDonna, Solo Fontova is a gangster. Okay, I've never seen him kill anyone but I don't know that he hasn't. I've seen a woman he beat up because she didn't want to see him any more. The end of that story, according to Jack, is he kept her a prisoner in his house until he decided to throw her out. Then he told her she had ten minutes to bounce or he was going to let Ernesto work out on her face with a razor blade. Now Jack tells me he lets Ernesto cut out their tongues. If you let him invest he's going to assume...let's just say he figures he's buying you."

"Shit, girl. That's not a pretty story. Jack told you that? But Jack's a pathological liar."

"I wouldn't say pathological. He likes to exaggerate."

"I already told Solo this is strictly a business arrangement. I said if he couldn't live with that he needed to walk away."

"And you trust that he will? I don't."

"We need this money, Karen."

"How much?"

"He said fifty up front and there was another fifty if we needed it."

"Yeah, well there's Jack exaggerating again. He says Solo told him a quarter mil."

LaDonna threw her head back and laughed. "We probably won't need a hundred. Quarter mil?" She laughed some more.

Karen frowned. "I don't know. I think Solo would like to see Ramon out of the movie too. Maybe he thinks he can buy him out."

"What's he think? He can direct it? It still isn't a quarter million dollar movie. Fuck, Honeycutt, these men are worse than a bunch of tongue-waggin women. You *know* what they waggin."

"I know but I don't find that exactly reassuring. Look, LaDonna, here's the thing." She took a deep breath. "I stole something around fifty thou from Jack, which Jack stole from one of Solo's rigged poker games. Solo wants it back. He wanted it back anyway but now I think it's for your movie."

"And what? You don't have it?"

"No, I have it. It's in a safe deposit box. See, I told Jack I'd give it to him but he won't take it. He says Solo keeps raising the amount on him. He wants me to give it to Solo, the fifty that's left."

"So what the fuck, Honeycutt? Give it to him."

"I don't want to."

"What you mean, you don't want to? You telling me the asshole's a vengeful gangster and his sidekick's a slicer. You telling me not to deal. What the fuck are you doing?"

Karen sat back and stared out into the office. "I'm thinking…" She sat up again, looked at LaDonna. "You take the money for the movie. Then you don't have to deal with Solo."

"That doesn't get *you* off with Solo. Hell no I ain't taking that money."

"Why not? Jack and I will figure out how to play Solo."

LaDonna got up and started pacing the office. She stopped and looked at Karen. "No," she said and started pacing again.

Karen said, "Look, I just don't want to give the money to Solo. Anyone but Solo. In fact, I'm dying to give it away."

LaDonna stopped again. "Why's that?"

"Fuck," Karen said. "My mother."

"Your mother? You want to make sense here?"

"She says it's tainted."

"Wait a minute. You telling me your mother knows about this money?"

"Course not. She was just talking about money. Christ, it's all she ever talks about."

"So let me get this straight." LaDonna sat back on the sofa. "You don't want to keep the money 'cause it's tainted but you don't want to give it back to the person who tainted it. Tainted? What kind of fucking shit word is that?"

"You know. Judy."

"Yeah, yeah. Well I don't want no tainted money neither. Don't try to give me your problem."

"Goddamn," Karen said, "you don't think every dime Solo Fontova ever touched isn't tainted? For Christ sake, it's just fucking money..."

"Not to you. What I think, you want the money. That's why you took it to begin with..."

"It's more complicated than that."

"Oh, no doubt," LaDonna said, "but the bottom line is..." she raised her voice "...you want the money." Then louder, "So get over your mother!" She went to her desk to check the time on the computer. "Speaking of Solo Fontova, he's going to be here any time."

"Oh yeah? I'm kinda getting an idea here, LaDonna..."

—⁓—

Karen went downstairs to meet Solo when Luc called up to say he was there. Luc raised his eyebrows at her as she passed him. LaDonna was right—he was a busybody. Too bad, with those looks...those hands...

"Solo," Karen said. "Come on up. LaDonna's waiting for you."

Ernesto hung back.

"It's beans and rice day, Ernesto," Karen told him. "Grab a table, they'll fix you a plate."

He didn't move except to fold his arms and stand there in the middle of the room like a goon.

Karen leaned over the bar. "Where's Buddha?"

"Not till four," Luc said with a wag of a finger in his voice that pissed her off.

Solo was carrying a brushed-aluminum briefcase. Karen led him up the stairs, turning back to say, "Ernesto gives me the creeps, Solo."

"That is his job, Karen."

She smiled. "Of course."

They were out of sight of the bar now. He put his hand on her arm to stop her as she reached the doorway. "Now that I am investing in your friend's movie, you will have no trouble giving me the money, Karen. I am right?"

"We'll talk about that. LaDonna's waiting." She went through the door into the hallway.

LaDonna threw open her office door. "Solo, how nice to see you." She air-kissed him, first one cheek then the other. "Please, come in, get comfortable."

Solo laid the briefcase on the coffee table and sat on the sofa. Karen sat behind the desk. LaDonna pulled a straight-back chair up to the end of the coffee table.

LaDonna's eyes gleamed at Solo. "Is that——" her eyelashes fluttered as she looked down at the briefcase and back to Solo "——the money?" He sat back in the sofa, a man feeling important, and started to speak. LaDonna held up a finger. "First, I asked Karen to explain the tax credits to you."

He looked at Karen the way a Komodo dragon might. He blinked and his eyes were back on LaDonna, dismissing Karen. "The Louisiana tax credits? I know the state will pay back twenty-five, thirty per cent of the cost of the film."

"And you know," Karen said, forcing him back to her, "that if the documentary is not made for any reason, you can sell the credits to a tax broker for eighty cents on the dollar."

"Yes. I know that."

"Jack tells me that you intend to invest a quarter of a million into this project."

LaDonna let out a small shriek. "A quarter of a million dollars?

Is that what's in here?" She put her hand on the case. "Oh, how fabulous…"

Karen began talking over her. "Did Jack speak out of turn, Solo?"

Solo held up a hand. He said to LaDonna. "I have some new ideas I want to discuss with you. Over lunch. Alone." He glanced at Karen.

"But maybe Ramon should be here. Should I call him?" LaDonna smiled sweetly.

Karen could see exasperation ready to pop out all over Solo like sweat. She watched as he contained himself.

"That is not necessary at this point, for Ramon to hear."

Karen said, "I know Ramon is a pain in the ass, Solo, but he really is a great director."

"Please," said Solo. To LaDonna: "I have never said this— pain in the ass. What I think, he is not worthy. I think you will get tired of him. Do not misunderstand. I respect Ramon. He fights for his woman."

"He does," said Karen. "It's very sweet but he's maybe a little naïve. Getting back to the tax credits, the way this works is…" Karen reached for her purse and pulled a sheaf of papers from it "…I have the law right here if you want to see it. Anyway, the expenses and spending on the documentary have to be reviewed by a certified auditor. Of the producer's choice."

"Your point here, Karen."

She spread her hands, palms up. "You're the producer."

"The executive producer."

"Exactly. LaDonna is the star, Ramon the director. I do the paperwork. The paperwork can say your investment was more than two fifty. It can say it was, oh, let's say double that. The auditor signs off on it, you collect a hundred fifty in tax credits… my math says that means your investment is only a hundred big ones."

He still looked reptilian, his face immobile, but Karen knew him well enough to know the wheels were spinning upstairs.

LaDonna clapped her hands softly. "Tell me, Solo..." She patted the briefcase.

"Fifty thousand, LaDonna. Another fifty soon." He said that to Karen.

"The money's gone, Solo."

He began turning red, a slight heave to his chest. LaDonna reached out and put her hand on his knee. "Solo," she said, "Karen gave me the money. The bank called my loan after the hurricane and I had to borrow from...I might as well call them what they are, loan sharks. When Karen found out what they were charging me, she gave me the money. I paid them off."

He cooled off before he took LaDonna's hand from his knee and held it. "If it helped you..." he looked at Karen "...I forget about it."

"Solo," LaDonna said, "you are quite a man. Come on, let's eat. I'm starving." Solo followed her downstairs.

Karen counted the money in the case, wrote a receipt for it, and a duplicate for the records. She brought the receipt to Solo. Upstairs again, she occupied herself with Costa Brava work schedules and invoices.

An hour later LaDonna burst through the door. "Oh my God, Honeycutt, I couldn't wait for him to leave. While you were talking, I kept thinking, how do we pull this off? The paperwork..."

"Calm down, LaDonna. There will be two sets of paperwork. The salaries will be inflated except—where's the money? It won't be in your bank account, or mine or Ramon's, because there's only that money." She pointed at the brushed-aluminum briefcase. "That's all we ever got no matter what Solo's paperwork says. You see?"

LaDonna went over to the case. She opened it and gazed at

fifty thousand dollars stacked neatly inside. She closed it.

"You know, Honeycutt, you are wicked. There's only one problem I see and it's a big one. How do we get rid of him?"

Karen smiled. It felt like LaDonna's cat smile but on her face. "I think Ramon can take care of that problem."

"Ra*mon*?"

Karen nodded. "We let Solo get his tax credits in hand. Then I bet Ramon would take a great deal of pleasure siccing the state of Louisiana dogs on him and that Bullmastiff of his."

TWENTY-THREE

Pascal couldn't get out of the restaurant until almost ten o'clock. Karen waited for him at the bar. A half hour earlier she'd walked in, saw the buttoned red leather counter and missed Raynie. She sat at the bar and wondered what it would be like to sleep with Jimmy Johnpier. Harley Sands breezed into the bar just in time.

"Heard from Raynie yet?"

"She only left this morning, Harley. I'm sure they're still out celebrating..."

"Think she can keep him out all night?"

"And then what?"

"They get in his plane and fly home."

"And then what?"

Harley closed one eye, his face screwed up. "Eventually he takes his boat to tuna town. I can't stand it, I swear I can't..." He shook his head hard, shaking loose the images. "I'm taking over from Pascal in a few minutes. Things are trés in-ter-es-ting around here. Beware the brother."

He turned to go. Karen caught him by his apron strings. "What's that supposed to mean?"

"He keeps paying *someone*..." he leaned in and whispered, "the sous-chef...to give him a new key every time he loses it. It drives Pascal mad. And just so you know, Pascal's real interested in what happened Saturday night. He seems to think that just because I left here early, I know something about it. Gotta go." He wheeled out.

CHRIS WILTZ

—ᴍ—

Pascal had dinner brought to them in his office.

"I had plans for us," he said, "dinner uptown, show you my house, but Raynie's absence is messing up the works. I've got to hire someone fast."

"Johnpier sent a limo for her this morning. I helped her pack. It took all of half an hour and it's like she never lived there. Her stuff fit in the trunk, room to spare."

Pascal took the last forkful and wiped his mouth. "Give Johnpier a month. He'll lavish her with clothes, jewelry, things. Johnpier likes things. Wait till you see his palace." He took their plates to the bar. "A little port? I find it resolves the meal."

She smiled. "Is that quaint or worldly?"

"Hell if I know." He poured two small glasses of port. "Jimmy likes to say things like that."

"He has a profound effect on people's speech. Raynie came in last night talking...different...she said it was because she'd been with Jimmy all day."

He handed her a glass and sat beside her on the sofa. "You're worried about Raynie, aren't you—what, that she'll get eaten up with the money?"

Karen stopped the glass an inch from her lips. "Why should I worry? I'm sure she will. That's what she's in it for."

Pascal nearly lost the nip of port he'd taken. Karen smiled, took a sip of hers and ran her fingers up and down the long stem of the glass. "Haven't you talked to Johnpier?"

Pascal concentrated on swallowing before he said, "No. He called this morning to tell me they were off to Vegas. It was all news to me."

"It was? You told me he wanted to marry her."

"Right, but I had no idea he actually would, and so fast."

"When the woman says yes, you move. I guess."

248

"Wait, back up." Pascal put his glass on the coffee table. "He took her out yesterday, asked her to marry him, and she said yes. Just like that?"

"Sort of. He took her out, told her he wanted to marry her and said she could look at it as a business proposition."

"A business proposition? What, like a merger? I got a wedding invitation once from a couple in business who called their marriage a merger. Like that?"

Karen slid her glass on the table too. She crossed her legs, turning more toward him. "Pascal, where's the romance, the passion in that? Johnpier's in love with Raynie. Apparently he's not like a lot of men who think they can profess undying love and the woman will swoon into their arms." He laughed and she realized she wasn't nervous with him the way she'd been last night. "He told her he was marrying her for love—and her looks—and her youth, although I don't really remember that being part of the equation—and he couldn't imagine why she'd be marrying him for anything other than his money. Unless, of course, it was for his scintillating humor, which, as it turned out, kind of, um, closed the deal." Karen was into it now, letting loose, improvising.

"His scintillating humor. That sounds like Jimmy. So that's it? She says yes?"

"Well, I think there were a few other stipulating factors, but you're Johnpier's confidant. I think he should give you the details."

He reached across what had become a small distance between them and grabbed both her hands. "Uh-unh, you're not getting out of here alive unless you tell me."

"But Raynie told me in confidence."

"Did she say that? She said don't tell anyone?"

Karen tilted her head. "No. She didn't. I think it was just understood, you know? Given the nature of the talk. Women know when they can spill and when they can't."

"You're killing me here. What if I tell you Jimmy and I had a bet. Since I lost the bet, which means Raynie gets my dearly beloved '76 gold Eldorado convertible as a wedding present, I ought to get some kind of consolation prize. Tell me how the man did it. He's a conniving bastard, you know."

Karen started laughing. "He is. He's smart. He wanted her bad enough that he asked her to commit to three months and if she leaves, he'll give her whatever she thinks is fair."

He let go of her hands, took one and held it between them. "Son-of-a-bitch. So that's how you get a woman to marry you."

"Well, one way…"

He angled his body more toward her, edged a little closer. "That wouldn't work with you?"

"It might but it strains my imagination."

"What would it take, good old-fashioned love?"

"I don't know. I'm not sure I ever loved anyone enough to marry him. I thought so one time but…" She shook her head.

"I had one of those too, a couple, but I've got a few years on you."

She would have liked to ask him how old he was but he leaned in and kissed her, tentative at first, as though he wasn't sure she was ready for it. She stopped thinking about it, about anything, only the way his mouth worked with hers, his arms coming up around her…

She froze when she heard the knock on the door. Pascal pulled away slowly, ran his hand down the side of her face before he answered it. She heard Harley say through the partly opened door, "Sorry to interrupt, boss," and Pascal closed the door. He crossed the room, carrying a white canvas bank bag around its gathered-up neck. He unlocked a cabinet under some bookshelves at the side of the big desk and she saw him put the bag in a safe. He spun the dial, locked the cabinet. When he came back he held out his hand and walked her into the room next door.

—⅏—

This went straight to the heart, the kind of connection that made all the fireworks with Luc nothing but sport, not that there was anything wrong with that. This made you want to do the whole ride-off-into-the-sunset thing. Karen sighed deeply and Pascal touched her hair and kissed her then put his hand over hers, the one that rested on his chest and could feel his heart finally beginning to slow down.

The restaurant elevator started to move.

"People still here?" Karen murmured.

"No. That would be my demented brother." Pascal started to get up but leaned back toward her. "Don't move. I won't be long."

In the moonlight coming from the unshuttered bedroom window she could see him grab a pair of sweat pants from the back of a chair. The elevator had stopped. Pascal went out to the hallway, leaving the door open a crack behind him.

"Where did you get the key, Avery?"

"Oh, I uh, had an extra."

"Give it to me."

"Come on, Pascal. This is my building too."

"I live here, Avery. I don't have a key to your place, go barging in on you in the middle of the night. I can't believe I'm trying to use reason. Just give me the fucking key."

"What's happ'nin, brother? Gittin a little nookie?"

Karen heard them moving into Pascal's office. The thick plaster walls of the building muffled their voices so she couldn't understand what they were saying. She got out of bed and grabbed Pascal's shirt, opened the door enough to get through it and stepped into the hallway, hoping she didn't hit a loose board.

Pascal's office door was open.

"What are you going to do, Avery? Pull a gun on me?"

Karen stopped short.

"I'm clean, I swear. Said I was sorry 'bout that. Didn't I?"

"I don't remember either. Did O'Leary take your gun too?"

"I want to kill the motherfucker."

"I keep telling you, the Cuban's your problem."

"You think the Cuban's got my money?"

"I don't really know, do I, Avery?"

"Can you just give me some cash? I know you've got it."

"Not in the middle of the night. Why didn't you come over today?"

"I been busy all day."

"All day."

"Look, I got some new eyebrows."

"I couldn't help but notice."

"They okay?"

"Better than the real ones."

"Shee-it, Pascal."

"Out. Now. Come back in the morning."

Karen slipped into the bedroom. The elevator started. Pascal must have gone down with him. She sat in the middle of the bed, still in his shirt, and stared out the bedroom window, a nice view of moonlight on slate-covered rooftops, if she'd been paying attention. She wasn't; she was thinking that the money Solo gave LaDonna in the brushed-aluminum briefcase was Avery's money, that Jack stole.

When he saw her in his shirt he said, "You heard all that?"

"Most."

He got in bed and sat crossed-legged opposite her. "My brother, my half-brother actually, is a parasite and that may be the best thing I can say about him. He owns this building with me. He won't let me buy him out because then he'd have to take care of his own money. He's low wattage but bright enough to know if I don't dole it out to him, he'll gamble it away in no time."

"The gun—would he use it?"

"I don't know. Maybe. If he's pushed hard enough. He got pushed pretty hard Saturday night."

"Sounds like it."

He put his hands on her knees. "I think you know it. Tell me…" He rubbed his palms over her kneecaps "…did he rape Raynie? Is that the real reason she married Jimmy Johnpier?"

Raynie looked at herself one last time in the full-wall mirror of the ornate dressing room in the honeymoon suite at Bellagio. Her emotions ran high and confusing and she wasn't having much luck sorting them out. Fear was easy enough. Then there was a bunch of stuff having to do with Daniel that was quite unsettling. And a nagging little voice saying something along the lines of selling her soul to the devil, which she swore she didn't believe. She recognized curiosity too but that was more about her immediate future with Jimmy in the bedroom.

The champagne-colored peignoir was beautiful, though she preferred wearing a camisole and her underwear to bed. As soon as they'd arrived Jimmy had taken her shopping. They must have hit every designer boutique in the casino. With his encouragement she got dresses, shoes, two purses, jeans that cost almost four hundred dollars a pair, blouses, a jacket, beautiful lingerie as well as the peignoir, makeup, and a new set of luggage to get it all home. She fluffed her hair and opened the door to the bedroom.

Jimmy sat up in bed reading one of his huge collection of books about war and history. He had on navy silk pajamas with light blue piping. He took off his glasses and put the book aside.

"Raynie, you take my breath away."

She put one knee on the bed and sat close to the edge. He seemed very far away from her on the other side of the king.

"I'm never going to lie to you, Jimmy. You can always count on that. So I'm going to tell you that I'm not a virgin but I'm scared to death."

He smiled and looked a little goofy the way he did when he tilted his head and she could tell he was full of love for her. "You don't have to be, precious. What I haven't told you yet but suspect you'll be relieved to know is that I can't get it up any more."

"I'm sorry, Jimmy."

"You don't have to be sorry either. I had prostate cancer, rather advanced, and I thought I was going to die some time ago. Yet here I am with you and you are my wife. It's all so amazing that if I die tomorrow I won't be inclined to make much of a fuss about it."

"I don't want you to die any time soon."

"I believe you." He held out his arms. "Come on. Let me hold you and we'll go to sleep. Unless you want me to make you happy. I can still do that."

He lifted the covers and she slid under them. "I might like that some time," she said, "but I'm not ready yet."

He switched off the light and she nestled into the crook of his arm. He sighed with contentment.

All those mixed emotions swirling inside Raynie earlier dropped away and something she hadn't recognized, maybe because it hadn't been there yet, began to emerge—how safe she felt here with Jimmy. It occurred to her that she was still curious. Her curiosity would never be fully satisfied now. Was she relieved?

She was tired and lying with Jimmy was comfortable. As she relaxed up next to him and began to drift off, she said, "I'm not relieved, Jimmy."

TWENTY-FOUR

Pascal finished writing out a check to Avery. He'd taken his time because he didn't want to look at Avery's face, which was flaming red and appeared painful. Under the baseball cap, his eyebrows were bushy and unnatural, maybe not so bad if you'd never seen Avery, though one hung askew.

"You need to see to your left eyebrow," Pascal said handing him the check.

Avery reached up to feel it and it came off on his fingers. "Needs a little glue." He pulled a tube out of his front pants pocket and went across the hall to the bathroom.

Pascal followed him as far as the office door. "What happened to your face?"

"Emergency dermabrasion," Avery said slowly, concentrating on his glue-job. "There. Better." He walked out into the hallway.

"Don't come back for more," Pascal said. "As it is you're two months ahead with what I gave you last time. You know, the time you brought the gun."

"Judas Priest, Pascal. How many times I gotta tell you…look, my money got *stolen*. I'm gonna get it back."

"How are you going to do that?"

"I don't know yet. I think you're right—the Cuban's got it. I just gotta find him."

"That should be easy enough. If the Cuban's still in town."

"You think so, huh?"

"Sure, find O'Leary."

"He hangs at Molly's but I never see him with the Cuban."

"But he can take you to the Cuban."

"He isn't going to take me to the Cuban." He said it like Pascal had a walnut for a brain.

Pascal's patience was in short supply. "He will if you follow him. Eventually. Even if it means you get on a plane to Miami."

"And then what?"

"For fucksake, Avery. Then you deal with him."

If they don't deal with you first, he thought as he watched Avery retreat down the stairs so he could sneak out the back way.

—∿∿—

"Talk me down, Honeycutt. I beg you, talk me down."

LaDonna had been sobbing. She wiped under each eye with the Kleenex Karen handed her. Ramon stood watching, his arms dangling uselessly at his sides. They had found out from one of the lunch patrons that Spike Lee had been in town, making a documentary that sounded like theirs, people talking about what happened to them during and after the hurricane. He'd come and gone; his show already had an air date in August on HBfuckingO.

"Can you believe that, Honeycutt? All this work, all this money, and we got to find out from somebody eating lunch downstairs after I been talking it up big, the fuckin *definitive*—" she lifted her eyes menacingly at Ramon "—Katrina movie."

Ramon lifted his hands, looking at Karen, let them fall. LaDonna started crying again.

"Come on, LaDonna," Karen said. "There's always another idea. I'm sure you'll be able to use some of what you've got. You're just going to have to come at it a different way."

LaDonna flipped her hand at Karen.

Karen tried again. "No, really, LaDonna, you've got the money and I'm pretty sure there's more where that came from."

Hadn't Jack told her that Avery walked out of the game with eighty grand? Not that Jack would have handed all of it over to Solo. Where would he have stashed it? She needed to find the Thunderbird and pop the trunk.

"You know what my mother says, LaDonna: the money will come from wherever it is. And it's the same with ideas. They come from wherever they are too. Once you get over the shock…"

LaDonna put her hand over her eyes and motioned Karen to stop. "Okay, okay, you talked me down enough." She uncovered her eyes and looking at Ramon she said, "I let this punk convince me I was gonna be a star." Ramon lifted his useless arms again. "It's okay, honey, Karen's right, there's always another idea. How about this? We raise the money to build a community center in the 9. We can go outside New Orleans, go to L.A., raise corporate money, money from celebs…how's that for a way to get yourself known? We build a park around it—basketball court, playground for kids, picnic tables, barbecue pits, we even put in space for a police command center. And counseling. Video everything— how we get the money, the building of the center, the kids, the people, everything—and go for a mini-series. Now we talkin' about more than just what happened; we talkin' about recovery. We leave Spike in the dust."

Silence hung for a moment before Karen and Ramon rushed her, mauling her with enthusiasm and affection, congratulating her on her great idea. She made a face and pushed them off her. "For Christ sake, let me breathe. Now all I got to do is find the energy for it, ask myself for the millionth time if this is what I really want to be doing."

Ramon spread his arms wide and said with passion, "Oh *muchacha*, of course you want to do this. What could be better?" He smote himself of the forehead. "And look, get this great idea—we can sell chunks of the levees to the celebrities—you know, like the Berlin Wall or something. They'll pay thousands for that shit. We put it in a pretty box, a receptacle of some kind they can show on their coffee tables..."

Both Karen and LaDonna screamed, "No!"

Karen said, "*Your* idea, LaDonna, it's too good...once you get started you won't have time to ask questions like what do I really want to be doing."

"Yeah, yeah. You know what, Honeycutt, all this positive thinking, quoting your mother, it doesn't sit real well on you."

"You scared the shit out of me, crying like that."

"Yeah, that's some scary shit," Ramon said. "Maybe you'll like my idea for the Food Network—new New Orleans recipes, like spicy cookies called Cre-Oreos..."

"Shut up, Ramon. I'm telling the two of you, and you better hear this, Ramon. This isn't my idea. Solo came up with it. Not the police command center. I came up with that."

"You got to be kidding," Karen said. "I had no idea he had that much imagination."

"Honeycutt, haven't I ever told you that a man's greatest ideas come when he's got the hots for some woman?"

"Fuck me," Ramon said.

Avery Legendre stood in front of his bedroom mirror and put on his new creamy ten-gallon Stetson. Oh yeah, that was the look, his best one. He wore it down low and it put most of his face in shadow. Eyebrows—hardly noticeable. He didn't have on the whole cowboy outfit tonight—he was keeping a low profile, stick with regulation jeans and a short-sleeved black shirt but he had on his lizard cowboy boots. Just like a lizard, slide out from under his rock and wait for O'Leary to slide out from under his. He grinned at himself in the mirror.

Showdown at the midnight hour.

Now for the most important part of the show. He tucked the Walther into his waistband at the back. The summer weight sports coat, check the profile—nice.

He thrust his pelvis forward and cocked both his index fingers at the mirror. "Where's my fucking money, motherfucker?"

With the speed of Jackie Chan and the cool of Clint Eastwood, he pivoted toward the window and aimed his right finger. "Bam. You're dead." He saw the Cuban fall, clutching his heart, right where the bullet hit the target.

Shee-it. It might be worth eighty fucking grand.

Only, by the time he'd been waiting two hours at Molly's, sitting at the bar stacked two-people deep, getting jostled, trying not to drink too much but drinking too much, listening to a bunch of wise-offs—like he gave a shit about their asshole opinions—Avery didn't feel so cocky. He was getting more aggravated by the minute. The only other place he knew to look for O'Leary was over on Frenchman Street.

He went to the bathroom at Molly's and did some blow. Cockiness restored, he hit the street. He crossed Esplanade into the Marigny. Half a block away he saw Jack O'Leary come out of the Spotted Cat and cut obliquely across Frenchman. Avery waited until he went into La Costa Brava then he followed.

What he saw when he stepped into the place stopped him cold. O'Leary was sitting at the bar with Pascal, both of them talking to the woman bartender from Saturday night, and coming from the back was the Cuban with the woman LaDonna who owned the place. Behind them was another man, a hip-hop type, serious bling on his ears and around his neck, and the Cuban's thug, refried bean-breath. They started toward the bar as O'Leary stood, though Avery couldn't quite pick up what he said over the

CHRIS WILTZ

loud music.

He went around to the dining room side and ducked into the bathroom. He needed enough blow to put some steel in his nerves, because O'Leary had led him straight to the Cuban all right, but that's where Avery's plan stopped. He had no idea what in hell's nation to do now.

—w—

The band had packed up and cleared out, which left two couples still drinking at the side tables and Pascal at the bar. He glanced at his watch. Karen had been surprised when he offered to come to La Costa and wait until she got off, but he was looking weary. It was after two.

Zachary was cleaning up, filling the refrigerator with beer. She was about to tell him to make a last call when Jack walked in, boisterous as always, calling out to her over the music before he had cleared the doorway. Pascal turned his head. Jack didn't seem to notice him.

"I knew I should have locked the door," Karen said.

"Aw, sugarpops, you know you're always glad to see ole Jack."

"You remember Pascal Legendre."

Jack's smile froze but only for a second. "Sure. Pascal. Long time no see." He moved the bar chair next to Pascal's to put some distance between them, and sat on the edge of it.

"How's Miami?"

"It's good, man, great place. Yeah."

"When are you going back?"

Jack didn't seem to know what to say and Karen wondered if this was going to get weird. He was first to turn toward the noise on the stairway and stood up, grinning at LaDonna and her new entourage. He made a great show of greeting them; he clapped Solo on the shoulder, shook Ramon's hand vigorously.

260

LaDonna motioned to Karen from the end of the bar. Karen said to Pascal, "Soon," and went over. They leaned in and LaDonna said up close to her ear, "He's going to put the whole two fifty in."

"Did he bring it?"

"Not yet. Another fifty in a couple of days."

"Acting possessive yet?"

"Maybe a little, but, what, I'm gonna turn it down now?"

"That's a choice."

"Not tonight. Maybe tomorrow. I'll see how I feel then. Why don't you close it down for the night, come on over and we'll talk about the project."

"I'm going out with Pascal Legendre."

LaDonna reared back to take a look at Pascal. She waved at him. He waved back.

She leaned in again. "He's some hot shit, Honeycutt. Supposed to be a real catch."

"Yeah? I'll let you know."

"Shit, girl. Attitude like that, he'll stand up on his hind legs and beg." She looked after the group, Jack attached, going into the dining room. Not trying to be quiet now, she said, "What the fuck is O'Leary doing here?"

"Wandered in a few minutes ago. He is Solo's sometime partner, you know."

"Not on this deal he's not. I better go make that real clear. Zachary, bring over a bottle of champagne. Three flutes." She headed off to the dining room.

Zachary got the champagne from the refrigerator, and Karen asked the two couples if they wanted last drinks. He came back and told her to hand him another flute. He gave a laugh. "Jack's telling LaDonna he wants nothing to do with her movie so she's letting him drink champagne with them." She handed him the flute.

"What movie?" Pascal said.

"LaDonna's hurricane movie. It used to be Ramon's movie—he's the blinged-out boyfriend—but not any more."

"Who's the big guy? In the suit?"

"That's the Cuban," Karen said. "Solo Fontova."

"He's in on the movie?"

"Looks like it."

"I see." He nodded. "I get it now."

"What?"

"Avery's money. It's in the movie."

Zachary ducked behind the bar. "I'm ready to go. Okay?"

"Grab the keys," she said, lifting four full go-cups. "I'll lock up after you."

Ernesto was lurking in the foyer. He backed into the short passage to the dining room, something creepy about the way this big wide guy could move so fast, so silent on his feet like slabs of rock. Karen held open the door for the two couples as she searched for the key on the big ring.

Zachary motioned to her to step outside with him. "Where's Buddha?"

"I told him to clean up the music room."

"You better get him. I saw that cowboy dude go in the bathroom a while ago but I never saw him come out."

—⁂—

Pascal was standing behind the bar chair, stretching. Karen walked up to him, his arms still over his head, his eyes closed, and locked her arms around his waist. He smelled good. She decided she shouldn't dwell on that. He came out of the stretch, running his hands over her shoulders and down her back. He kissed her.

"Ready?" he said.

"Almost...Zachary said he saw Avery go in the bathroom."

"When? How did I miss him?" He was surprised, as though he'd been looking out for him.

Karen lifted her shoulders and pulled herself into him, taking a deep breath. She let her arms fall. "Gotta close out the register then we can go."

He nodded and headed off to the bathroom.

He still hadn't come out when she finished. She decided to take everything upstairs and check on Buddha when she came down. Several minutes later, though, she came around the stairway wall to see Pascal following Avery, in his flashy cowboy boots and ten-gallon hat, as he stomped off toward the dining room. She bypassed the door to the music room.

Pascal stopped at the wide opening to the dining room and leaned against the wall with his arms folded. As Karen came up beside him, he tilted his head toward her, lifted his eyebrows and a shoulder, and resumed watching as Avery went straight up to the table where Solo, LaDonna, Jack and Ramon were sitting. Same as he'd practiced in front of his mirror, he said, "I want my fucking money, motherfucker." His fists opened and closed at his sides; his body was wired to explode.

Solo stared at first. His face showed nothing, but the horror of Avery's dermabrasion and the big fluffy eyebrows, showed on Jack, Ramon and LaDonna. When Solo stood up, the force sent his chair back so hard it fell over and skidded. "How dare you," he said with quiet menace. "There is a lady present."

In answer Avery bumped the table. All the champagne flutes toppled.

"Shit!" LaDonna, along with Jack and Ramon, jumped up. "Buddha!" she shrieked.

Karen started to turn, to get Buddha, when out of her peripheral vision Ernesto appeared, coming from the foyer. Avery saw him too. He pulled his gun. "Right there, bean breath," he said. He backed away so he had all of them in sight.

Jack took a step away from the table. "Avery, Avery," he said, a slight laugh in his voice, a grin on his face, "come on, man, let's talk about this…"

He aimed at Jack and stopped him. "Nothin to talk about. I want my money right now."

Jack held out his hands. "Man, nobody has any money here."

"You stole my money and you gave it to this fuckin Cuban."

Jack laughed. "Naw, man, nobody stole nothin…"

Avery moved the gun back to Ernesto and squinted one eye. "I can start by blowing off bean-breath's knee caps."

Pascal pushed himself away from the wall, his weight centered on both feet. Avery saw the movement and glanced at Pascal.

"Avery," Pascal said, rather quietly, though clearly Avery heard him.

The music pounded in Karen's ears. Hadn't she turned it down?

"Okay," Avery said, "this is what I want. I want one of you motherfucker's to tell me where my money is. Then we can go get it." The gun was still on Ernesto.

No one said anything. Karen could feel the bass thumping in her chest. She looked over at LaDonna for a second, catching her expression of wide-eyed terror before she turned her eyes back to Avery.

Avery lifted his gun arm, holding it out straight. His left hand came up to clasp his right wrist, to steady his gun hand. He squinted again. "I really would like to watch bean-breath after I shoot his knees out."

Karen could hear every word though the music seemed to have gotten louder, throbbing against her eardrums. The sound of a chair scraping on the rough wood floor broke the tension. Ramon yelled, "The money's upstairs—okay?—upstairs."

Avery looked over at Ramon. Karen caught a glint coming off Ernesto as Pascal said, much louder than he had before, "Avery, the Cuban."

Karen eyes shifted to Solo. Avery turned the gun. He fired at Solo then dropped the gun as if it had been shot out of his hand. He clutched his chest. The shiny black and silver handle of a knife stuck out of his breast bone. Ernesto was already running when Solo hit the floor. The whole building shook. Avery looked at Ernesto with total disbelief before he fell.

—ɷ—

In the music room Buddha lifted the large ear phone away from his tiny ear. He'd been sweeping the stage, singing along with his favorite group of all time, the Supremes, volume up max. He turned Diana down and listened for a moment. Nothing but Brazilian Girls wailing out there but he'd heard something, or maybe he'd felt it more than heard it. Somebody must have dropped something heavy. He snapped the ear phone back in place and let the Supremes rip. He swept the little dirt pile into a dust pan, emptied it into the garbage can he'd brought in with him, and balanced the broom over the top of the can. He stepped down off the stage and walked over to the door, his eyes squeezed shut, his voice high-pitched and tinny as he sang into the handle of the dust pan, *"Baby luh-uhve, my baby luh-uhve, I need your love, oh-oh I need your love…"*

—ɷ—

Ernesto knelt on one side of Solo's body, Jack on the other. Ernesto was weeping and doing something that sounded like praying in Spanish. Jack was digging in Solo's suit coat pockets.

Karen went up behind Jack and shook his shoulder. "What are you doing?" Solo's blood was pooling in her direction. She stepped back. "Look," she said, "you're kneeling in his blood.

Get up."

Jack stuck his hand way down in Solo's pants pocket.

"What are you doing?" Karen yelled.

He whipped his head around. "I gave him all the money. I'm going to get it."

Ernesto looked up, tears smeared on his cheeks. His face twisted and he said something to Jack in Spanish that sounded quite vicious. When Jack didn't stop looting Solo's body, Ernesto pushed him.

Jack almost lost his balance. "You snot-nosed sniveling little bastard. *Comemierda*." He pushed Ernesto.

Ernesto caught himself on one hand and started yelling at Jack. Karen shook Jack's shoulder and kept shaking it. "Stop it, Jack. Have some fucking decency. Get up. Get up, goddamnit!"

LaDonna started yelling for Buddha, full-lung hysteria.

Buddha heard that as soon as he opened the door to the music room. He ripped his earphones off and charged like an elephant toward the dining room. He saw LaDonna, her hands at the sides of her face, taking in the scene over Solo's body, screaming for him. He pushed Pascal, who was standing over Avery, kicked at Avery's cowboy boots, shoved Karen to the side, grabbed Jack by the back of his shirt, threw him to the ground and sat on him. He still had his dust pan clutched in his hand.

—⚭—

By post-hurricane time standards the police arrived faster than a speeding bullet. Not until seven in the morning did they finish questioning everyone. The coroner's staff took the bodies away but couldn't tell Pascal or Ernesto where autopsies would be performed or when the bodies would be released. The coroner's offices and labs had been flooded and bodies from the storm were still waiting at sites all across southern Louisiana. Jack got hauled off to University Hospital, where charity cases were being taken, to see how many of his ribs were cracked and if there were internal injuries.

Karen sat alone at the bar, drinking another Coke. She pushed it away. Her mouth tasted like stale sticky candy. LaDonna and Ramon had gone upstairs. Buddha left when LaDonna told him to. Pascal said a few words to one of the detectives then they left, taking Ernesto with them. She heard the front door close. Pascal came over and sat next to her.

"We can go," he told her.

She nodded. "I'm not finding it in me to be sorry about your brother but then I don't think you are either."

"He wasn't one of the good guys. Truth is, I didn't know until tonight how dangerous he was."

"Is that right?"

"Come on, let's go."

"I don't think so."

"What—why not?"

"I'm not sure what happened tonight but I guess I'm wondering how dangerous you are."

Pascal smiled. "You're kidding, right? I'm a little tired…"

"I'm not kidding. When Jack came in, I think you were looking for Avery to be right behind him. I think you expected him."

"I did, sort of. He told me he was following Jack around looking for the Cuban."

"Right. You told him last night the Cuban was his problem."

"What's your point, Karen?"

"I think what bothers me most is the way you cued him tonight."

"What in fuck's name are you talking about?"

"You saw the knife just like I did but that's not where you wanted Avery to look. You said, 'The Cuban.'"

Annoyed, Pascal said, "The thug isn't Cuban?"

"Yeah, but he's the thug, Solo's the Cuban."

"You think I was telling him to kill the Cuban?"

"I don't think you cared one way or the other. You just wanted his attention there, not on Ernesto."

"I had no idea he was that good with a knife."

Karen stared at him.

"Come on, Karen, what do you want me to say? I'm glad he's dead? I'm not trying to hide that from you. Come home with me."

She wanted to touch his face, as though what was troubling her could only be explained by feel. "What you did was risky; some of the good guys could have died too."

"Like everyone in that room wasn't already at risk?"

"It's all about money, isn't it? You wanted him out of your building, out of your finances."

Pascal's mouth tightened into a thin straight line then he nodded. "I did."

"What did you say to him in the bathroom?"

"I didn't tell him to go out and kill the Cuban, if that's what you think."

"But you saw the chance and you took it. You know, I thought I knew something about risk. I don't. Or not enough. Or I never thought it all the way to the end, when somebody gets killed."

"We're too tired to have this conversation. We can talk about it tomorrow. Today. Later today."

"I'm not ready to talk about it. I want you to go home now."

He stood up. Karen thought he might be struggling between anger and something else. Finally, he put his hand around the back of her neck. "Will you call me? Soon?"

"I'll call you when I'm poor again and when I'm ready to tell you why that's a good thing. And when I think there's a rat's-ass chance you might understand."

TWENTY-FIVE

Raynie Johnpier sat on the silk-covered sofa in the living room of the St. Charles Avenue mansion. Her home. Except Jimmy was right—the place was more of a museum than a home. The only rooms she felt comfortable in were the bedroom and sitting room upstairs. She loved the kitchen and had cooked almost every night since they'd returned from their quick honeymoon. And she loved the summer house.

Her eyes moved from one beautiful object to the next but she wasn't really seeing them. Karen had been right—she'd gotten bit on the ass, and they'd only been married a week yesterday, but it wasn't the way Karen meant. Or she didn't think so. It wasn't Jimmy. She liked Jimmy; maybe she loved him. She definitely thought she could. She didn't want to walk away from the marriage. But she missed her old life, missed it badly. It had all started when she heard about the shooting at La Costa Brava. Okay, strange, but she wished she'd been there. She missed the action in the restaurant, goofing around with Harley, living with Karen, keeping up with LaDonna and Ramon, and the Quarter and all the characters. She thought about Luc the bartender, maybe too much. She missed Jimmy coming to Le Tripot to see her.

That morning Jimmy had left for Houston, not sure for how long. Maybe she'd go downtown and see everyone, see if she really missed it all. Maybe she'd just go out to the summer house and think about all the things life with Jimmy offered her. It popped into her brain, another one of Uncle Dudley's old saws: It's hard to see sometimes when you have a seat in the front row.

She sighed as the doorbell rang. She looked out the front door to see the postman waving what appeared to be a manila envelope. "Registered mail," he called to her.

She went down the marble steps and around the old Cadillac sitting in the curved driveway. Jimmy had told her Pascal bet him the car she wouldn't marry him. Too bad for Pascal; she loved the car. Maybe she'd take a spin around the park later.

The postman handed her the form through the iron fence. She signed it and took the envelope, surprised to see her name on it. The return address was Le Tripot, but that was Jimmy's handwriting, wasn't it? Her heart began to race.

She stood in the foyer and ripped open the envelope. There were several sheets, the first a handwritten letter.

Dearest Raynie,

You need an explanation from me for everything that's going to happen.

It all started when the big C decided to settle in my nether regions. I suppose you could say I went a little insane. I'll spare you the boring details and give you the outlandish highlights.

First, I stopped paying taxes. I never liked paying them anyway so I used Uncle Sam's cut to help buy myself a mansion and an airplane, and I used the airplane to run around the world buying up as much art as I could to fill the mansion. It was a glorious time. I stopped paying attention to business and spent the short time I thought I had left to surround myself with beauty. All my life I have craved things of beauty and refinement. More on that in a moment.

They have caught up with me. My becoming a pauper is not enough for them. I am going to be indicted and they are going to send me to jail.

If I had met you a few years earlier perhaps I wouldn't have been such a foolish man. That I have had the astounding luck to meet you at all and have you agree to be my wife, short time though it must be, will fill me with joy for whatever time I have left in this world. You are the ultimate in beauty and refinement, dear Raynie. Your sweetness and kindness are not qualities I've seen much of in the world I inhabit. It would be a further crime for you to have ever been married to a felon.

You will find a suitcase on the top shelf of your closet with $150,000 in it. Enclosed with this letter is a copy of LaDonna Johnson's note. Which is worth more than $50,000 with interest, another item I released from Pascal's possession. That should pay your rent for a few years. My lawyer has the original. Keep in touch with him in case there is anything left after the jackals finish with our possessions. Don't remove anything other than your personal belongings, the money and your car from the house. And don't tell anyone, including the lawyer, about the money. The contents of the house have already been inventoried and if you take even one item, they will have an excuse to hound you.

The names and particulars of my law and accounting firms, along with a few suggestions about the money, are on the next page. With this, my darling girl, I set you free. Leave quickly, don't look back, have no remorse. Your presence in my life has changed me into a better man. Ah, and in such a short time…

I hope I have insured that you never have to cook frog legs again as long as you live, unless you want to, of course.

With my undying love,
Your frog prince,
Jimmy

She was stunned then her eyes filled and her brain went into rapid-fire confusion. What did he mean, it would be a crime for her to be married to a felon? Where had he said he was staying? The Hyatt? Curse the man for refusing to carry a cell phone. She went to the kitchen to call, waiting for the number and the phone to ring at the front desk at the Hyatt, barely keeping herself from getting frantic.

When the young woman answered, she asked for his room. "This is his wife," she said, "and it's urgent."

"Oh, Mrs. Johnpier, just a moment..."

The man who came on wasn't Jimmy. He was with the Houston Police Department. Were they arresting him already? "Mrs. Johnpier," he said, "I'm very sorry to inform you that your husband checked into the hotel a little while ago. Then he went up to the roof. I'm sorry, Mrs. Johnpier. He jumped."

Raynie clutched her stomach; she felt sick. A voice rang in her ears, Judy Honeycutt saying, "Think about money and it will come." All she'd done was think about her old life and she had it back. She ran for the bathroom.

—⁓—

On a balmy Saturday afternoon Peewee Meeker strolled along Park Avenue in downtown Eunice, on his way to the tuxedo rental place. His wedding was in three weeks and every few days Alice Roy gave him a list of things he needed to do. Then in the evenings he'd go over to the Pendergast's house and Alice Roy would check off what he'd done on her master list and tell him what she'd done, and they'd microwave popcorn and watch a movie until her parents went to bed. After that they'd neck for a while and Peewee would feel her up and kiss the baby through her tight smooth abdomen, but Alice Roy had decided no more sex until after the wedding. He could hardly wait for the wedding.

Guitar riffs filled his head so he didn't notice the pickup truck pulling up almost next to him. The tuxedo store was two doors away when a large hand clamped down on his shoulder and he heard a voice he'd hoped never to hear again in his life say, "Hear you gittin hitched, penis."

Raymond Dick stood there grinning at him, with the Hulk's vice grip on his clavicle. He expected to be lifted and tossed down the street any second.

"Uh, yeah," he said trying to laugh.

"Does that hurt?" With his thumb Raymond pressed into the hollow at the base of Peewee's throat.

Peewee coughed and choked on, "Yes."

"Cut it out, Raymond."

Someone had come up on his other side. Peewee turned only his eyes, finding Earlene's boyfriend Daniel. He coughed again.

"Let him go."

"Don't want the little penis to run off, do we?" Raymond said but he let go, his hand resting on Peewee's shoulder.

"I'm not going to run off."

Daniel took his other shoulder and turned Peewee toward him. "Just tell us where Earlene is, Peewee. You told everyone at Savoy's you went fishing at David Pecot's camp in Venice…"

"But guess who we just happened to talk to?" Raymond's grin was turning dangerous. He always grinned like that before he beat someone up. "Everyone knows David Pecot but David Pecot doesn't know you."

Daniel said, "I need to know where she is, Peewee, that she's safe."

Peewee could see the pain in Daniel's eyes. Daniel was okay

except he was friends with Raymond. He wanted to tell him; he thought Earlene had let this go way too far, but she was his friend.

"She's safe, Daniel, I promise."

"I guess that means you know where she is." Raymond's thumb found the hollow and gently stroked it.

Peewee talked fast. "I promised her I wouldn't tell. Don't ask me to do that. She said she was coming home soon, maybe for the wedding." His eyes begged Daniel.

Daniel shook his head. "I'm not waiting any more."

Peewee was close to panic now. "What are you going to do?"

"I'm going to go see her. That's all, Peewee, I'm just going to go see her."

Peewee hesitated and Raymond said, "It would be a shame if you were all messed up for your wedding."

Peewee flung Raymond's arm off him with his forearm. He kept his voice as steady as he could. "You're a bully, Raymond. You always have been. Why don't you grow the fuck up?"

Daniel said, "He's got a point, buddy." He moved Peewee away from Raymond. "You stand over there while Peewee tells me where Earlene is."

So Peewee told him.

—⁂—

Karen and Luc got over trying to avoid each other. They were too busy. After the shooting La Costa Brava had been closed a couple of days. When it reopened it seemed as though everyone in town started coming in. LaDonna was going to have the floors refinished in the dining room since it had been impossible to wash all the blood out of the worn wood, but part of the attraction was the stains. As Luc said, people liked to rubberneck while they ate.

Karen came from upstairs at five o'clock and Luc got the cappuccino machine going.

"How's Raynie?"

"She stopped being sick around noon yesterday. You know, I think she loved him."

Luc said, "Shock."

"What, you don't think she could have loved him?"

"I mean she's still in shock. I don't know if she loved him. I guess at some point she'll be able to tell us."

"Maybe. She keeps saying, 'Watch what you think about,' whatever that means."

They were silent for a while, Karen sipping at her cappuccino, Luc straightening lines of glasses he'd already straightened.

"So you got her all moved in?"

"She's in but Jimmy bought her a new wardrobe. We don't know where to put it. I think we're going to look for a two bedroom."

Luc nodded. "Too bad, though, that's a good place. So...what's Raynie going to do? About work, I mean. Or maybe she doesn't have to any more."

"She's already talked to Pascal. She's going back to work at the restaurant sometime next week."

"That's good."

A few uncomfortable moments passed.

Karen said, "She might come over later. She's having trouble sleeping."

It seemed as though they'd stretched the conversation to its outer limits until Luc said, "This has been a full tilt black-rock week."

Karen put her cappuccino down. "Did something happen to you I don't know about?"

"You know about it." He put his hands on the bar and assumed his stance.

She picked up the cup again and said over it, "I'm not sure

what you mean."

"Sure you do. Look, I wish I felt different about everything but you have to admit, it got scary, way too scary."

"I admit it."

He leaned on his forearms and smiled at her. "You remember what you told me about Jack taking risk over convenience and Solo taking risk over inconvenience? Did I get that right?"

She nodded.

"Well, what about you? What side do you fall on?"

The feeling she was going to blow passed in about two seconds. She smiled back at him. "Neither. For me, it's risk for risk's sake."

—∿—

Daniel and Raymond consulted their map, found a parking space, and walked to St. Philip Street. They found the address on a rickety wood gate with no door bell.

"This looks bad, Daniel. My sister's living in a rat trap. I say we wrap my shirt around her head and haul her off."

"That gives me some insight as to why she left, dickhead."

"What does that mean?"

Daniel knocked, rattled the gate by its handle, then started yelling, "Hello? Hello?"

Raynie was in the shower and Karen had Cassandra Wilson at top volume but she finally heard the commotion. She opened the gate to two guys in jeans and cowboy boots. One of them held his hat in his hand. It seemed as though there were too many cowboys in New Orleans these days.

The one holding his hat said, "I'm looking for Earlene Dick."

Karen stifled a laugh and started to say she didn't know anyone named Earlene Dick but something clicked. "Are you Daniel?"

He said he was and Karen let them in. Daniel introduced her to Earlene's brother. She told them to wait in the courtyard.

The water was still running in the shower. She knocked. "Raynie?" She opened the door a crack. "Can I come in?"

"Sure," Raynie said.

Karen walked into the steam. "Hold your horses, okay? There's someone here asking for Earlene Dick."

Raynie's head popped out from behind the shower curtain.

"The man of your dreams—Daniel."

—⁂—

Raynie and Daniel sat at the courtyard table. Karen had left for La Costa and Raymond had finally been banned to ESPN after he'd gone on a rant—nothing but a guilt trip about Earl, who asked for her all the time, and Bernie, who would never forgive her, and all the gossipy speculation running around Mamou, people saying she'd been murdered, went chasing after a man, was pregnant, and everything in between.

They talked quietly, Raynie trying to explain why she'd had to leave. She knew Daniel would never quite understand when he said, "Okay, you've had your adventure. Come home with me now. We have children waiting to be born, Earlene."

She had told him every other way she knew. "The thing is, Daniel, I'm not Earlene any more. I'm different...things have happened...I can't live that life."

"People don't change, Earlene. Not really."

"You're right. They don't. I've known I can't live that life for a long time. I guess since my mother died. I could ignore that, marry you, have all those children you want. But, Daniel, I would never be happy."

He looked away. "So you're happy now?"

She had decided from the moment Peewee called her yesterday that she wasn't going to tell Daniel and Raymond about Jimmy Johnpier even though that was part of her new identity, her new history, what made her not Earlene any more. "Yes, I am. I'm happy now."

She reached across the table for his hand. He looked at her. "There's something for me here, Daniel. I have to stay for it."

"Maybe after you find it you can come home."

"It's not about finding anything. It's about being comfortable here, recognizing it as the place I belong. Don't wait for me, Daniel."

"So that's it? I'm out?"

She didn't know how to answer his anger. He took his hand from her and picked up his hat.

She watched him and Raymond walk away. He didn't look back, although Raymond did to holler, "You better come see Earl, or I'll come git you, li'l sister."

There was a moment that she wanted to run after Daniel, a moment of doubt. She closed the gate. She could sit here and cry and go through it all for the hundredth time or she could get on with it.

—⟋⟍—

Karen, Raynie and LaDonna were sitting around LaDonna's office at La Costa Brava.

"One thing about it," LaDonna said, "Ramon's his happy old self again." She laughed. "He hated Solo but he sure wanted that money bad. Girl, I ain't never seen a man so conflicted." She shook her head. "Money. You try to get it, you got it, you don't got it, it's sitting right in front of you—no matter where it is, it makes you crazy."

A short rap at the door and Ramon opened it. "Hello you beautiful women. You ready, LaDonna?"

"Just a minute, honey, wait for me downstairs."

He closed the door and Karen said, "Where's all his bling?"

"I told him lose it for a while. We're off to the 9 to talk to what people are down there about the community center. He's not going around raising money like that neither."

"As long as we're talking about money…" Raynie took some folded papers out of her purse and handed them to LaDonna. "Don't forget about this."

LaDonna looked at the note, the fifty thousand dollars she owed to Jimmy and Pascal. "I haven't forgotten. I thought I owed Pascal now. You inherit this?"

"Not exactly. Pascal and Jimmy had a little bet. Jimmy won."

"So, what, I owe you now?"

Raynie took the papers back. She tore them in half. "You don't owe nobody nothin."

LaDonna looked from Raynie to Karen, back to Raynie. "I'm sure he meant for you to have this money. I mean, girl, there's nothing left."

Raynie shook her head. "For the film, a parting gift from Jimmy."

—m—

After LaDonna and Ramon left, Karen took Raynie to one of the tables across from the bar.

"That was a real act of generosity, Raynie, but I want to pay LaDonna's loan off."

Raynie considered that a moment. "With what?"

"With money Jack stole from Solo that I stole from Jack."

"Fifty thousand dollars?"

"I think it's a little less than that now."

"You took it but you don't want it any more?"

"Something like that. And LaDonna's note—don't give me that Jimmy's parting gift crap. That money was for you."

"I want LaDonna to be free of it. She lost her house, everything.

I'm okay. There'll be some money left after the IRS gets theirs, a fair amount, the lawyer thinks. I'll be okay."

"You sure?" Raynie nodded and Karen said, "Why don't you sleep on it a few days."

"I don't need to. I'm okay, really. You keep your money. For a rainy day."

"I don't know. It's the way I got it—bad karma."

"Who's that, your mother talking?"

Karen sighed. "I've been indoctrinated. What do you want to drink?" She started to get up.

Raynie put her hand out. She sat down. "I went over to see Pascal yesterday. He said to ask you if you're poor yet and tell you he's ready for his rat's-ass chance if you are. Does this money have anything to do with him?"

Karen shook her head slowly. That wasn't the right question. The question was what was he willing to do for money? What were any of them willing to do for it? And then, if they got it, what did money do to them? You did have a choice about that, didn't you?

"You should go talk to him, Karen. Jimmy thought the world of him, and he's always been good to me. Maybe he can help you with this whole money thing."

"Maybe, but he doesn't know about it. It's just money in general. Like LaDonna said, how it makes people crazy."

"You really don't want this money? Give it to LaDonna for the community center. What's the money club mantra—share the wealth, create more?"

Karen looked up with disbelief. "You say money club and..."

Raynie paled as Judy and Kirk walked into the bar, Kirk on crutches, his leg in a cast.

"There she is! You don't come to see us any more so we came to see you." She kissed Karen then Raynie. "By the way, Jack's at your house. I thought you and he were..." she pointed her thumbs away from each other.

"Easier said than done." She said to Kirk, "What happened to you?"

"Fell off a ladder. Your mother, she's been unbelievable, taking care of me, making us money…she's an amazing woman." He smiled at Judy and she beamed.

"Show us the scene of the crime," she said.

Karen took them into the dining room.

"You know, darling, I really worry about you down here, all this violence…"

"Mother, please. There are the blood stains. Business has been booming. Let's go have a drink."

The bar began to fill up, with the first jazz show starting in less than an hour. Buddha sat on a stool at the door to the music room, collecting money and showing off his new ink, a body with a knife in it and a cowboy hat over its face. Zachary said he'd work a double so Karen had him make her a Matador. She had a few Matadors. She noticed Luc paying a lot of attention to Raynie. Later she heard her mother talking to Raynie about the money club. When Kirk told Judy he was tired, Karen walked them out and let her mother fast track through all the don't-be-a-stranger routines, which now included a sales pitch for the money club.

She was weary when she sat next to Raynie at the bar. "For fucksake, my mother. Maybe if she started a how to get rid of money club, I'd go."

She polished off her Matador and Zachary asked her if she wanted another. She shook her head. "I'm bouncing." She said to Raynie, "I'm going home to deal with Jack."

"You do that. I'll hang here for a while."

—◠◠◠—

Jack was lounging on the sofa, watching highlights from college football. "Hey, sweetstuff," he said when she walked in. His eyes floated back to the TV, his hand into the bag of Nacho Cheese Doritos he was eating.

"Jack, I'm getting dangerously tired of asking what the fuck you're doing here."

"What?" he said with his mouth full. His eyes never left the screen. "Oh, man, did you see that?" He wiped the Doritos hand on the sofa.

"Hey, that's my sofa, you prick."

"Oh, sorry." He tried to turn to brush the sofa off with his clean hand, groaned and lay back, rubbing his hand over his rib cage. "I'm almost out of pain pills. You got anything?"

"No, I don't."

"A bourbon would be real nice, babes. These ribs are killing me."

She brought him a drink and sat in the big chair where Jack couldn't see her without twisting his head.

"Oh, this is a good one," he said, not about the drink, but gesturing at the TV. "Check this play."

Karen stared at the screen.

"You see that?" He twisted his head, winced and said, "Sumbitch is like a fucking locomotive."

He never noticed when Karen didn't answer. She sat a while longer, a few more plays, Jack yelling at the TV, a commercial break, more plays, Jack stomping his foot at the TV then complaining about his ribs, and finally, a new announcement from the National Weather Service about predictions and hurricane preparedness.

She couldn't take it any more.

She got up and went into her bedroom. Inside her closet was the gym bag with the money in it. She'd gotten it from the box at the bank with the idea of giving it to Raynie. Or splitting it.

The two of them living on it. Or something. Easy come, easy go. She brought it into the living room and dropped it between the chair and the TV. Jack either didn't hear or decided not to turn his head again.

She went over to the commode and reached under it. The gun was still there. She knew Jack had searched the apartment more than once. She tore at the duct tape holding the gun to the bottom of the commode. The liquor bottles on top rattled.

"What are you doing, Karen?"

Making too much noise, she guessed. "Nothing."

She went and sat back in the big chair. She flicked her wrist the way she'd seen guys do in the movies and the cylinder opened. She spun it. Yep, still loaded.

"What..." Jack struggled into a sitting position. "What the fuck are you doing, Karen?"

"Well..." she said. She aimed and shot the TV. The bullet blew it backwards but the wall stopped it then it toppled on its face. It smoked and popped and lay silent.

"Jesus H. Christ!"

"Guess we don't need cable any more."

"Give me the gun, for Christ sake, Karen." He started to get up. She motioned him down with it. "Don't point it at me."

"Calm down, Jack."

"What the fuck? Do you know how much that screen cost?"

"Nope. Recognize that bag down there?"

He looked. "The money."

"No, the chump change. I was thinking about giving it back to you."

Jack was rallying. He gave one of his little laughs, a snigger, really. "I could use it, sugarcakes, I really could. You know, laid up and everything."

"I know. But I don't want to give it to you. I think I'm going to give it to LaDonna for her movie."

"That's a real nice gesture but that would kinda be like throwing good money away. I don't think you want to do that."

"Good money. Hm. Maybe not." Karen aimed the gun at the bag. "That's not good money. That's bad money." She shot it.

"Karen, for fucksake, you outta your mind? Give me the fucking gun. You're gonna have everyone on the block calling the cops."

"Oh, come on. Just once more." She shot it again. "That's really fun. I'd let you try it but I don't think you'd get off on it the way I do."

"Fuck me on a bike, Karen." Jack sat back, whipped.

Karen flipped out the cylinder. "Three bullets left." She closed the cylinder, sighted down the barrel of the gun at the dead TV and said, "I thought about giving the gun back to you." She glanced at Jack from the corner of her eye. "But I'm not going to." She lowered the gun. "I'm going to keep it in case you ever come back here. If you do, I'm going to shoot you three times."

She saw the gate open. Raynie slammed it and rushed in through the French doors. "Did y'all hear those gunshots? What's that smell?" She looked at the TV. She looked at the gun Karen was holding in her lap. "What is going on here?"

"We don't have ESPN any more so Jack's leaving. And I figured out something about money."

"You did? What?"

"Sometimes you just need to shoot it."

CPSIA information can be obtained at www.ICGtesting.com
Printed in the USA
LVOW12s1805261013

358656LV00002B/10/P